Wyld Witch Weather

Wyld Lands Academy Book 1

Janna Ruth

Janna Ruth

Wyld Witch Weather

Wyld Lands Academy Book One

For all the wild ones,
who never felt like they belonged.

You are loved.

A Note about Sensitive Topics

Dear Reader,

Thank you for picking up Wyld Lands Academy. This series is great fun, full of elemental action, romance and surprises. I don't intend to hurt you with any of these surprises, so I want to give you a heads-up about some of the darker themes and scenes in this novel. If you don't want any spoilers and are happy to take whatever I throw at you (I promise nothing freaky) then skip this note and start reading!

Here we go!

There's a lot of teenage angst, especially in Book 1. Milena has had a tough life, dealing with abandonment issues ever since her father left when she was young. Her mother is overwhelmed, and she's experienced a lot of bullying. Wyld Lands Academy is a fresh start for her, but learned behaviour isn't easy to shed. She can be self-sabotaging, mistrusting, and doubtful of her self-worth at times. She has a lot of complex emotions and, unfortunately, her magic is linked to them.

Even worse, she now has a supernatural bully.

Playing with the elements is dangerous. There'll be injuries, and Milena will suffer a severe asthma attack. Magic goes wild, a big storm breaks out, and a fire gets out of control.

At the very end, we catch a glimpse of where the series is headed, with a potentially disturbing scene involving a line-up, aggressive police action, and brutal arrests. Without giving too much away, I can tell you this series deals with themes of minority oppression, unfair persecution, and fascism. Although it's dark, I hope the series will leave you feeling hopeful that people *will* stand up and fight for freedom. There are many good people in the world, and Milena is one of them.

It's time to enrol at Wyld Lands Academy! Have fun!

Love,
Janna

1

The wind, the wind—the heavenly child...

There's nothing heavenly about the wind. If it's a child, it's a wilful one; never listening, gleefully destructive, doing whatever the hell it wants. Like me.

It's gone now, that storm deep inside of me, all those emotions that I can't control, no matter how hard I try. Not the slightest breeze is blowing around me. I have nothing left to give.

But boy, have I given.

The chemistry lab around me is literally in pieces. Every glass is shattered, even the windows. Chemicals are dripping from the tables, reacting with each other and the dust on their way down. Luckily, it's a poorly equipped school lab, but leave it to me to accidentally start an explosion. Not that it's needed with the constant storm inside of me.

I wish I could control it. But then again, I know I never will. Because when I let go of all the sadness, all the longing, and all that pain inside of me, it feels *so* good. For a few precious minutes, I feel free. Like the wind.

And then reality blows in and I realise I'll be expelled before the day is out.

Again.

2

Endless white fields float by as the car travels down the highway. I lose myself in the sight of the snow, ignoring the signs that tell me we're closing in on Prague—our destination. There's something soothing in this sea of white as it covers the bare ground beneath, hiding its ugliness. Snowflakes whirl in the wind. Oh, how I long to be out there under the sky with the cold breeze on my skin.

Instead, I'm stuck in a car with my mother, who won't shut up about my recent failures and what awaits me if I fail again.

"This is pretty much your last chance, Milena, and you've chosen to wear *that* to the interview?" She throws me a quick glance before turning back with a disdainful huff.

I can't help but check my offending clothes. Is it the *Alia Tempora* band shirt I'm wearing over a tank? Compared with some of the others I own, this one is harmless. Or maybe it's the short, tattered skirt that's not covering enough of my legs for my mother—or the cold season. Then again, my legs are sufficiently covered by ripped tights. Probably it's all three in combination.

In comparison, my mother is well put together in one of her many pencil skirts and matching jackets. Her hair is pulled back tightly into a bun, not a lock out of place.

"You know, you might have to colour your hair," she continues. "Private schools have notoriously tight rules about which colours they allow."

"Why am I going to a private school again?"

My hair will definitely not pass a colour-code as it is. I like it, though. The bright purple almost matches Markie's signature tresses—she's the lead vocalist of *Alia Tempora.* I had it coloured last week, just in time to ruin my mother's Christmas.

My mother glares at me. "Because it's the only school willing to take you."

And we're back to square one. My failure to keep from getting expelled.

"Seriously, child. I don't know what's wrong with you."

My mother knows exactly what's wrong with me. She just doesn't want to admit it. It's the wind. When I get upset or angry, the wind follows my cues. I don't know why it does that. It's not like it's dependent on me. It'll blow up a storm when I'm happy and relaxed or be completely calm when I wish there was a little breeze, like on a hot summer day. But when I get really angry, when I want to scream and shout, it's always right there at my side.

Of course, no one believes me, not even my mother. *The wind doesn't blow indoors,* they say, as if I don't know. It's not just a stupid excuse, though. I'm not making it up to hide my "violent tendencies" or whatever my teachers like to call it. I'm not vio-lent—at least, I try not to be.

The wind blows in and destroys everything in its path. I just happen to stand at the centre of it, too upset to rein it back in, basking in the destructive force that mirrors what I feel inside so perfectly. At least, until it dies down, and I'm left with the pieces.

"It wasn't my fault," I mumble, trying not to think too hard about what set off my latest outburst.

They had to close the school for the day to deal with contamination in the school lab—apparently, there was a risk of explosion or combustion or whatever other reaction might've happened if left untreated. It was a costly operation and I feel like that played a much larger role in my expulsion than the fact I destroyed the lab in the first place. If you'd heard the headmaster, who also happened to be my chemistry teacher, you'd think I'd taken a baseball bat to it. That's not what happened, but my mother has long since given up on asking for my reasons. There's only one thing that matters to her.

"You need to take this seriously. No more outbursts. No more tantrums. This might be your last chance to graduate with a higher education." She laughs sharply. "And believe me, you don't *want* to enter the workforce just yet. They won't be as lenient as school."

I guess expulsion is a sign of leniency now.

"It was a good school, you know?" Once again, she glances at me, waiting for approval. When she doesn't get it, she groans. "I don't get it. Why can't you be—"

"Normal?" I suggest.

Another glare. "How about a little less teenage rebel and more respectful student?"

Ouch. My mother's opinion of me seems to have hit rock bottom. Not that it was ever very high to begin with. I've always fallen short of her expectations, and in recent years, I've proven myself a proper nuisance.

Because of my weird wind affinity, we've had to move five times in the last six years, and I've changed schools twice as much. She had to find new jobs—fortunately, she's so competent, it never takes her long—and new homes. Especially the two times I managed to wreck the rentals.

When I was younger, she called me a force of nature. Now she just sighs heavily and massages her forehead. Unfortunately, she's stuck with me until I'm eighteen. Or at least she was until she found this new school: *Wyld Lands Academy — International School of Prague.* A boarding school. Someplace where she won't have to see me every day. *If* they agree to take me.

According to the sign we just passed, there's only twelve kilometres left to Prague, which means it's only a few more to the city boundary. Already, more and more houses replace white fields, the heat of vehicles and humans turning the pristine snow to ugly mush.

I don't care much for the city. Yes, it's a very pretty city with a beautiful centre, a fairytale castle, and a host of red roofs currently covered in snow, millions of tourists flock to the streets every year, and sure, it's nice on a school trip, but I'm not much of a city girl.

My favourite memories are from the time when we lived in the Krkonoše Mountains. The school there was a very small one and I had to ride my bike down and up the mountains to get to it. Even though it took me forty minutes, I enjoyed the wind in my hair and nature around me. Life felt easier there.

Big cities on the other hand always suffocate me. The smog makes my asthma play up and there are too many people around. And the wind... the wind feels unnatural as it's forced through the high-rise buildings, blocked and diverted at every turn. It can't breathe freely, either.

I don't want to disappoint my mother yet again, but I don't really see much hope for me studying in Prague. Especially not at a prestigious private school. *The son of the prime minister recently graduated from there*, I was told, as if it was motivating and not greatly intimidating. My mother might wish we were part of high society, but we're lower-middle class, not too bad off, but not wealthy enough to mingle with the rich and famous. Which makes me wonder how we're going to afford a school that's good enough for politicians, diplomats, and celebrity offspring.

We pass the city boundary and my mother enters the address to navigate the unfamiliar streets, too busy now to berate me any further. I look outside the window again, taking in the boring buildings on either side of the street. This certainly isn't Prague's good side. But then, I catch a glimpse of the Vltava and the trees covered with a thin blanket of untouched snow alongside it. The water glistens in the rare winter sun, speckled with boats that pass under bridges. Above the white roofs, I can see Prague Castle rising, and I have to admit, it looks postcard chic.

The view is obliterated soon enough by more houses. My mother curses at the trams in her way and the clogged-up streets. She's not much of a city girl, either, even if she likes to pretend otherwise.

Wyld Lands Academy is located on the outer skirts of the Old City. I imagine it squashed in with the rest of the buildings, but once we get close, the street opens up, and I see a big snowy park. Behind the trees, a castle-like building rises, complete with red-roofed turrets. I know it has to be the school, because young people in unflattering grey uniforms with green details walk on the brushed paths, noses buried in green scarfs.

One look, and I can already tell I won't fit in.

Historical buildings, fancy school uniforms, prestigious alumni… There's no way they'll even consider taking me once they have a look at my record. Or at my sorry self.

I tug at my ripped tights, suddenly wishing I'd worn a different pair, but I know it doesn't matter. Nothing I own is good enough for this school. This will be a very short-lived stint.

We pull into the parking lot. My hand flies to the handle, eager to get out of the confines of the car, but my mother roots me to the seat with a stern glare. "I want you to be on your very best behaviour."

Something knots in my stomach. There's a barrage of words fighting to get onto my tongue but I swallow all of them. In my mother's eyes, I'm nothing but a troublesome teenager, slave to my hormones—or rather slave to my unruly nature. "I'll try my best."

There's another intense stare, as if she's trying to say my best isn't good enough. At last, she nods and a rare smile slips onto her face. "This is going to be good."

I finally get to leave the car. Instantly, a soft breeze caresses my cheeks, and I feel the knot loosen a little. I close my eyes and try to let go of all my thoughts and fears, concentrating on the whisper in my ear and soft tug on my hair as I take several deep breaths.

The air isn't as bad as I thought it'd be. The open space and trees definitely help make this place feel less like a big city and more like nature. It's still not enough, though. I feel the houses loom nearby, as if waiting to wrap their stony embrace around me and anchor me to the ground.

"Milena!" my mother calls sharply. "They're waiting for us."

Annoyed, I open my eyes and click my tongue. Surely, a minute or two won't mess up anyone's timeline. "I know, I know, you can't wait to get rid of me."

She stares, exasperated. "That is not what's happening here."

"Isn't it?" It honestly feels that way.

"No," she snaps. "I'm just trying to make right by you. Make sure you get a good education, so you're well equipped to make a life for yourself."

I walk past her with an eye-roll. "So, the long game of getting rid of me."

My mother huffs indignantly, not deigning me with a reply. "Ms Martínková is waiting for us." I can only assume that's someone from admin.

People watch us as we make our way across the park to the wide building ahead. If my art education isn't failing me, I'd say it's a gothic style, complete with little gargoyles under the roof. The windows are tall and pointy, making it look more like a cathedral than a school.

A wide set of marble stairs leads to a double door, which has been opened to the rare sunshine. Students slip in and out, carrying their books with them. Next to the door a brass sign carries the school's name: Wyld Lands Academy.

We enter a huge hallway that used to be the foyer of a mansion, dominated by two wide flights of stairs. In between the stairs are a number of movable boards which boast information for visitors and students as well as student successes and notices. Large windows brighten the hallway on either side.

On our left is a surprisingly modern glass cubicle that seems to be the secretary's realm. Or maybe they have a separate person to monitor the comings and goings in the hall. It's where my mother's headed to get directions.

While she talks to the person in the cubicle, I hang back and continue to take in the marvellous architecture of the Academy. Looking up, it has this cathedral-like quality with curved beams supporting a high ceiling. From the look of it, the main building has three or four upper floors. When I lower my gaze, I start noticing helpful signs at either of the corridors on the side. To the right is the dining hall, stage, and library, while the left leads to the sports field, training rooms, a swimming pool, and a sauna.

Come again? Is this a spa or a school?

The stairs lead to classrooms. I wonder where the sleeping quarters are since they're not labelled anywhere around the hall.

"Milena!" my mother calls, leading the way. "It's down here."

The headmistress' office is just around the corner. We're spared the awkwardness of an introduction by the secretary who announces us before leaving us alone.

"Mrs Šimková and... Was it Milena?"

When you think of a headmistress, you'd probably imagine an old stern lady. Not so Ms Martínková. She's got a wide, open smile and is not a day older than my mother, which puts her in her early forties. Her hair is blond and wavy and there's a soft smattering of freckles on her nose. She's quite pretty for a teacher, and I wonder if that's a rich and famous thing.

"Yes, this is my daughter, Milena." My mother tries to mirror the headmistress' smile but fails to do so convincingly. The lines of worry are etched too deeply into her face. "Come on, darling. Say hello."

I throw my mother a glance that hopefully lets her know I'm not a toddler and shake Ms Martínková's hand. "Hello." Internally, I've started the countdown to when this model-turned-teacher will realise she's made a mistake and can't offer me a place.

"Sit, sit." She waves us to two chairs before turning to a little table that holds a water boiler, a coffee machine, and a water tumbler. "Would you like a drink?"

"Oh, yes, please." My mother's slowly warming up. I don't fault her. She should enjoy the amenities while it lasts.

Personally, I decline the drink, instead settling sullenly in the annoyingly soft chair. The office is pretty but also surprisingly bare. There's a big wooden table and a computer, and the obligatory book shelves with nothing but educational books. From what I can tell, Ms Martínková has the same boring taste as every other educator in the country. But her copies are probably signed.

"So, Milena," the headmistress addresses me, "you're currently in Year 11?" When I nod vaguely, she continues, still way too friendly for my taste. "What do you enjoy most about school?"

Are students supposed to enjoy school? I exchange a look with my mother, and she makes it very clear that I'd better come up with something impressive. So, naturally, I shrug. "I dunno, art, perhaps."

My mother laughs, as if my teenage answer is particularly droll. "Milena has always been quite interested in the natural sciences—Biology, Geography, Chemistry. She's my little scientist."

I side-eye my mother. After the incident with the school lab, she told me I'd better not step into another lab ever again. To be fair, she also said that about trophy cases, libraries, and greenhouses.

While my mother sings a rare song of my praises, I hold my tongue, trying my best to keep a straight face. It's not like I'm a bad student. My grades are alright, especially in written exams. Orally, I've been told again and again that I need to show more engagement. It's what holds me back from truly excelling in any of the subjects, according to my teachers. Personally, I prefer it that way—there's much less attention if you're just cruising by.

From time to time, Ms Martínková's gaze settles on me. It gives me the impression she'd prefer to talk to me, but my mother is not leaving anything to chance. She's giving the pitch of a lifetime, artfully skirting around the exact nature of my frequent school changes. As if Ms Martínková doesn't have access to my reports.

At last, there's a chance for her to get a word in. "Look, I'm happy to give Milena a chance. That is if she passes our physical requirements."

What kind of fresh ableist hell is this? Is this a sports' school? Will I have to join a team, or worse, do track and field? If so, I'm so screwed.

"*Physical* requirements?" My mother sounds equally confused. "What exactly does that mean?"

"Oh, it's nothing to worry about. I'll send Milena to do some tests while we continue our conversation about her potential future at Wyld Lands Academy."

As if on cue, there's a knock at the door. Ms Martínková stands to introduce us to the new entrant. "Ah, Grisha. Right on time. This is Milena Šimková, a new applicant, and her mother. Milena, this is Grisha Spotnek. They'll be supervising your exam." She makes a little gesture as if I'm supposed to get up and leave.

Once again, I'm surprised by the youth of the staff here. It's hard to say exactly how old Grisha is. They could be in their mid-twenties or as young as me. It doesn't help that they keep their hair so short it barely classifies as stubble. It distracts me so much I don't notice the obvious clue until I take a second look. They're wearing one of the grey school uniforms—long pressed trousers and a tailored blazer with green details on the cuffs and lapel. A fellow student, then.

Their brown eyes are full of warmth. "Nice to meet you, Milena." They nod their head towards the door. "Let's get you tested."

My gaze searches my mother's and I give the slightest of shakes, hoping no one else picks it up. I don't want to get tested, much less on my physical abilities. Is there anything more mortifying than failing an entry exam because you start wheezing after half a round of running?

My mother has no compassion. "Come on, don't keep everyone waiting." Her voice is slightly tense, as if she smells the whiff of rebellion in the air. "It's just a little test."

Unable to hold back a heavy sigh, I push myself out of the chair.

"I'm sure you'll pass with flying colours," the headmistress says, her tone almost managing to convince me.

If there was even the slightest chance, I might believe her. Instead, I drag my feet as I follow Grisha to my doom, ready to embarrass myself in front of a fellow student.

I snort. As if anyone here would be my peer.

3

"Don't worry," Grisha says as soon as the door closes behind me. "It's less of a test than a series of physical exams."

Now we're going to the doctor? "Why?" slips out before I can hold my tongue.

"Why?" They seem confused.

"What's the point? I mean, are you guys big on sports or something?"

They lead me down the corridor to an indistinct door at the end, weighing their head as if to consider how to break the news to me. "There's a huge physical component to our daily schedule. The school believes in strengthening both body and mind, but it's not necessarily sports per se."

Well, that cleared up pretty much nothing. Who knew all these privileged kids had to be star athletes on top of their already impressive resumes? "Cool." Then, after rethinking my answer a bit, I add, "Full disclosure, I've got asthma. It's often triggered by physical exertion." And the pollen in spring, animal fur, and laying down in bed, because my lungs don't appreciate lying flat.

"There'll be other areas for you to excel at." They open the door and wave me inside.

As I enter, I try to make sense of their answer. But no matter how I turn it, there's no sense to be made. Unless excelling at not having asthma is now a thing. I wonder what other chronic diseases I could excel at not having, and snort softly. I take a look at the room and freeze. It truly looks like a doctor's office, reminding me an awful lot of my asthma specialist and her stress test room, complete with an airlock cabin and home trainer. But there's other stuff, too: something that looks like a whirlpool, and a selection of weights.

Grisha pulls out a tablet and moves their fingers across. "Let's start with the basics. Please take off your shoes and step onto the scale over there."

Yep, this really is a medical exam. One I didn't consent to. Fortunately, I'm not conscious about my weight—it's pretty average for my age and size.

Grisha finishes up the basics before appraising me with a long glance. I have no idea what they're looking for, but after a while they nod and lead me to the cabin. Once I get closer I notice it's not quite like the asthma test machines I'm used to. For once, there's no mouthpiece to breathe through, just a chair.

"Just sit inside and breathe normally. Let me know when it gets too hot."

My confusion is at an all-time high. What kind of test is this? How long I can sit still? Are they testing my tolerance for tight spaces?

I sit on the swivel chair while Grisha operates a couple of switches on a panel next to the closed door. Sudden heat falls onto my shoulders, and I glance up, discovering an array of infrared lamps above me, their elements glowing orange.

At first, it's kind of nice, just warm and toasty, but the temperature keeps rising, and soon I feel like I've been standing in the sun for too long.

Let me know when it gets too hot.

That's the test. They're actually testing how well I can withstand the heat. What for, I have no idea, but short answer: I'm terrible with heat. There's a reason I love the wind so much, especially in summer. This kind of dry, unrelenting heat quickly brings me to my limits.

I try to keep a straight face, but when it starts to feel like I'm breathing in a furnace, I'm unable to cover up the distress. My neck prickles and I can feel sweat beads forming on my forehead. How long do I need to endure this to pass? I'm starting to feel like a rotisserie chicken.

Five minutes and a whole lot of gasping later, I give up. Without waiting for Grisha's approval, I push the door open.

The relief is immediate. Fresh cold air washes over me, cooling down the sweat on my skin and filling my lungs. When I've caught my breath, I ask, "Did I pass?"

Grisha frowns at the readings, clearly not impressed. Well, sorry, I didn't know I was being tested on how well I'd do in a desert. And by "desert" I mean the Martian desert during the day.

"Let's move on to weights." They lead me to a bench with multiple kettlebells. "You can skip the light ones and pick up one you think you can manage. Then we'll work ourselves up to find your limit."

I wish they hadn't said I should skip the light ones because, honestly, the small one at the end is the one I would've picked. Self-consciously, I pick the third smallest kettlebell. That's skipping two, right?

Unfortunately, the weight is a lot heavier than expected. I know I'm not strong, but surely I can lift a medium weight off the bench. "How heavy is this?" I ask when I manage close to an inch before my arms give way.

"That one? Thirty kilos."

Thirty? I look along the lines of bigger and heavier weights. Assuming they're going up in ten-kilogram increments, they go up to one hundred and twenty. And no, they don't look like it.

"I can lift this one," I say, preparing myself to lift twenty kilos with a big jerk of my muscles. I can only hold it for a bit but I prove my claim at least.

"You sure?" Grisha asks.

"Am I sure if I can lift this one?" I ask, slowly getting annoyed. "I just showed you, didn't I?"

Apologetically, they quickly shake their heads. "No, I meant are you sure you can't go higher?"

"Yes. I might look like it but I'm not a fitness junkie." For the record, I do *not* look like it.

Grisha smiles softly, apparently amused by my sarcasm. "The next one should be it, then."

With *it*, I assume, they mean a test I'll pass. Only I no longer have any clue about what we're actually testing here.

It only gets weirder as they lead me to the whirlpool. It's filled with water about two hands deep. Grisha drops a marble into it, close to where we're standing, and gives a flourished bow. "All you need to do is move the marble across the pool without touching it."

I stare at them. Then I blink. "Come again?"

"Try moving the marble through the pool without lifting it or anything like that."

It doesn't make any more sense when repeated. "Can I use a tool?"

They smile at me as if to encourage me. "Just the water."

"Just the water," I repeat slowly, then stare at the marble. This particular test sounds more like a puzzle than a physical exam. How can I make the marble move in the water?

Physics lessons come to me, and that one section about wave types we did in geography. The water isn't too deep. If I move the surface, some of that energy should translate to the bottom.

I feel incredibly stupid as I kneel and put my hands in the water, then give it a big push. Sure enough, a wave forms, or rather a ripple. The marble, however, looks as if it gives in to the movement for only a moment before deciding to stay put.

I try again from a different angle and with more force, managing a millimetre at best. The body of water completely swallows my mechanical force. The waves crash against the walls of the pool and I splash myself, but the marble barely moves at all.

My movements grow more frantic as anger rises in me. This is stupid. Surely, they're messing with me. There's no way this is the actual test. Where's the true nurse? And what have I done to deserve all this ridicule?

When a wave breaks on itself, splashing me in the face and down half my shirt, I finally give up. "Please tell me there's a trick to this." Clearly, I'm doing it wrong. So much for Mummy's Little Scientist.

"There is," Grisha admits freely. "But clearly, you're not capable of it."

I gape. Did they really just say that? I'm not good enough for the trick? "Wow." I just embarrassed myself for this student nurse's amusement.

"Don't worry. We've still got one test left. Here's a towel." They hand it to me and I struggle immensely with accepting the offer. At last, I snatch it from them and furiously rub my face and dab at my T-Shirt.

Grisha waits until I drop the towel unceremoniously on a chair and catch my breath. "Alright. This is the last one, I promise." And then they hand me a slightly oversized peak flow metre, replacing the mouthpiece with a fresh one. "Just do a couple of those for me."

Once again, I find myself staring. After all of this, they want me to prove to them my lung volume is practically non-existent? First, I get roasted alive, then I fail to lift any of those impossibly heavy weights and embarrass myself in the water, and now I need to show them I'm serious about my asthma?

Screw this. This is ridiculous. I don't want to go to this stupid school with their weird physical expectations. These tests are clearly designed to make fools of people they don't want, and it only took one look at me to decide I wasn't a good fit.

I close my lips around the mouthpiece, still stewing. The knots in my stomach are back. It's so tight I want to scream. Instead, I blow.

The whole peak flow metre flies out of my mouth and hits Grisha in the face. At the same time, my friend the wind blows in. The door of the heat cabin slams open and shut and the water in the pool is whipped into a frenzy. The blasted marble finally starts to move, though it only rolls back and forth on the bottom with the waves.

Its motion captivates me enough to snap me out of my little tantrum, and the wind settles. Stone-cold reality slams into me. I've done it again. I've lost my temper and blown my chance, as small as it might have been.

Without any regard for Grisha, who's holding their nose and moaning, I jump off my chair and flee. Tears sting in my eyes as I find my way back to the headmistress' office. Before I can overthink it, I burst through the door, startling the two women enjoying a cup of coffee and laughter.

"Milena!" My mother looks instantly panicked. Her lip quivers as she takes in my slightly bedraggled sight. "What did you do?"

I try not to let the question get to me, but it's hard because my feelings are already in turmoil. "Nothing, I..." I close my eyes and take a deep breath, trying to keep the storm in me at bay. "Can we go?"

"Uhm..." Irritated, my mother checks with the headmistress. "I'm sorry." She laughs nervously. "I guess we'll wait for the test results?"

"There's no need," Ms Martínková says with a gentle smile. She looks at her computer, which must have come alive with a new notice. It obviously doesn't take long to type in *'FAILURE'.* The smile deepens, and I feel like I'm going to be sick. She doesn't have to be so damn glad about it. "It's just as I thought from looking at the reports from your old school."

All that hyping up from my mother for nothing. She knows I mean nothing but trouble.

"I'm pleased to offer you a place. Welcome to Wyld Lands Academy, Milena."

4

After those weird-ass tests, I no longer want to stay—not that I ever did. But of course, my mother is so relieved *someone* is willing to take me off her, there's no discussion about it, especially not when I'm offered a scholarship. A good school, no fees, and they're willing to take a chance on me; it's everything my mother's dreamed of.

"I don't like it here," I tell her when we have some privacy at the car.

She unloads my luggage from the trunk, wasting no time in ridding herself of me. "Don't be ridiculous. What's there not to like?"

"Uhm, those physical requirements, for example?" I don't really want to tell her how badly I messed up, which means I can't tell her how ridiculous they were in the first place.

My mother laughs, the sound so incredibly weightless and free. "You passed," she reminds me. "I've always said you need to trust your body a little more. You can't just use your asthma as an excuse for not trying." She gives me a delightful one-shoulder shrug. "As you've just proven, you're perfectly capable of passing a physical exam."

She lets the tail gate slam down, locking me out. "Besides, Ms Martínková told me about the school's concept."

"Yes, yes, a sound body supports a sound mind," I say quickly before she can repeat the bullshit. A terrible thought comes to me. "Do you think that's what'll fix me? The piece I've been missing all these years?"

Judging by the guilty look on her face, it's exactly what she's thinking. "I don't see how it could do you harm."

"Mum!" I want to tell her how horrible it makes me feel like she's going to abandon me here, but I can't force the words over my lips. My mother has suffered a lot through the years because of me. She's done everything in her power to keep me safe and on a good path, not allowing me to give up when the going got tough. "There must be some other school."

"It's this one or else you'd better start working on your CV." Her harsh words are immediately followed by a gentle hand on my cheek and a warm look. "I know how hard it is for you to settle into a new place, but I've got a really good feeling about this school. It's a huge plus the headmistress isn't holding your past against you. She told me we all make mistakes, and I love that." She smiles softly. "I know you're not a bad kid."

"Do you?"

"Oh, Milena." She pulls me into a hug that eases a little of the tension I carry inside. My mother lets go of me and puts her hand on my shoulders instead. "Promise me you'll try to stay calm. Don't let people get to you like they usually do. Just ignore them and focus on yourself."

So basically, don't worry about making friends, just please manage to hang around until graduation. "Sure."

"Once you're settled in, send me a list of everything you need." She heaves my bag closer to me and out of the way of the car. "This should get you through the first couple of days. Now…"

The moment of goodbye is here. My mother won't help me get settled or hang around any longer than she needs to. That probably means I'm a big girl now. I just need to suck it up and get it over with. "Drive safe."

"I love you." If only I could allow myself to believe she means it.

I grab my bag and take a step back, watching as she gets into the car and slowly pulls out of the parking lot. Our eyes lock, and she blows me a kiss. I hope she's not looking for a smile because my face is completely frozen. It's either that or yet another tantrum. And I've promised to behave.

When the car's taken from my sight by the trees, I heave a big sigh, grab my luggage, and turn around—straight into someone.

"Woah," a male voice says, as strong hands catch and steady me. A laugh punctuates the chill winter air. "Sorry about that."

I take a step back to orient myself. Then I look at him. Like everyone else, he's clad in the grey school uniform, but where it looks drab and boring on everybody else, he looks as if it was tailored specifically to accent his muscular build and cool paleness of his skin tone. The angles of his face are as sharp as the suit, and his surprisingly grey-green eyes match the colour of the details. His black hair has been shaved on the sides and the back but is long enough on the top to move in the wind. With his tall, slender features I could easily see him walking in a Paris fashion show just as I could see him taking over the world as some junior politician.

He gives me a short bow that betrays his Japanese heritage more than his features do. There's a warmth in his eyes as he regards me. "You must be Milena. I'm Jin Čermák. I'm the Head Boy at Wyld Lands Academy and here to give you a quick tour."

Of course he's the Head Boy. I bet he's on all the brochures.

"Shall we?" he asks, the smile still lurking behind his gently curled lips.

Oh, gosh, what am I doing staring at his lips? How about responding to him instead? If only I could remember what he just asked me.

"Milena?"

"Yes." Would you look at that? I've got a voice.

Jin flashes me the kind of grin that'd have the world falling at his feet. "Let's get going, okay? Do you want me to take your bag?"

I appreciate him asking instead of assuming I need the help of a strong man to lug my belongings around. "If you don't mind." I have no idea how many stairs we'll have to take, so this is a mere precaution after failing so miserably at the weight test.

Together, we set off on the white paved path under the trees. Jin strikes up polite conversation. "So, are you the first of your family to study here?"

Should I tell him about my illustrious history of expulsions? Not wanting to start off on the wrong foot, I settle for a simple, "I am."

"Oh, wow. That must a big change for you, then."

What's that supposed to mean? That I'm not used to walking among the rich and powerful? Way to rub it in, fancy Head Boy. "Sure."

Jin isn't deterred by my monosyllable answers and keeps smiling at me. "What's your element?"

Don't tell me he's into astrology and such. I stare, while trying to remember what Aquarius was. Not water. "Air?"

"Cool, me too. We'll see a lot more of each other, then."

I glance at Jin from the side, hoping he doesn't notice my stare. "Will we?"

Despite all the weirdness so far, my heart surges at the thought of spending more time with him. I have to mentally slap myself to remind myself he doesn't mean it in a romantic way. Why am I even thinking about romance? I'd be lucky to make a friend around here. I sure wouldn't mind having Jin as a friend.

"Yes, I'm assisting with the air and water classes."

"Come again?" Did he just say *air* and *water* classes?

Jin smiles encouragingly at me. "Oh, it's not a big deal. I just run the drills at the beginning then walk around, helping people with their stance or any other issues that might arise."

He's saying words, but they don't make up sentences in my head. I stop short of the big stairs and stare. "What kind of classes are they?"

His eyebrows crawl up as understanding blooms on his face. "Oh, uhm... did Martínková not tell you yet?" He pulls up his phone, looks at a message, and pulls a painful grimace. It's kind of cute how flustered he seems. "Right, she wants to see you for a... *proper* chat after we finish the tour. You really *are* the first of your family here."

"That's what I said." This is all getting weirder by the minute.

"Sorry. I'm making a mess out of this." He rubs the back of his neck and tries for a hopeful smile.

I can't help it. I have to smile back. "Is this your first tour?"

"Pretty much. I was only appointed four months ago and the new entrants had their proper tours a month before that. We usually don't have someone starting in the middle of the school year. Though, I guess it makes sense, in your case."

The smile dies on my lips, and my stomach twists itself into knots. "Did they tell everyone?" So much for leaving things in the past and giving me a new chance.

Now Jin looks confused. "Tell everyone what? I... Look, I'm not the right person to tell you. I think." He struggles to find the right words, and I start to think that maybe there's something else creating this weird communication barrier between us. Once again, he tries for a hopeful smile. "Shall we just do the tour? It'll all make sense when you speak to Martínková."

"Sure. Show me the air class," I quip, having no idea what that'd even look like.

He laughs softly. "There aren't any on right now. Everyone's at study time or training in the back. But I can show you the classroom, make sure you don't get lost tomorrow morning."

We decide to leave my luggage with the secretary before we make our way through the many corridors of Wyld Lands Academy. As Jin said, classes are out for the day, so we encounter only few students. Many of them know Jin, and I quickly get the impression he won the Head Boy election by a landslide.

The classrooms are fairly standard, lots of tables, chairs, cupboards, and digital whiteboards in the front. Some rooms are devoid of any furniture, which makes me assume the college isn't at capacity. Air class turns out to be just a fancy name for the location, as the class is held outside behind the school—even in winter. It must all be part of the physical focus of the school. We're all going to be so healthy when we graduate.

The only class we come across is happening in the courtyard close to the air class. Spread out around a wide fountain, about twenty students go at each other with sticks. "Kendo?"

"Something like that." Jin looks as if he wants to explain more, but his lips remain shut in a thin line. Abruptly, he jerks his head to the building behind the courtyard. "Those are the sleeping quarters. I don't know which room you've been assigned to, but it's likely going to be on the first floor to the left. The rooms are usually shared between two people."

That's not too bad. Maybe I can make a friend out of my roommate.

"Anyway. The library and dining hall are in the East Wing over there, and that's as much as I can show you right now."

All in all, it's a pretty school with huge grounds. There are water features and gardens, and even an outside training and rock-climbing area. Full-body statues and busts are placed along the pathways, inviting people to linger.

A small building near the East Wing catches my eyes. At first glance, it looks like a mausoleum, but its copper cupola shimmers in the sun, surprisingly free of snow. The doors are closed and, as far as I can see, barred. We're too far away but I notice elaborate carvings in the wood.

I nudge Jin, trying not to focus too much on the jolt of electricity that runs through my arm at the touch. "What's through there?"

"Which... Oh, uhm..." He's thinking way too hard about how to answer me. The lie comes out eventually. "It's been closed for a while."

I raise my eyebrow at him. "Right."

Jin deflates slightly. He doesn't seem very used to lying. "We should get you back to Martínková. I promise this'll all make more sense then."

He leads me back to the main building via a stroll through the student hall. We're still way off when we come across a familiar face. Grisha calls out to Jin and clasps hands with him, then they take a look at me and their face falls. "Oh, it's you."

I can't help but notice the bruise under their eye where the peak flow metre hit them. "Yep, it's me." They're probably not my biggest fan at the moment.

"What happened to you?" Jin asks.

Inwardly I cringe, waiting for the moment when Jin's opinion of me takes a turn for the worse.

Grisha shrugs. "The risks of helping with the tests."

Definitely cringe. I wish I was already in Ms Martínková's office so I didn't have to listen to them rehashing my embarrassing performance in the exam room.

Jin looks at me, amused. "You did that. With air? Huh!" Somehow he sounds triumphant. "And they always say we're the softies."

I don't know why but the way Jin says it makes me feel included in something I don't yet understand. He's not making fun of me. He sounds proud.

My cheeks flush with heat and I have to tell myself this won't last. Soon he'll be looking at me with the same contempt as everyone else. My little accident may seem droll now; it won't when the wind gets out of control.

"Well, I'll leave you guys to it," Grisha says, already half turned away. "Welcome to Wyld Lands, Milena."

It still surprises me they don't seem mad about what happened in the exam room. It might be the most chill reaction someone's had to my stormy outbursts so far.

"See you later!" Jin calls after them, before leading me up the stairs. "Let's get you back to Martínková. I'll ask her which room you're in and bring your luggage over."

"Thanks." He truly is the kindest. Popular and beautiful, but not an ass.

We walk up the stairs along a beautiful gallery. Instead of portraits and lists of previous students and teachers, the walls are covered with giant landscape paintings, each more beautiful than the last. I see waves whipped into a frenzy in front of a crumbling coast, high mountains hidden in the clouds, and glorious thunderstorms across jagged landscapes.

The paintings fill me with an irrational sense of longing for the mountains I used to call home. How I long to stand right there under that heavy rain cloud, the wind whipping my hair this way and that while the electricity in the air makes the hairs stand up on my arms. I can taste the tension in the air just before it explodes.

A soft breeze carries through the corridor, picking up my purple strands just enough to make them dance.

Next to me, Jin clears his throat. His mouth is hidden behind his fist, staring anywhere but at me. He swallows, then audibly lets go of a breath. "There's the office."

He points ahead at an unfamiliar door, and I frown. "No, it's not." It doesn't look anything like the office before. We're not even on the right floor.

"Oh, this is the *real* office."

"The *real* office?" What's going on?

Jin shrugs with a helpless smile. "The one you were in is the outside office. This is the... normal office." He knocks on the door. "Just don't freak out, okay? I'll see you around."

"Don't freak out" is not the kind of advice that instils a lot of confidence in me. My heart beats rapidly when I hear steps behind the door, and I miss a beat when it's opened.

Ms Martínková looks as friendly as before. "You're here. Thanks, Jin." She smiles at me. "Come on in."

With a head full of worries, I step inside.

5

The *real* office is wildly different from the one downstairs. I have so many questions. The first thing that draws my gaze is the closed glass sphere on the desk which has a fire burning inside—not a candle or one of those digital displays, but a real, flickering, burning-hot fire. How it doesn't melt the glass, I have no idea. But it's far from the only odd display in the office. Near the window is a row of potted plants that I swear look different every time I glance at them. I try to ambush it by looking out of the corner of my eye, but nothing seems out of the ordinary until I look to the right, and the plant there is suddenly higher than those on the other side. When I check again, the middle one's blooming. I swear, it didn't even have buds before.

More landscape pictures adorn the walls inside, though while the ones outside are masterfully painted, these are more sketches, and yet, they encompass the same intensity, the same wildness. The graduation certificate hanging alongside them, awarded to Ilona Martínková more than twenty years ago, almost feels out of place, mundane as it is.

There are a lot of files and books in this office, too, more than downstairs, but whereas the books in the fake office were the standard tomes of youth education, not a single title here feels familiar. Instead, I see the word "element" pop up surprisingly often, almost as if I'm staring down an alchemy collection. Between the books are handwritten journals, and my fingers itch to pick one and explore its secrets.

It takes a lot of effort to settle my gaze on the headmistress. Ms Martínková watches patiently, a soft smile on her face. "Excuse me for being so vague earlier," she says from her chair. "I know you have a lot of questions. When I talked to your mother earlier, she seemed quite oblivious, which makes me wonder how much your father told her."

"My father?" I haven't seen my father since I was four years old. One day, he dropped me off at a friend's house and never returned to pick me up. He's been missing ever since, which is a fancy way of saying he abandoned us and left the country to evade child support payments.

Ms Martínková nods. "He and I were acquainted in our youth. We went to this very school together."

So much for being the first of my family here. I swallow as her careless words tear open the mixed bag of feelings about my father I keep closed most of the time. He left us with no warning or excuse. It made life so hard for my mother, and I can't help but think he left because of me, because it storms when I cry. And yet, I miss him dearly. When a rare memory of him floats to the top, it always leaves me with deep longing and the most painful of doubts: that he *didn't* leave because of me and instead was the only person who loved me for who I am. It's an annoying thought, because the chance it's true is practically non-existent, but the fantasy is too much to discard for good.

"Do you know where he is?" I ask, more confrontational than I probably should be.

The headmistress shakes her head. "He's been out of touch since... since about the time he went missing."

I can't do this. I can't sit here and listen to a fairy tale. My father is a lowlife who ran when the going got tough. I don't care if he was the Head Boy of Wyld Lands Academy or the captain of the Kendo team, he has no relevance to me and my life.

Ms Martínková watches me, nodding slightly as if she knows exactly how I'm feeling. "Let's talk about the wind, shall we?"

Once again, I swallow heavily. "The wind?" My heartbeat is as light as a butterfly's wing. She can't possibly mean what I think. Was there a mention of the wind in my report? Surely not. Everyone who's ever heard me talk about it thinks I'm crazy.

Please don't let this be a mental health talk.

"It comes when you summon it, doesn't it? A harbinger of destruction outside of your control."

I blink, stare, then swallow. "Are you saying...?" How do I word this without getting myself instantly expelled?

"It's magic," Ms Martínková says with a wistful smile, then laughs. "I know it sound outrageous, but that's what it is."

"Magic," I repeat, thinking maybe it's not me who's lost her mind.

She nods again. "Mhm. The wind comes when you summon it because you're an air mage. And because I can see you're about to run out of my office, relax. Everyone here can control one or two elements. Mine is fire."

To demonstrate her point before I actually do run away, she splays her fingers, summoning a flicker of flames that mirrors those swirling in the glass sphere on her desk. The dance on her fingertips is mesmerising. If it's a party trick, it's the best I've seen.

"Everyone is a mage?" I find myself saying, shocked how little keeps me from accepting this outrageous claim. "Jin...?"

"Oh, Jin is one of our most talented students. He's a rare dual mage, controlling both air and water magic. You'll see a lot of him when you join the air class."

"He mentioned that." I don't know why I'm even engaging with this ridiculousness. Perhaps because it's the first time someone's offered an explanation instead of brushing me off as wilful and a chronic liar. Or because there's little else that could explain how the wind responds to my anguish, always making a bad day worse. "So, this school…"

Ms Martínková nods. "This school teaches elemental magic in addition to the regular curriculum. Besides Maths, English, Physics, and all that, you'll learn about Elemental History, its different applications, and most importantly, how to control your element."

The sudden burst of hope I feel makes my voice quiver. "There's a way to control it?" Why did no one tell me that before?

"Yes." A crease appears between her eyebrows. "Milena, I'm going to be honest with you: you've shown vast potential, both before coming here and during the elementary test with Grisha. It's absolutely vital you learn how to control your power."

Her intensity really drives the words home. She makes it sound as if we're talking about life and death. And maybe we are when I think back to what happened in the lab before Christmas. Or just earlier today with Grisha.

Ms Martínková reaches for my hand across the table. "I'm sorry it took us so long to find you. I would've brought you here earlier if I'd known."

"Because I'm a danger to people around me." Speaking the words feels like I'm forced to swallow poison. *A troublemaker. Violent tendencies. An absolute menace. Freak.*

"Would it help if you knew you're not the only one?" Ms Martínková asks kindly. There's a glint in her eye that makes me believe we have something in common. It's a disconcerting thought. What could I have in common with a beautiful successful woman who could be my mother?

Her throat bops, a tiny hint she also needs to gather her courage. "When I was your age, my fire was frequently out of control. As I'm sure you can imagine, it was a bit of a disaster. Several people were hurt because of me—a boy was burnt so badly, he needed a skin transplant."

I swallow. Memories press against my conscience, almost spilling over into my awareness. "It was an accident, right?" My voice is hardly more than a whisper.

She nods. "Oh, yes, very much so. My emotions got the better of me and a minute later, there'd be a fire. My school back then still holds the record for most call-outs to the fire brigade in a year." While she tries to make light of it, the pain still colours her voice. I know it so well. "It wasn't until I came here and learned how to control my element, and most importantly"—she locks me down with a stare—"my *feelings*, that I found peace. This school can help you, too. I really hope it does."

Forget about the fact there's magic in the world and how ludicrous the thought is. If this school can help me get my outbursts under control, I won't let it get away from me. This first glance of hope steadies me. "My father was the same?"

"Oh, yes. He produced glorious storms." There's a twinkle in her eye. "Gave new meaning to '*storming* off'."

I laugh at the image. That he's not the monster of my mother's laments or the saint of my wishful thinking but a moody teenager just like me makes him seem a little bit more real.

"What about Jin?" Apparently, I'm obsessed with him.

Ms Martínková's face falls. "I can't tell you about other students' struggles. Teacher-student confidentiality, you know?"

I nod. This means she'll keep my secrets as well. It's probably not a good idea to go around asking for other people's traumas, anyway. If anything, Jin's success has shown me this is possible: I can truly learn how to harness my wind.

"So, what happens after school? I mean, is this the only one? How many people are elemental... mages, was it?"

"In terms of global population, only a handful. There are a few other schools like ours, but ours is the best."

"Of course."

The headmistress chuckles, and I feel an unfamiliar warmth spread in my chest. It feels so nice to have a grown-up relate to you instead of judging. "Well, most of our students are from wider Europe, but we get a high proportion from other continents as well. As for what life looks like after school, that's a conversation for another time, maybe next year when you've grasped the basics and had enough Elemental History lessons to understand our peculiar trials."

It seems like a loaded answer and I'm suddenly very keen to start Elemental History. I mean how cool does that sound? Not a boring reiteration of this war and that war with the occasional world-changing invention thrown in, but a history that reads more like a fantasy novel? It seems like it'd be much less of a chore.

"There are structures hidden in the fabric of the world that allow our alumni to use their powers for the better. If you're interested, you might want to talk to your fellow students. Find out what their parents do and what they plan to do later in life. You could start with Jin." The suggestion is followed up by a delightful giggle.

And I'm grinning. *Grinning.* What's happening here? Is this what acceptance feels like? If so, I'm hooked.

"Now, if you don't have any immediate questions, you should head to your dorm room and unpack."

My head is *full* of questions, and while they all feel urgent, I know better. Most of them will probably answer themselves on their own once I've spent a little time here.

The headmistress hands me a folder which contains a key to my dorm room, as well as the number and a plan of the school. A curious peek at the other papers shows me my schedule. My heart leaps when I see Elemental History, Air Weaving, and Elemental Defence classes among the usual subjects. There's even a spot for Nature Meditation on there.

I head towards the door, excitement bubbling in me so much my limbs feel impossibly light, and I can't stop grinning at the information pack. Just as I'm about to open the door, Ms Martínková calls out one last time. "Oh, Milena."

"Yes?"

She smiles warmly. "My door is always open for you, okay? This is a safe space for you and your peers."

I'm feeling so fuzzy my cheeks flush. "Thank you, Ms Martínková."

My head full of crazy ideas and hopes, I bounce out of the office, for once ready to take on the world.

6

One thing I'm very curious to find out as I cross the courtyard to the dorms is what's truly behind that building in the back. Checking my new plan, the answer is both intriguing and ominous: *Wyld Lands Portal.*

There's a freaking portal in the building? How cool is that? No wonder they named the school after it. If only I knew *what* the Wyld Lands were.

I throw a glance at it, confirming the door is very much under lock and key. Access is obviously restricted, whether permanently and forever or only for certain people—like students.

Speaking of students, I must've been focusing too much on Jin before to notice anything. Now I know what to look for, I see the elements in action. A group of students have planted themselves on either side of the long fountain, pushing a boat back and forth between them. The group on the side closer to the entry are air mages using the wind to move the boat across, while the group at the far end are doing weird things to the water.

As I watch, a wave grabs the boat, *literally*, and pulls it underwater before carrying it to the end. Instantly, there are crude jeers and swearing from the air side who can't do anything to stop the advance. Calls of cheating arise. The water mages respond likewise, taunting the others for not having a more nuanced approach.

I laugh at the good nature that permeates this rivalry. The laughter sticks in my throat when someone calls for Jin.

I hadn't noticed him before, but now I'm hyper-aware of his presence. He's with the stick fighters, but more importantly, he's changed out of his uniform and into an equally well-fitting black uniform that leaves his arms bare from his shoulders. Sweat glistens on his skin despite the cold air as he turns his head. "What?"

His current opponent sees his chance. Alarmed, I take a step closer, opening my mouth to yell at him to watch out, but before I can, Jin spins around with surprising agility. I can't even look fast enough to make out his movements. All I see are the bulging muscles of his upper arms and the way his staff connects with his opponent's, until he's pushed the poor guy against the fountain.

From behind, a wave rises and seizes the hapless fighter around the waist. A second later, he's dragged into the water to the cheers of the assembled water group.

I'm in awe of this display of water magic. The wave almost looked like a giant hand. What impresses me even more is Jin's display of camaraderie. Instead of basking in the glow of his adoring followers, he reaches out to the fallen student and pulls him from the fountain, then a wind rises and blows his opponent dry.

Ms Martínková told me he was a rare dual mage but seeing it in action is definitely something else, especially seeing how he calls the wind and manages to harness it so perfectly it doesn't even upset the water leaves me speechless.

This is what it might look like if I succeed here.

Jin claps his opponent's shoulder and appears to be laughing. Suddenly, his gaze meets mine. At first his face freezes, but then he gifts me with one of his beautiful smiles, and I blush. His attention is quickly diverted by others in the courtyard, and I seize the chance to hurry across the last stretch.

The doors to the dormitories are closed to keep the warm air inside, and I sigh when the warmth hits me like a soft wall. It takes a moment to orient myself. There are a couple of common spaces where students hang out that I need to navigate before I find the right staircase leading to the first floor—on the left, just as Jin has predicted.

The corridor is covered in a soft carpet that makes this section of the school much cosier than the rest. The room I'm in is a quick find, my luggage dutifully delivered to the door. Curious, I locate my key and open the door.

The first thing I notice is there are two beds, one on each side of the room. I've got a roommate. And whoever it is has made themselves home everywhere. Their clothes cover both beds, despite the cupboards assigned to both sides. There are two desks, one for each of us, but my chair has been moved to the other side of the room, and a box blocks half of the table.

Obviously, no one's told them yet about my arrival and subsequent need for space. I don't worry about it. We can sort it as soon as they return. Instead, I focus on the overall feel of the room. To my great delight, a row of potted plants fills most of the window space. Beside the bed and workspace assigned to either of us, there's a couch and a bookshelf, half of which is taken up by a surprisingly well-sorted rock collection. I suppose that means my roommate is an earth mage.

I carry my luggage inside and leave it next to my bed until I've made a decision about what to retrieve and what to leave until there's a bit more space. I open the window which looks out over the park surrounding the school. Below, I can see students playing in the snow, forming snowballs and having a play fight. The stakes are heightened when a fire mage makes the missiles melt just before they hit their target.

Since it's too cold, I close the window again. My gaze falls on the selection of pictures displayed on my roommate's desk. Turns out she's a girl about my age with long brown hair that's braided a bit matronly in at least half the pictures. There's one with each of her parents; the one with her mother tells me she's going for a mini-me look with that hair style. I don't know how old these pictures are, but she truly is miniature sized, though the confidence on her face gives her a massive boost. Her features are a bit edgier than most girls would prefer, but she carries them proudly.

From the looks of it, she has two supportive parents, which makes me a bit envious. And friends. Loads of them.

My heart skips a beat when I recognise one of them. Jin.

I reach for the picture to take a closer look. He looks a bit younger here, maybe fifteen or sixteen. He and the brown-haired girl are standing in front of the Grand Canyon, one arm around each other and the other stretched to the side, grinning widely as the wind whips their hair around.

"What are you doing there?" A harsh voice calls out from the door.

Startled, I turn around. The girl from the pictures is standing in the doorway, though in reality, she looks a lot sharper than in her pictures. Her square chin and small size—she's almost a head smaller than I am—makes her look like a pit bull. And judging by the tone of her voice and icy stare, she's going to act like it.

"That's *mine.*"

"Sorry." It takes me a moment longer to realise she expects me to put the picture back on the desk. "I was just drawn in by Jin. I've met—"

"Of course you were." There's something condescending in her voice that brings back a barrage of ugly feelings.

Unless I manage to turn this around quickly, we won't be friends. I step away from the desk and smile at her. "I'm Milena, your new roommate."

The girl crosses her arms over her chest and raises an eyebrow. Her gaze sweeps over my body, from the tips of my purple hair to my ripped tights to my dirt-covered boots. "No, you're not."

We are *not* going to be friends.

"I don't share," she declares haughtily.

"Uhm, yes, you do." If I can't win them over with kindness, attack becomes my second nature.

Her eyes narrow. "Says who?"

I stare at her coldly. "Do you want to see the official assignment? No problem. I have everything right here."

As I open my folder to take out the sheet of paper with the room information, she marches over and snatches the whole thing from me. One look at it and her nostrils flare. "I'll lodge a complaint and see that it's rectified."

"Okay, Princess."

"What did you just say?" I didn't think it was possible, but her voice has managed to drop a few more degrees.

Pointedly, I take the folder back. "That you'd better get used to sharing your room, because I'm not going anywhere."

Her face distorts and then she starts laughing. It's an ugly sound that grates on my skin. "You think you stand a chance in here? That is the most hilarious thing I've heard in a long time."

"Is that so?" I ask in an unaffected voice, not particularly interested in her act.

"You obviously come from nothing." She spares another glance at my clothes. "A feral mage they found in the wild. Let me guess, you've only just found out about magic."

Since she's bang on the money, I keep my mouth shut tight.

A disgusting show of pity softens her face for a moment. "That's what I thought. This must be so exciting for you." The fake sweetness gives way almost instantly. "Well, here's the truth: this is an elite school, and you're nothing but a freak of nature who has no business studying here. You can try of course, but you'll never keep up with us legacy students."

"You and...?" Right now, she's just one single mean girl. I can't *wait* to meet her stupid posse.

She smiles smugly. "Me and Jin. I hope you didn't get your hopes up or anything—every stupid girl does. I've known him all his life, and we were already playing with magic while you were still struggling with wooden blocks."

So many insults in so little words. She's an expert at this. Unfortunately, I'm an expert at being the target of insults. To be fair, the ones about my magic prowess are new. I hadn't had enough time yet to worry about how demanding the lessons might be, but apart from that, I've heard this kind of speech countless times before. It doesn't surprise me Jin grew up in a magic-filled household, but I truly hope she's overestimated her pull on him, because he doesn't seem like the kind of guy who'd hang out with the likes of her. Then again, I hardly know him.

"Great, then maybe you could use your magic to move your crap off my bed."

"Are you dumb? I'm an earth mage. My magic doesn't work like that. It's more like this." She stomps her foot.

A sudden tremor beneath my feet makes me jump. I try to keep my balance but end up on my ass instead. Outraged, I look up at the other girl. The window clatters in its frame, and it takes me moment to realise it's not due to this very localised earthquake but because the wind is begging to be let in. A slight breeze inside makes the curtains rustle. If this earth mage thinks I'm going to back down, she's got another thing coming.

No! I can't allow this to happen. I need to shut the wind out again. Calm. Settle. It takes so much from me, my whole body shivers, but I manage to push the anger back down and the curtains settle.

The worst thing is seeing how satisfied she looks. She knows she's won this round, even if she has no idea how close she came to getting seriously hurt. Her earthquake was a surprise, but it had nothing on the raw power of the storm inside of me.

"On the floor, in the dirt," she says smugly, "where you belong." Then she steps over my legs and picks up her clothes from my bed and dumps them on hers. "If I catch you touching my stuff again, I'll bury you six feet deep."

The storm rages in my head, but I force it down. I won't let her take this from me. This might be the only school where I could ever be me, and I'll fight tooth and nail for my place, even if it means I have to suffer through her bullshit for the rest of the school year.

7

I'm the plucked paradise bird in a crowd of stylish grey geese. When I make my way to the dining hall later this evening, everyone stares. Some dismiss me instantly, others start whispering to their friends as I pass by. When they're not busy judging me for my appearance, I hear laughter and excited chatter. There's a lot of magic happening over dinner: a group of fire mages barbecue their meat right there at the table, while two water mages throw a ball of water back and forth. One loses control, and the water splashes over the head of a girl, who jumps up screaming. A handful of earth hits the perpetrator in the face, throwing him off-balance. Satisfied, she sits again and dabs her face dry with a napkin.

At the other end of the line to get food, I spot Jin. As before, he's surrounded by a group of friends, laughing at something. I see Grisha in the crowd, keeping to the edge of it, but not my roommate. It comforts me a little that her supposed friendship with Jin won't be constantly in my face.

Unfortunately, their big group is a little too intimidating for me. They're all older and taller than me and joining them feels too much like intruding. We're not friends. Jin only guided me because it was his job, nothing more.

He doesn't notice me in the line, and soon the group breaks away to occupy a couple of tables in the middle of the room. I stave off the sudden bout of loneliness and distract myself by looking at the food.

Apparently, it's a free for all, a bit like the conference catering my mother gets sometimes. There are a few options of hot dishes in deep aluminium trays, salad with a bunch of toppings and dressings to choose from, fruit and cups filled with pudding, yogurt, and jelly.

I pick some bread-filled dumplings and pour meat sauce on top, enough to soak each bite in later. The salad options are a bit overwhelming as I want to try all of them, but I figure there'll be a similar offering tomorrow. Lastly, I pick a green jelly cup.

Then it's time to decide where to sit. The tables are all big enough for six to eight people. Unfortunately, none are unoccupied. The few people who meet my gaze make it quite clear that there's no space for a newcomer at their table. I wander around for quite a bit before I find a table with a single girl with shoulder-length ash-blond hair, reading a book while absentmindedly picking at her food. The only personal adjustment to her uniform is a necklace made up of painted wooden pearls.

"May I sit here?" I ask, as meekly as I can.

The girl looks as if I've asked her to strip naked in front of everyone, her watery blue eyes are that big. But then she nods hastily and gives me a shy smile. "Of course."

I make sure to answer her smile with one of my own. "Thank you." With a chair between us, I take a seat. "I'm Milena, by the way. As you can probably guess, I'm new."

"Ester," she whispers, then clears her throat. "Are you a transfer?"

"Yes. Though I came from a normal school. Without magic and all that."

She glances at her book, clearly contemplating whether she's done enough to appear sociable or not.

To keep her attention, I ask, "What are you reading?"

"Book three of the Spirit Seeker series," Ester says with another smile. "It's a really fun story about nature spirits, not too different from what we have to deal with." She sighs longingly. "I wish our nature spirits were as friendly as these ones, though."

"There are nature spirits?" I thought it was us who were the magical ones here.

Ester sways her head back and forth. "We call them elemental beings, and they're not native to our world. But from time to time, one escapes from the Wyld Lands, and then it's usually a big disaster. Unless the guardians capture and return them before the shit hits the fan."

My jaw must've fallen open, because Ester giggles adorably. "Sorry, I didn't want to scare you."

"No, no, keep talking," I assure. "I find all of this highly fascinating. Does it happen often?" I think of the building in the courtyard, the portal to the Wyld Lands. It must be where those elemental beings come from. No wonder it's locked.

"I don't actually know, but I suppose so, because there's a lot of guardians. We're all trained in the basics, but if you're serious about joining them, you can sign up for extra training."

It must be one of the jobs available once I graduate. I have to admit, it sounds much more interesting than the options I previously had. It definitely beats the odd jobs I'll have access to if I don't make it through school.

I glance around the assembled students. "So, who's going to join the fight?"

"Jin Čermák, obviously," Ester says, with a nod to the popular kids' table. "He's going to follow in his father's footsteps to keep his legacy alive."

"Legacy?"

"His father was Alexej Čermák, one of the most notorious guardians. He became the captain of the guardians at only twenty-four and made hundreds of captures before his untimely death about ten... no, twelve years ago."

"Did the elemental beings kill him?" If it's that dangerous, being a guardian might not be my new dream job.

Ester leans over to whisper the next piece of gossip. "He was murdered by a witch."

"What's a witch?"

"A magic user with an unnatural connection to the Wyld Lands. They're said to commune with the elemental beings." Ester smiles suddenly and picks up her book to show me the cover. "Kind of like Rika here, although she's not a crazy magic addict like our witches."

I like Rika's hair and decide to check out the books myself sometime. Anyone with turquoise hair deserves my attention.

"So, witches are addicted to magic?" All of this is very confusing, but if I can get my head around it, there's less of a chance I'll embarrass myself in front of someone else. Like my roommate.

"I think so. They use way too much and can't control themselves," Ester explains, her nose wrinkling with distaste. "They're a hundred times more dangerous than an elemental."

"I see." A witch murdered Jin's father and now he's supposed to follow in his footsteps. I don't know if I find that brave or incredibly stupid. Maybe a bit of both.

As I look over yet again at his table, I see my roommate approaching him. To my annoyance, she hadn't lied about knowing him.

"Can you tell me more about the girl talking to him now? She's my new roommate and not a fan of the arrangement." The more I know about her, the better I'll be able to defend myself against her barbs.

Ester's eyes widen. "Oh, dear. That's unlucky. She's Pavlína Sokolová, the daughter of the current captain of the guardians. Her mother was Alexej's second-in-command, though she's a bit older than him."

That explains why she and Jin grew up together. I try to recall the picture of her mother and remember how much Pavlína looked like a mini-me. I suppose she's another prospective guardian.

"You must be an air mage, then," Ester guesses correctly. "They always try to put opposing elements together. It helps us with balancing. I'm a water mage."

I regard the explanation with a frown. "Is that safe? Putting two opposing elements together?"

"Like I said, it's to balance us out. It actually keeps us safer that way. The rules are a bit more lax in the upper classes once you've passed the first few tests."

While I can at least hope I won't be stuck with Pavlína for the rest of my time at this school, it still strikes me as counter-intuitive. "I meant safe in terms of personalities. She already hates my guts."

"That's just Pavlína for you. They let her have her own room because there weren't enough air mages and she's already quite advanced in her control." Ester smiles, slightly amused. "But there's no such thing as elemental personalities. I've got a fire mage roommate, and they're the most chilled-out person I know."

When she puts it like that, Pavlína doesn't really strike me as what I would've assumed a typical earth person would be like, and I guess I don't necessarily qualify as an air person either. Not when I fly off the handle so easily.

I laugh nervously. "Sorry, I'm just trying to make sense of everything."

"Oh, you will soon. It took me a couple of weeks as well. When I started—" Ester suddenly freezes. The smile slips off her face.

Confused, I glance around until I find Pavlína. Her attention is on our table and she's glaring at Ester.

"Excuse me," Ester mumbles. She grabs her book and her tray.

"Wait." What kind of shit is that? One mean look from Pavlína, and my new acquaintance has to run?

Ester regards me absolutely horrified. "I can't. Sorry, Milena, but I'd rather not be seen with you." She scurries off before I can change her mind.

Great. I wonder if Ms Martínková thought about that when she put me up with Pavlína. Of course, I won't immediately run to her—open door policy or not. This is a battle I have to fight on my own if I ever want to find a foothold.

To make matters worse, my food has gone cold. There was too much exciting stuff to be learnt to remember eating. That won't be much of a problem going forward, seeing as Pavlína will keep me isolated for the foreseeable future.

The dumpling seems to expand in my mouth and I only manage to get down half of it, leaving the second completely untouched. Instead, I devour the salad, before poking at my jelly until it's turned into a complete mush, the only way to properly eat it.

The entire time I sit there, not a single person dares approach me. The frustration comes in waves. I'm fine with it one minute, then struggling with tears the next.

This is *fine*, nothing new to me, though it seems particularly malicious this time around. But I want it to be *different* for once. My previous attempts at socialising have all fallen to pieces because of my air magic. It was too different, too scary and weird. Now, I'm surrounded by people who are like me. And here I am, still the one eating alone. I'm starting to hate Pavlína with a passion. How dare she ruin this for me? What did I ever do to her?

The familiar knot in my stomach returns, and I need to breathe through my nose before I start a storm in the middle of the dining hall. I have to keep this wind in until I've learnt how to control it. I don't want to be expelled from this world, especially not over yet another bully.

When I've calmed enough to trust my legs, I return my tray to the kitchen. By the time I turn around, my table's been snatched up. Ridiculous.

I decide I've had quite enough of people for one day and walk back to the dormitories before Pavlína can get there. If I'm lucky, I can pretend to be asleep and avoid round two. For today, at least.

When I return to the room, my school uniform's been delivered. I know it won't help much, but at least, I'll stick out a bit less tomorrow. I sigh, blinking away tears. Who am I kidding? Even if I look exactly like everyone else, I won't fit in. It's incredibly hard to get accepted into an already-existing community, and everyone here's had at least a few months together, if they don't already know each other through their illustrious parents.

I'm suddenly terribly homesick for my mum. I want to call her and tell her to pick me up. I know it's ridiculous, and my head plays out how that conversation would go: *you have to put in some effort. Give these people a chance. You might be surprised by them.*

Too bad everyone else's mothers haven't seemed to dish out the same useless advice, because nobody's been giving me a chance. Apart from Ms Martínková. Is it too early to use her open-door offer? I shudder at the thought. Definitely too early.

In the end, I don't call my mother, and I don't run to the headmistress, either. Instead, I get into bed by eight thirty and blast music directly into my ears. As I curl up on my side, I hug tight the tattered flying squirrel toy I've had since I was a little girl and swear to myself that I'll turn this around starting tomorrow, before feeling endlessly sorry for myself.

8

In my dreams, I'm back in the mountains, but these are much higher than the ones I grew up in. Their jagged peaks tower over me, poking holes in the incoming cloud cover. The wind increases. It blasts through the valley, wiping all the tears away.

Not that I'm crying. I might've been in whatever dream came first, but within a minute of being exposed to the elements, the previous dream has been wiped clear from my conscience. Instead, my heart rejoices.

One thought and I'm on top of a rim, looking down on the valley. The wind is even stronger here, tugging and tearing at my clothes, my hair, and even my limbs. I lean into it, marvelling at how it holds me. Without its strength, I'd be tumbling down this hill, my body battered by the rocky outcrops and gravel chutes.

Instead, I get an even better view of the valley, which now holds a raging river that cuts into the mountain as I stand and watch. On the other side, the peaks disappear into thick grey clouds. Lightning dances around me in a mesmerising display of primal power.

I feel the electric tension in the roots of the hair on my arms and head. There's danger in the air. And I laugh.

My laughter echoes through the valley, bouncing off the shimmering rock faces as the wind whips into a frenzy. Lightning strikes below and fire bursts from a grove of trees. They're quickly consumed in the roaring flames. A few minutes later, torrential rain pours down.

The crack of thunder rattles my bones and I shake in my boots with exhilaration. Then the storm is upon me, and I know I shouldn't be standing here on this ledge, an easy target for the lightning, yet I don't move, eagerly awaiting the strike that'll set my veins on fire.

The rain quickly soaks my clothes and a shiver runs down my spine. The wind glues the wet clothes to my skin. The next clap of thunder splits neatly above me. I think I've gone deaf. But no, there's a roar. The storm is nearing its peak. And then a gust lifts me up and throws me off the cliff. Only instead of falling, I'm flying. I float through the air, one with the wind and the turmoil around me.

Something hard hits my cheek as I collide with a rock face. But there's no rock face. I'm way too high for the earth to reclaim my body. Until the wind loses its grip, and I fall.

Gasping, I shoot up in my bed. There's not enough air in the room to fill my lungs, and for a moment, I panic. All the glorious air has gone. My body feels heavy and I still can't breathe. What's going on?

I blink and see Pavlína kneeling next to my bed. She has her hand raised, watching me anxiously. "What are you doing?" she asks, struggling to sound as annoyed as she wants to.

"I can't..." My lungs seize up, and I finally realise what this is. "Inhaler. I... Please."

Pavlína wastes no time rummaging through my bag, finding the inhaler I always carry around with me. She hands it to me, and I rip it out of her hands, eagerly breathing in two puffs. For a few more minutes, my lungs struggle. They don't come right completely, but I'm not about to drop dead.

I've never had an asthma attack so severe. My asthma is annoying at best, a chronic condition that leaves me breathless and wheezing when I do anything strenuous. It kept me from competing in the annual athletic competitions, but mostly because it provided an easy excuse, not because I was truly unable to. I did hike a lot in the mountains, after all.

But this was different. For a few moments, I truly couldn't breathe. It also felt much longer than it probably was, and it was likely I *had* been able to breathe after all, but it hadn't felt sufficient. The memory of it makes me feel claustrophobic in my own body. Gone is the light-weight freedom I tasted in her dreams.

"You're done with the drama?"

I almost forgot about Pavlína. Her momentary kindness in not letting me die has reached its limit. Her voice is as sharp as ever and she glares.

"Drama?" I whisper, still wheezing.

"Well, you went totally ballistic," she launches into a tirade. "Look what you've done to the room."

I hadn't had time to take in my surroundings yet. When I do, my heart sinks. The dream. I'd called the wind in my dreams, and it brought as much destruction as always. Paper and stones litter the room. The chairs have been knocked over. One is broken into pieces, the other crashed into Pavlína's bed. Her collection of photos have been smashed, and I've uprooted at least three plants, soil scattered from the windowsill to the middle of the room.

I feel like I'm going to be sick. I wish I could say this has never happened before, but it's not even remotely true. I've absolutely wreaked this much destruction and more before.

"I was asleep," I mutter meekly.

Pavlína scoffs. "Which only shows how pitiful your control is." She huffs and shakes her head. "You'll never make it as a mage."

It's hard for me not to believe her at this point. "I'm sorry."

"I don't care." She picks up a stone, some kind of transparent crystal, and purses her lips when she notices it's chipped. "I hope you're not as poor as you look, because I want everything tidied up and replaced."

In order to pay for anything, I'll need to tell my mother. It sounds like Pavlína won't report me, so I might not be expelled before I start classes, but she'll still be disappointed. I promised her to be better.

"Okay," I whisper meekly.

Pavlína rolls her eyes at me. "This is exactly why I don't want to room with an air head."

"I thought you were best friends with one."

She laughs haughtily. "Are you trying to compare yourself with Jin? He's never lost his shit like this. In fact, he's a top student and has masterful control. You'll never be like him. Now, chop, chop. They do inspections on Thursdays. You have about two hours before they come in."

Obviously, she's not going to help, and why would she? I'm the one who's turned this room into a battlefield. I'm as dangerous and unpredictable as ever. The devil child. I've never hated the wind more than this moment.

9

Cleaning up the room took so long I almost miss breakfast. I quickly grab a leftover croissant and an apple before racing to the main complex where the classes are. My Thursday starts with Elemental History, followed by English and then Physics, but I have no idea how to get there. I thought it'd be straightforward, that 206 means it's on the second floor, yet when I go up the stairs, it somehow only leads to the first floor.

Soon, I'm completely lost. How do you get to the second floor? Does it even exist? Am I even in the right building?

I'd ask someone, but the few students I see are quickly hurrying to their classes, vanishing behind doors like bees in their hive. A bell rings, telling me I'm officially late. What a wonderful, fantastic day it's been so far.

For five more minutes, I go back and forth along the corridor before I decide to run back down the stairs, intent on asking the secretary for directions. But naturally, when I need it, the cubicle is empty.

I eye the big stairs and remember they definitely had another staircase leading higher, yesterday. And there it is, the coveted second floor. It takes me another precious minute to figure out which direction the classroom lies since the numbers somehow fall in both directions. But it's the even numbers I need, so I turn left.

Like in the corridor with the headmistress' office, the walls are hung with portraits from what I assume are the Wyld Lands. I come across one that looks vaguely familiar: a storm over a mountain valley. Instantly, I'm transported back into my dream. The painting is so vivid I can feel the wind tugging on my hair. I must've been transported there after seeing the pictures yesterday, and I'm suddenly filled with a distant longing for that portal in the courtyard.

But then reality crashes in, and I realise I'm very late now. Fortunately, the elusive room is close. There's no window in the door to see what's going on inside. For a moment, I contemplate skipping class, but then shake my head. Regardless of how it'll look to my new teachers, I'm not going to miss *Elemental* History.

Meekly, I open the door, which is located close to the teacher's desk in the front, which means everyone notices me straightaway. I recognise Pavlína in the first row, looking as smug as ever.

The teacher is an older white man with tufts of greyish hair above his ears and long horizontal creases across his forehead. His grey-blue eyes look at me with instant disapproval. "You must be Ms Šimková. Nice of you to join us."

There's the predictable giggle to such a public reproach.

"I got lost on the way." Surely, he can cut me some slack here.

"Next time you should take more time to familiarise yourself with your surroundings."

Sarcasm burns my tongue, but I manage to keep it down. There's not even the slightest breeze in the room, and I'm damn proud of that.

"I'm Mr Reisz. Now, don't stand there. Go find a seat." He hurries me along and picks up the thread I interrupted.

On the screen at the front is a painting of a medieval town in flames. It's vaguely familiar, but I can't put my finger on it. The only empty seat is in the back on the wall side. My heart longs for the window, but that's probably not a good idea after this morning's disaster. Everyone around me is furiously writing or taking notes with a tablet. They all have the same book open, so I guess it was issued for this class. I only have a tattered college pad and no idea where to start. It takes me about five minutes to realise we're talking about the Great Fire of London in 1666, even longer to understand it was started by an elemental being that'd escaped the Wyld Lands, or rather, a small group of them.

It turns out Elemental History isn't nearly as exciting as I thought it'd be. It's still events and boring facts, such as the breakdown of minutiae and actions against the outbreak and where human intervention failed. The obvious questions like, 'Was everyone aware of the elemental beings?' or 'How did they get to London?' aren't answered, either because I missed them in the ten minutes I took to find the room or because everyone knows the answer.

I take notes occasionally, but because I was thrown into it without any context, it's damn hard to tell what's truly relevant and what isn't. I'm still struggling with breathing freely this morning, and so my attention wanders to my dream. Instead of notes, pictures of mountain ranges appear on my notepad. Beautiful high mountains battered with wind.

"...until the follow-up investigations revealed a human hand in the fire elemental's arrival. Martha and Prudence Carrigan, two notorious fire witches were later proven to have aided the fire's progress after multiple records turned up of the two women dancing gleefully in the ashes."

The words drag me out of my trance. Suddenly, I'm wide awake. I can get on board with elemental beings escaping into our world from some mysterious primordial dimension, but those witches are a different manner. Did they really start such a devastating fire and *enjoyed* it?

Apparently so, because Mr Reisz starts to detail the biographies of the two sisters, which include several proven and unproven charges of arson. Apparently, the Great Fire of London was their masterpiece, an act of terror that sent both to the executioner's block, or rather, the executioner's lake. Martha and Prudence were both hung with a stone, then drowned. No fire for these two witches.

The lesson comes to a close and Mr Reisz announces homework for next week. "I want each of you to write a 1,000-word essay on a similar witch act of terror between 1550 and 1850. I expect a detailed analysis into their motivations and how their acts changed the course of history at their time. If you don't know where to start, I'd suggest *A History of Elemental Witchcraft* in the library."

Hopefully, not everyone needs the book, because I have no idea which historical catastrophes were freak weather events and which were caused by witches.

The students rise at the sound of the bell and make their way out of the room. When I try to follow, Mr Reisz holds me back. The last students glance at me but decide I'm not interesting enough to linger.

Mr Reisz opens a cupboard on the side and takes out a book: *'Part One of Elemental History Year 11 — Origin of Elemental Beings and Notable Appearances throughout Human History'*. "We're almost through with this one, so I expect you to read up on what you missed.

We have midterms in three and a half weeks, and I expect you to at least try and pass. Since I understand you're starting with little to no knowledge about elemental beings, I'll keep you exempt from other homework for two weeks. After that I expect you to have caught up."

Two weeks to catch up on nearly four months of lessons, and just a week later, I'll have to sit an important exam that might decide my future here. "O-okay."

"You've chosen a bad time to join this school," he says, as if I had any choice. "Now where do you have to go next?" He nods towards my schedule, a lot kinder than in his initial moments.

"Physics. Which is apparently in 233."

"That's in the side tract. Go down the stairs and down the left corridor. There's a connecting stairwell at the end of it, before the gym."

I can't help but comment, "That sounds overly complicated."

His bushy eyebrows crawl up disapprovingly. "It's an old building, Ms Šimková. You'd better get going if you don't want to be late again."

Uh-oh, never question old buildings in front of the history teacher.

I thank him, stuff the book into my backpack, and hurry out. Hopefully, my streak of bad luck will end now. But who am I kidding? I'm the poster child for bad luck.

10

Fortunately for me, the mundane subjects, as I've dubbed them, aren't as bad as the special ones. My education's been interrupted far too much, but I've managed to keep up with the standard curriculum. English is a lot like Czech, which isn't taught at this school, being all international and all. It's a shame, because I really enjoyed working on Czech writers and poets. My English on the other hand is only mediocre, but that seems to be a common problem, because the students truly come from all over the world. The teacher never utters a word in Czech, but he's patient with us.

Physics is the easiest class so far. The unit we're currently looking at, resistors and capacitors, is something we already covered at my previous school and that I'm confident in. That and electrical currents in general will be the main topic of the midterm, which means it's one subject I can neglect in my studies.

After Physics, it's another subject I'm quite familiar with: Chemistry. I can't help it. Just the thought of going into another lab after what happened last time scares the shit out of me. What if I destroy this one as well?

With an uneasy feeling, I enter the room that has been refurbished to hold a state-of-the-art chemistry lab. Instead of simple rows of benches with gas outlets for the Bunsen Burners, there are proper fume cupboards on every bench. There are even safety rules beyond 'maybe you should wear glasses for this one'—we all have to wear lab coats and glasses as well as closed shoes.

Part of me is excited about doing real chemistry instead of the same old boring experiments, but the bigger part of me is scared about how much it'll cost to replace everything when I inevitably destroy it.

Nervously, I shuffle into the back, where I'm delighted to see Ester again. As soon as she notices me, though, she puts her head down, using her hair to shield my view. It's a flimsy barrier and I decide to ignore it. "Hey there. Looks like we're sharing Chemistry."

Silence.

"Look about Pavlína—"

"Please don't talk to me," Ester says in a rushed but pointed whisper.

What kind of terror reign has Pavlína established here? I look around to find her among the same group of earth mages she's been running around with all day. Apart from one girl, who seems to be Pavlína's chosen lackey, the rest are all boys. Loud and boisterous, muscle-packed boys. They look more like her bodyguards than friends.

"Fine." I resign myself to being the loner I've always been. It would've been nice to have friends for once, especially after Ester and I struck up such an easy connection yesterday. I want to ask her more about the books she reads and maybe ask her for help with Elemental History, but if she doesn't want to dare Pavlína's ire, I can respect that.

"I love your hair." A very pointed statement for what's supposed to be a compliment.

I lean back to meet the eyes of another girl on Ester's other side. A cheeky smile greets me. Her own dark brown hair is braided with colourful strands of green and orange.

Ester looks up startled. "Jamila!"

"What?" Jamila asks, looking amused. "Are we really going to let some musky dirt slinger dictate who we talk to?"

Okay, sign me up for that friendship!

Ester, meanwhile, looks utterly horrified and hushes Jamila eagerly, throwing nervous glances at Pavlína, who's busy holding court at the front. "I don't want to get in trouble."

"Look, I understand that. You don't have to talk to me if you're afraid of Pavlína."

"Are you afraid of Pavlína?" Jamila asks, raising her eyebrow in a challenging way.

Ester's turning red. "She's intimidating."

"No. Fire is intimidating. Pavlína is all bark and no bite." Jamila shrugs. "We're already outsiders, what's the worst she can do?" She leans back around Ester again and offers me her hand. "Jamila Leviná, she/they, fire mage."

"You're Ester's roommate," I note, then take their hand. "Milena Šimková, she/her, and apparently, I'm an air mage."

"Figures." Jamila smiles as they shake my hand. "Anyone who can rile up Pavlína within a day is someone I can see myself hanging out with."

"I'm flattered," I say with a giddy laugh.

Unfortunately, the sound draws Pavlína's attention. Her nostrils flare as if she were a bull getting ready to charge. The way she sits amid her muscle-packed boyfriends, she looks like a queen. A queen who's used to getting what she wants. I understand now what Ester meant by "intimidating".

True to their word, Jamila pokes out their tongue. Outraged, Ester slaps their arm, but it's too late, Pavlína's already narrowing her eyes. Then she huffs, dismissing us with a flick of her head.

Ester lets out a sigh. "We're so screwed."

"As long as we're a 'we', we're going to be fine," Jamila says, totally relaxed.

Now I'm the one blushing. Could that be true? Could we become a "we"? I've never had friends, I've certainly never had friends who were willing to stick up for me in the face of my bullies.

"You in?" Jamila asks, a dangerous grin on their lips.

"Of course," I say, with only a hint of hesitation. I don't know if they're right about Pavlína. The earth queen might totally destroy us—especially me—but I'm willing to risk it if I get some friends in return.

With a smug smile, Jamila bumps my fist behind Ester's back. "Nice."

There's no time to deepen our acquaintance as the lesson begins. Chemistry is taught by a French woman, Madame Guerineau, whose accent shines heavily through her English. She's a delightful ball of energy, though, who's really excited about teaching. Once she's set us all on the course for a saponification experiment where we'll create our own soap, she walks through the room, answering initial questions, and slowly makes her way to me.

"Hey, Milena." She greets me with a smile. "Ms Martínková told me you enjoyed Chemistry in your previous school?"

"I did." At least until the day of my expulsion. I wonder if Madame Guerineau knows about that.

So far, she's still smiling. "That's wonderful. I always love it when I see girls passionate about science. Now listen, I'm not sure what exactly you've done so far, but why don't you come to my office after class and we'll check what you need going forward. I'll make a little list of all we've gone through and what to focus on for the midterms."

"Alright, sure."

"Okay. Good luck with the soap. Just put your hand up if you need anything." With a last smile, she leaves us to the experiment and hurries to a student with a question.

I check with Ester and Jamila. "She seems nice."

"Nice, yes, but also very, very strict," Ester says with a sigh. "Are you really good at Chemistry?" When I nod, she pushes the provided box with chemicals towards me. "Please. I've got two right hands when it comes to this stuff, and Jami is a bit... fire-happy."

Jamila snorts, her hands already around the beaker with olive oil and red crayon. Apparently, we're not going to use the supplied heat plate. "I know what I'm doing."

"Me too," I say to Ester and start measuring out the sodium hydroxide for the next bit of the experiment.

"Wonderful, I'll take notes for the report, then." Apparently, Ester has resigned herself to our decision of being friends.

Just then, someone knocks me in the back. A split second later, I hear glass burst on the floor and completely freeze. My breath catches in my throat as I wait to feel the liquid seep into my clothes. Sodium hydroxide is corrosive and can cause destruction of clothing, burns to the skin, and irreversible eye damage. I should know because—

"Can't you be a bit more careful?" Pavlína's bitchy voice sounds in my ear. "You don't have to destroy *everything*."

There's no sodium hydroxide corroding my pants. The beaker that broke was completely empty, sacrificed for a petty demonstration.

Pavlína sneers at Ester. "Figures you two klutzes would stick together. You deserve each other."

"Are you going to clean this up, Pavlína?" Madame Guerineau asks, but one of Pavlína's bodyguards is already on the ground.

A tremor goes through my bones, as I watch the shards twitch and pull together, neatly gathering on a dustpan. When he's finished, there's an extra jolt, just to make the three of us jump.

Jamila nearly spills hot oil across the boy's hands. "Careful there, earth diggers. You don't want me to spill hot oil over you, what with the three of us being such terrible klutzes."

Pavlína lets out a patronising snort. "Let's go, Mirko. We don't want to be here when it all blows up."

For the second time in a row, I freeze. Does *Pavlína* know?

"You okay?" Jamila asks once Pavlína has gone.

I nod shakily. She can't know. There's no way she'd have access to that kind of information, important mother or not. "Can anyone guess why she hates me so much?" I try to make my voice light and slightly sarcastic, as if all this doesn't matter to me.

But it does. I've had enough experience with bullies to know the only way to make them back off is to scare the living shit out of them. And by then, you've already lost.

"Honestly?" Ester asks. "I think she's just mad because she's got to share with... well, someone who isn't a legacy student she could buddy up with. If your parents aren't mages, too, you're a bit second class here." She sounds as if she's had some experience with it as well.

Jamila reaches over and puts their hand on Ester's arm. By the way Ester pulls away, I assume it's still a bit hot to the touch. "Sorry," Jamila says with a laugh, "but all that legacy crap is bullshit. It doesn't matter whether your parents were mages. A first-generation mage can be just as powerful if not more than those descended from an old elemental family. And some of the legacy students can be weak-ass."

Ester softens and reaches out. "You're good enough."

"Tell that to my parents and siblings," Jamila says with enough bitterness in their voice to make my heart go out to them. We obviously have something in common there, but I'm not ready to dive that deep just yet.

There's plenty of chance for this 'we' to break apart at the slightest amount of pressure, and I don't want to give that kind of ammunition to anybody. Not yet. Maybe never.

After class, I visit Madame Guerineau's office, where she gives me a quick quiz to determine where I stand before handing me a list of experiments and lessons completed so far, marking those that are especially important for the exam. She seems pretty happy with my showing, and so I leave her office with a bounce in my step.

Unfortunately, that bounce becomes a ball of nervous energy by the time lunch comes to an end. After the long break, I'm about to face my first air magic class. I've asked Ester and Jamila about what to expect and they've each ensured me I'll be fine. Elemental magic can be fickle sometimes, but everyone still struggles with control at our grade. And besides, I have a really good teacher. I'm going to see Jin again, and that only adds to my nervousness. What if I totally embarrass myself in front of him? He's supposed to be this super talented air—and water—prodigy. I've already seen him in action, and what I've seen was incredibly impressive. I bet he didn't struggle with his magic when he started out.

Slowly, I make my way to the outside arena reserved for air students. Near the fountain, the water students are gathering. From Jamila, I know the earth and fire students have arena-like facilities for training, which is good news, since that means I don't have to worry about Pavlína interfering.

My heart misses a beat when I see Jin again. Like before, he's exchanged his uniform for a sleek black training shirt. He stands next to the air teacher, both striking formidable figures against the cloudy afternoon sky.

This is a double period taught for all grades at Wyld Lands Academy. The teacher, Mr Vávra, divides us into year groups before taking over the older two, leaving Jin to deal with our anxious group. My stomach flutters when he gives me a smile of recognition.

Like everyone else, we start with a warm-up that includes a lot of breathing techniques. I follow the others, trying to concentrate on the flow of air through my body just as Jin describes. My lungs are still a bit sketchy from my earlier asthma attack, but I feel the exercise opening them up. My wheezing is almost undetectable now. Annoyingly, it's exactly what my doctor's always recommended but which I never had enough discipline to develop into a habit.

Once we finish the warm-up, Jin pairs us off. "We're going to start with a simple push exercise. Concentrate on the wind in your hair and the breath in your lungs, then push that air towards your partner. Let's see who can push the hardest."

Two guys are eagerly calling upon the wind to try and push not just the air but the other person away, too. I'm paired up with an Italian boy called Lucio. He's fairly short and stocky but makes up for what he lacks with a whole lot of swagger. "I'll let you go first. Show me what you've got."

I don't buy his macho attitude. It's too forced, like he's only doing it because it's expected of him. I also worry my performance will be a bit much for him. Unleashing the storm might push him straight into the Year Twelve group. If there's a gentler way to do this, I don't know it.

"You're not going to hurt me," Lucio boasts, making me wince.

"We should push each other," I say, trying to get him to at least protect himself from my inevitable onslaught.

"Yeah, yeah." He waves me off with a pompous gesture. "You start, I'll knock you over later."

His pretentiousness becomes grating and I feel the familiar anger rising in me. Fine, if he's asking for it, I'll show him what I've got. I close my eyes and reach for the wind as I've done so many times before, both by accident and because I can't resist.

There's no wind.

I feel the soft caress of the wind on my skin from the other students, but it's not the same, it doesn't feel like *my* wind, and when I try to reach for it, I might as well be trying to catch the clouds. My breath catches in my throat. I gasp for air and come up empty. Just like this morning, only this isn't an asthma attack. This is just wrong.

It's gone. My trusted connection with the wind has been cut.

11

My heart batters against my chest as I struggle to draw proper long breaths, just as we've just done. Again and again, I reach out to the wind, but it eludes me so completely, I might as well have gone blind. Black spots dance in front of my eyes, and I stagger, clutching my chest.

Across from me, Lucio is talking, but the words don't penetrate the rush of the pulse in my ears. I'm still gasping for air, while simultaneously blinking away tears. I don't understand what's happening. What happened to my wind? What's wrong with me?

Suddenly, there's someone else. Two hands grab me by the shoulder, steadying me. Green eyes look straight into mine. *Jin.* "Milena, I need you to calm down. You're having a panic attack. Can you breathe with me?"

I don't know if I can, but I nod anyway. My first attempt at following his lead is a colossal failure. I manage to draw in a bit of air before I hiccup and my throat tightens. Jin isn't deterred; he keeps modelling nice long breaths until I mirror him, shakily at first, then steadier.

At last, he nods and gifts me with a smile. "There you go. That's better."

"Look, I don't know what happened," Lucio whines across his shoulder. "We were just doing the exercise. She kept staring and not doing anything and then—"

"Lucio, please join another pair to continue the task," Jin says kindly but firmly. "Everyone back to your exercise!" I hadn't even noticed everyone else staring before they scurry back into position.

"Of course. Sorry." Lucio throws me an apologetic glance that doesn't quite fit with his previous act. "Hope you feel better soon."

Jin waits until Lucio has joined another pair and the three of them move the air between them before he stares into my eyes again. "What happened?"

"It's gone," I whisper. "The wind. I can't feel it." My throat tightens again, while my eyes burn with tears barely held back. I'm agitated, prime condition for me to call upon my wind, but there's nothing. Not even the slightest breeze.

Jin frowns at me. Before he can continue, Mr Vávra approaches us. "Is everything okay here?"

"Yes," Jin hurries to say, instantly straightening his back. "We're just having a few first-time nerves. If it's okay, I'd like to work with her on it."

The teacher claps his shoulder. "I'll take over the elevens, see how much they've learned so far. You take your time, Milena. It doesn't have to be much in the beginning. We're more interested in improving your control, rather than pure power."

"Okay," I manage to say, not sure that's my problem here.

Jin takes me aside, so I don't have to do this in front of everyone. Far too many people are still glancing over, and I know by tonight, everyone will have heard of my failure.

I'm a failure, I suddenly realise. All my life, the wind has been a constant companion—even if I didn't want it, when it ruined my life, it was always there. And now that people have given me permission to call it, it's abandoned me.

The wind's abandoned me.

"Breathe," Jin urges. Apparently, I've been slipping right back into a panic attack.

After a few more deep breaths with him, I've calmed down enough to say, "This has never happened before."

He nods, seeming a bit concerned. "Look, you've gone through a lot of change. You've only just learned about elemental magic. it's normal to be overwhelmed. We usually have an orientation week before the semester starts to help people come to terms with their magic. You're not the first to have a panic attack."

As comforting as that might be, it does nothing for me. I can't even focus on his words, still trying to reach out for the wind. I truly feel like I've lost a sense or somebody's cut off a limb. I'd never noticed how much the wind was a part of me until it was gone.

"What if I've lost it? If I don't belong here?" It doesn't matter if I catch up on Elemental History or pass the midterms, if I'm not an air mage, they'll send me home. "What if it's all a mistake and I can't really control the air?"

Jin laughs softly. "It's not a mistake. You *are* an air mage. Remember what you did during the test?" His expression sobers slightly. "And Pavlína told me how you called the wind in your sleep." He leans in, his eyes sparkling slightly. "You're not only an air mage, you're a damn powerful one, too."

I close my eyes, shakily breathing in. Of course, Pavlína would run to Jin and tell him all about my transgression. She doesn't want me to befriend him, so, naturally, she'd badmouth me at any opportunity.

"Milena." He draws my attention again. "Let's try this once more, okay?"

His voice forces me to open my eyes. Following his lead, we do a few more breathing exercises from the warm-up. I try to believe him when he says this is completely normal, but I *know* it's not. The breathing doesn't make it any better, meditating won't help me. I can focus on the air as much as I want, but when I try to seize it, it slips through my fingers, leaving me with nothing.

Throughout the two hours, Jin stays encouraging, endlessly repeating what must be extremely boring for him. About ten minutes before the bell rings, I manage to create a whisper of a breeze.

"That's it!" Jin claps excitedly.

I feel relieved the wind hasn't been completely taken from me, but it does little to lift my mood. This isn't even a shadow of what I was capable of before.

"Hold onto that feeling and try to replicate it with the next breath."

The breeze is snuffed out like a candle. Jin's forehead creases in response. He's about to give up on me. I can feel it.

"It's hopeless, isn't it?" I whisper, too tired to try again.

Jin shakes his head and forces a smile, but the wrinkles remain, giving the lie away. "Absolutely not. I think it's just a blockage. Maybe something internal."

"Are you saying I need to see the school councillor?" Do they even have one?

"It wouldn't hurt." Jin shrugs his shoulders apologetically. "Or you just need to give it time. You've obviously got it in you. I'm not worried at all."

Liar, I want to say, since his face tells a completely different story, but I appreciate the sentiment. Even if it's useless, it feels nice to know he's not quite ready to give up yet.

"Come on." His voice gains some confidence and his real smile returns. "It's just a roadblock. We'll find a way to break through it in no time. In the meantime, rest up, do the exercises I just showed you before you go to bed and when you wake up, and stop worrying about it." He looks deep into my eyes. "You *are* an air mage. I believe in you."

Who can hold on to doubt and self-pity when you've got an extremely hot and unbelievably kind guy telling you he believes in you? Not me. For the first time in two hours, it doesn't hurt so much to breathe.

12

Unfortunately, as soon as Jin returns to his many other duties, the self-loathing creeps back in. I suppose I should be glad. Without my wind, I'm just a normal moody teenager. My mother will certainly be happy to hear the news—no more violent outbursts or inexplicable mishaps.

A few months back, I would've killed for this normalcy, but now I've got it, the bar's shifted. Normal here means playing around with your element—I see the others doing it in the courtyard, in the dining hall, and between classes. They've developed all kinds of games from sneak-splashing (trying to drop a ball of water upon someone), to wind-throwing (no hands allowed for this ball game), to flame-holding (who can hold onto a flame the longest). They're having fun, freely being themselves.

Being me apparently means always being the odd one out. When I'm around normal people, I have weird wind accidents. When I'm around elemental mages, I can't even move a breeze.

Everyone keeps telling me I shouldn't worry. Ester and Jamila both shared their struggles when they first started here: Ester splashed herself frequently, which led to her outsider status, while Jamila had problems keeping her fire from breaking out at the most inopportune moments.

They're both much better at control now, though still a far way from how they'll be at the end of Year 13.

Jin continues working with me in class but he can't do constant one-on-ones, so I spend most of my time sitting on the side, going through the same exercises again and again, not achieving anything. And slowly, the encouragement dies down and pitiful looks and mocking begins. What's an air mage without her wind?

The other classes are being troublesome, too. Mr Reisz completely overestimated how much time I'd have to catch up. Since I can't call the wind, I spend every free minute in the library, but with all the homework and test preparation from other classes and two more elemental subjects I have to catch up on, only a fraction actually gets done.

I'm falling behind and there's no smothering the fall. Midterms are awfully close, and there's no way I'm going to pass. And if I don't—what then? I haven't found the courage to ask yet.

The worst thing is my breathing isn't coming right. I'm starting to think there's something I'm allergic to in this old building, because I've never had to deal with constant asthma before. Walking all these stairs and corridors leaves me breathless, and at night, I can't sleep because it feels like my lungs are seizing up.

I'm this short of giving up. Maybe if I just pack up and leave, I can vanish into the streets of Prague and won't have to face my mother for failing to stay at yet another school.

But then I remind myself my father went here and this might be the only place I can find out more about him. The thought of him leads me to the headmistress and her more than generous offer. After one and a half weeks of struggling, I'm ready to face defeat. It's practically like ripping off a Band-Aid. I'll confess my ineptitude and she'll set my expulsion into motion.

I don't tell either of my new friends I'm going to see her, instead slinking up there just when everyone else is eating dinner. I've never seen the headmistress in the hall, so I'm guessing she's a bit of a workaholic or likes to keep her distance from staff and students.

I'm in luck. Her door is half-open when I arrive and she's still sitting at her desk. Upon my gentle knock on the door, she looks up and instantly breaks into a smile. "Milena. Come on in."

My stomach is knotted painfully as I close the door behind me and take a seat in front of her desk. Today the big glass on her desk holds a miniature thunderstorm. Its crackling reminds me of all that's lost to me.

"How are you finding the academy? You've survived your first week, so—"

"I wouldn't exactly call it surviving," I mutter. Really, I might as well fall down the stairs and break my neck for all the good I'm doing here.

Ms Martínková frowns slightly. "I'm sorry to hear that. Is it all that catching up you need to do? It's a huge task. I wish we could've enrolled you sooner."

"Midterms are coming up," I say cautiously, hoping she'll write me an exemption. She can do that, right?

"Yes, they are. I suppose it's a bit soon."

I'm relieved she acknowledges the impossible task I've been given. "Does that mean I get to sit them out this time?"

Unfortunately, there's a head shake. "I don't think that's a good idea. But don't worry. First off, midterms only determine half your grade, or really a quarter, since most classes don't solely rely on written exams.

You can easily balance a bad grade with a good one at the end of the year. Secondly, there's the opportunity to resit any tests you've failed at the end of the break. And I think it'll be a good measure to see where you're at and where you might need tutoring."

While her explanation at least removes the fear of having to leave after my inevitable failure, it doesn't do much to lower my anxiety. I'll still have to study for the midterms, hoping I pass at least half so I can resit the others. I wonder if it makes sense to just throw away subjects like Elemental History instantly or whether I should risk barely passing and having a bad grade that I'll have to counter with better results at the end of the year, hoping I *will* get better results then. Right now, that's far from a given.

"So, the grades just make up twenty-five per cent?" That's still a huge number. I can do enough maths to know how much I need to apply myself afterwards should I fail.

"For most classes, yes. Obviously Air Weaving and Elemental Defence training are different. In that case, it's fifty per cent, but at least you barely need to study for those."

She sounds so hopeful when all I want to do is to cry. I try to hold the tears back, but a strangled sob escapes me. "I don't think I'm a mage," I confess in an awkwardly whiny voice.

Ms Martínková raises her eyebrow, instantly concerned. "What do you mean?" The question is so loaded my anxiety rises instantly.

Between gasps and barely held-in sobs, I explain how I'm struggling to connect with the wind now I'm here, that my asthma has got worse, and she must've made a mistake. "I mean it makes sense, right? Technically, I'm a legacy student, but I wasn't even on your radar for the last sixteen years because... because..." Tears finally spill over. "Because I can't do magic. It was all an accident after all."

Because crying isn't bad enough, my asthma's playing up and I have to take a few puffs from my inhaler. I hate doing it in front of anyone but there's little choice in this situation.

Ms Martínková holds out a tissue box to me, of which I make immediate embarrassing use. "I have to confess," she says, with a huge frown, "after your results in the test room and"—with a sigh, she adds—"the reports we had from your previous schools, I didn't expect you to struggle with that part of our education. Control, yes, but potential, never."

I feel awful for disappointing her. She's been so kind through everything, even offering me a scholarship, but it was all wasted on some pretender.

"I'm a bit at a loss as to what might've caused this block," she admits. "In the past, how did you feel when you called the wind?"

"Upset." It takes me a moment to realise what she's playing at. "As upset as I am, there should be a storm in your office right now."

The headmistress lets out a hapless laugh. "Yes, and while I appreciate that isn't the case, I'm worried."

"Maybe it's performance anxiety," I say with a little shrug. I've never had to call on my storm to demonstrate my ability.

Ms Martínková looks as if she wants to tell me that this isn't how it works, but after a while, she nods. "Yes, it might be. In that case, I think you just need to give it a bit more time. Relax and keep working on your breathing techniques."

"What if the wind never comes back?" I whisper.

"It will," she says confidently. "You're one of the strongest air mages I've seen enter this place. You will unlock your potential. We'll figure this out together."

I feel strangely comforted by her confidence in me. Just like Jin, she believes I can do this. All I have to do is trust them and hope the underlying problem, whatever it might be, will resolve itself. Maybe going to the school counsellor isn't such a bad idea after all. God knows I've got more problems than I can shake a stick at.

"So, let's find a day where we can try a few things." Ms Martínková consults her calendar, trying to work out when she can squeeze me in. I'm flattered she isn't going to pass me off to someone else but actually wants to help me herself.

Finally, she nods. "Right, let's do Tue—"

A loud noise blares through the room from multiple sources. Some kind of alarm. "Is there a fire?" There's one probably every other week, given the kind of students here.

Ms Martínková stares into space, unspoken thoughts behind her eyes. Then she stands abruptly. "Milena, I need you to return to your room and stay there until the alarm stops."

No fire then, if I'm supposed to stay inside. "What's happening?"

"An elemental being just escaped from the Wyld Lands."

13

I'm too curious for my own good. The smart, responsible thing would have been to follow the headmistress' orders, return immediately to my dorm and lock myself inside. But how can I do that when there's an elemental being on the loose in the courtyard? I've only heard about them and read a little, but what do they look like? What do they feel like?

Is it a fire spirit, water, or a creature of air? My heart beats faster, not out of fear but pure exhilaration. I want to meet an air elemental. A creature of the wind like—

My excitement comes to a complete halt. I'm no longer mysteriously connected to the wind, not like I was before. We're nothing alike. Unless... I hardly dare to hope. If it is an air elemental, meeting it might be what breaks through my block. How could I glance upon a wild creature like that and not want to fly with it?

With my excitement restored, I hurry down the stairs, following in the footsteps of those training to be guardians. No actual guardians have arrived yet, but I figure this isn't the first call-out for the senior students.

I push through the doors into the courtyard and freeze at what's in front of me. The sheer size of it is awe-striking, and while it's not the hoped for air elemental but a water creature, my exhilaration is at an all-time high. The being has gathered the fountain water, surging back and forth across the courtyard like a stormwater wave. Sometimes it's nothing more than that—a big giant wave—but other times, I can make out vaguely familiar shapes: a seal lodged on a rock, an albatross diving into the deep, a swarm of fishes, then nothing but raging water, eager to break out of the confines of the courtyard. I don't know what I'd expected from an elemental being but it wasn't this.

"Out of the way."

Someone jostles me to the side, a group of black-clad people who are distinctively older than the students. The one who pushed me aside barks orders, directing everyone in the courtyard to form a perimeter around the elemental being before moving in. Wind buffets the water, forcing it on itself, and the perimeter tightens. I stretch to see whether I can make out Jin, but he appears to be on the other side of the courtyard near the dorms.

Using the excuse I was told to return to my dorm, I slowly make my way around the guardians, edging ever closer to the elemental. It's so beautiful. Terrifying, for sure, when I see how high the waves build only to crash down on the being, but oh-so beautiful. This close, I can see into its depths, and it's as if I'm standing on a cliff and peering into the ocean itself.

The ocean fascinates me. Czechia is a landlocked country. We're surrounded by mountains, not water. There are lakes, of course, and the Danube runs right through the country, gaining width as it makes its way to the East, but those are only shallow waters. And while this elemental is nowhere as vast as the ocean, it carries its essence. I see secrets swirling in the deep, unspeakable terrors that aren't meant for the surface, the silence so removed from the turmoil of the heavens, the darkness where no light has ever shone, and the profound loneliness of a place where you're the only living being in miles and miles of water.

The ground shakes under a concerted effort of the earth mages. The elemental, which has towered so high it'd be visible beyond the roofs of the school, collapses. Too late to escape, the water crashes down on me and the guardians in my vicinity.

I hit the ground when the pure force of the water slams into me. For a moment, I can't breathe, but I don't care. My whole body trembles as the mystical energy of this being presses down on me. Its conscience washes over me, filling me with longing for the wide oceans when the Earth was young, when land was still a dream of the future.

Then someone pulls me up and I surface. Fresh air blows over my face, filling my lungs with much needed oxygen. It's one of the many women among the guardians. She shouts at me, but my ears are still filled with the silence of the ocean floor. I understand her urgent shove towards the buildings clearly enough without speech.

Oh, how I long to submerge myself in this glorious being again. I'm not a water mage, but if this is what the elementals are like, I can't wait to meet the wind. Maybe my dream of flying will become a reality.

I stumble away from the fight, watching as the mages use all the elements to constrain this glorious being. Wind buffets it from all sides, earth soaks in as much as it can, fire slowly eats away at it, turning what's supposed to be liquid to steam, and water moulds it, constraining it into a smaller and smaller space. It seems impossible to contain this vast being in anything as small as the fountain, but between so many guardians, it shrinks further and further.

The guy who jostled me steps in with what looks like a glass container. At first, it seems as if he's swallowed by the water, but then fire hisses and a blue glow grows stronger and stronger, as if the elemental's pulling all that it is into itself. When it's nothing but a glittering blue orb, the commander sweeps in and catches it in the glass container. Instantly, the water calms, splashing unceremoniously onto the ground. The fountain is half-drained and huge puddles cover the courtyard, ruining the practice yards.

Now the elemental has been captured, I feel something else. A wild call behind me, a siren song unlike any other.

Slowly, I glance over my shoulder. I'm standing right in front of the portal building. Something is different, though, and it takes me a full body rotation before I can lay my finger on it.

The *door*. The beautifully carved wings of the door have been opened. It's just a crack, really, but I feel the potential lurking behind them in the darkness. *My* potential. A wind sneaks through the crack, caressing my cheek, beckoning me to follow it to a place where we can both soar and nobody can stop us.

If someone asked me to call the wind right now, I know in my bones I could. This close to the source of my magic, I can do anything. I need to do it, need to prove to myself I'm no longer broken, that I belong here in this place.

"Did you open it?" Suddenly, there's Jin, looking at the door in horror.

"Of course not. I don't have the key."

He nods, incredibly tense, as if he expects another elemental to jump out from behind the doors. And then I understand what it means. An elemental has escaped, but somebody opened the door for it.

At last, he moves forward, closes his hand around the doorknob and pulls it shut.

Instantly, I feel as if my airways have been shut off. Without the strong wind from the Wyld Lands, I'm nothing again. Useless.

Jin pushes the bar down to provide another barrier before pulling out a walkie-talkie and reporting the issue. "I need someone to lock the portal up. The door was open when I arrived."

"Don't you..." I need to draw a breath before I can continue speaking. "Have to... return... the ele...mental?"

"They'll do that later. We analyse and categorise each transgression before returning the essence where it belongs." He puts the walkie-talkie away and looks at me. "Are you okay?"

"When was I ever okay?" I ask, clutching my chest as if it makes breathing any less painful. Dark spots dance in front of my eyes. I feel bereft, bereft of air, of the water elemental, the Wyld Lands, of everything.

Jin regards me anxiously. Then he seems to make a decision. "Come with me."

"Where to?" I gasp.

"Somewhere it's easier to breathe."

14

Sadly, we don't slip through the doors into the Wyld Lands—I have no doubt my breathing problems would be negligible there. Instead, Jin pulls me to the side first, where he dries me with a weird combination of air and water magic—his wind blows me dry, while the water simply drains from my clothes and hair on his command. I've seen him do it before with his fighting buddy, but it's something different to experience it; it feels intimate, as if his hands are on my body, wiping each drop from my skin with endless care. I never noticed how long his fingers were until they hover near my face, slowly outlining my features.

It's good I'm already out of breath because I would've held it if I weren't. Even so, I'm completely engrossed in his display of restraint. If I'd tried to dry him with my wind—back when it still came to me—I would've blown him over. In comparison, his wind is more like a whisper, its strength shielded expertly so it won't hurt me. "Tamed" comes to my mind, and it instantly feels right. This is what being a mage is all about. They aren't slaves to the elements, but their masters. In their hands, the most primal forces become compliant tools.

"Come," Jin whispers, and I notice my wheezing has calmed a bit. "I'll show you my favourite place."

His favourite place? This isn't his normal shtick, right? I mean, does he do that with every air student who needs a little extra help or is this a move he pulls around girls he might like? Assuming he likes girls. I don't actually know much about his private life apart from his father's untimely death, and that's something he never told me about so it feels a bit shabby to hold it over him.

Jin leads me up a side tract, climbing flight after flight. My heart sinks as I contemplate how tough this climb will be on my weakened lungs.

"We can go slow," Jin offers. Gifting me with a shy smile, he adds, "I promise it'll be worth it. I often go there when I can't breathe."

Jin, unable to breathe? He seems so infallible, so incredibly accomplished. Everybody loves him, even the teachers.

My tongue prickles with a curiosity only speaking can satiate, but I keep my mouth closed. I've got an inkling I'll learn about it quicker if I let him open up to me on his terms.

Slowly, but surely, we climb up the stairs to the top floor. Up there, Jin stretches and pulls down a ladder folded to the ceiling. As it unfolds, a trap door opens up. "It's the access for the chimney sweep who comes once a year to service the old funnels."

Intrigued, I follow him up into the attic. I hope this isn't the place where he goes to breathe easy, because it's blanketed in dust. I can already feel it coating my airways, my nose tickling in response. There isn't much light left in this day, so the attic feels dark and secretive, a little like the elemental before they captured it.

Jin pulls the trapdoor shut, enclosing us in darkness. By the time my eyes adjust to the low light, he's unfolded a rusty metal ladder right next to the trapdoor. Going first, he climbs it to open a small window that's so coated by decades of grime, it hardly functions as a window anymore.

"Be careful when you get up here—it's coated with frost and it's a long slide down." He pulls himself up and moves out of the way, freeing the view for me. A star's already gracing the evening sky.

I poke my head through the hole and take in a deep breath of icy air. A breeze picks up the strands of my purple hair and messes them up. I already feel a million times better.

Jin offers me a hand as I follow him onto the slanted roof, covered in snow. "Careful now."

With our heads low, we climb the short distance from the skylight to the surprisingly wide ridge. He sweeps the snow off with a short blast and assists me as I swing my legs over the edge and sit down. Then he sits next to me, infinitely more relaxed than I've ever seen him.

"Isn't it beautiful?"

It's already dark, but while I can't see the sea of red, I see an ocean of lights. The Vlatva is a black band threading its way through the city and the beautiful bridges that span it. Prague Castle rises in front of us with its spire and the St. Vitus Cathedral that houses the Czech Crown Jewels, and I can easily identify Old Town Square from here. Down in the streets, it feels full and suffocating, but with the snow and the lights, it looks like something out of a fairy tale.

But the best thing about it is the wind gusting across the roof, threatening to throw us off. It's not nearly as strong as the wind in the Wyld Lands, but its force buffets me, welcoming me as eager as a puppy. It's freezing, but I enjoy it too much to spare a thought for my poor fingers. Jin's right—it *is* easier to breathe up here.

He doesn't speak for a long time, just watching the city beneath us, feeling the wind on his skin. Then, when he's finally had his fill of the view, he says, "I used to get panic attacks, too, you know?"

Again, I'm stunned to find out how brittle his shiny surface truly is. It's not the greatest thing to have in common but it is something. A connection or maybe a secret, only shared between the two of us. "Why?"

"Why?" he repeats, bemused, then rubs his hairless chin. "You mean what could I possibly have to panic about?"

Ashamed, I look at the city. That was my initial thought, yes, but then I remember the darkness in his life. "I know about your dad," I confess in a tiny whisper that only carries to him because he's sitting in the wind.

"Everyone does." He sounds tired, and I know I've hurt him. It must be so exhausting for everyone to know his dad was killed by a witch. His shoulders tense slightly. "Who told you? Pavla?"

It takes me a moment to realise he called Pavlína by an affectionate nickname. "Oh, no, she hates me."

"She's not half as bad as she pretends."

"Don't."

Curiously, he looks over. "Don't what?"

"Don't defend her actions. I've dealt with bullies my entire life. I don't care for her sob story."

Jin purses his lips. I'm well aware I might've just lost him, but I won't take the words back. Pavlína has had it out for my blood the moment she laid eyes on me. The last thing I want is to hear Jin taking her side.

"Sorry," he says instead. "Would you like me to talk to her?"

"Oh god, no."

He chuckles softly. "I suppose it'd make it all worse?"

"Infinitely so." Then after a while, I decide to reward him by saying, "It was Ester." From his blank stare, I assume he doesn't even know her. "She's a water mage in my class."

Jin deflates slightly but nods. "Like I said, everyone knows. I get pitying glances wherever I go. I've learned to expect them. My mother says it proves people aren't assholes." He chuckles. "Forget that—my mother would never use such unkind words. She's all kindness and politeness. What she means is that their pity shows they care. And to be honest, it only bothers me sometimes, like when people can't get over it, when that's all they see or they change their entire behaviour around me and they only see me as the boy who lost his father."

Anxiously, he searches my face. I wonder what he's so scared of, but then I realise he's worried *I* could change my behaviour towards him now I know. "You're more to me than that."

I did not just say *that*.

Mortified, I sputter, "I mean, your father doesn't come to mind when I see you. It's all you. The Head Boy, the teacher, the future guardian."

At first, he seemed amused, delighted really, but at the last addition, he winces.

"Wrong again?"

Jin shakes his head. "No, it's just... I'm fine with pity. My mother taught me the grace to accept it and not think less of myself."

She sounds like a wonderful woman, strong and compassionate. I'm glad he's got a mother like her in his life, not one who can't wait to be relieved of her child-rearing responsibilities.

"The thing that drives me up the wall here are all these expectations. Anybody who knew my dad always tells me how I'm just like him, how proud he would've been, and how many great things they expect from me in the future. People think I'll follow in his footsteps, and sometimes it all feels like a giant trap. They lure me into it, and then I'll disappoint them."

He leans back with a sigh and closes his eyes. I recognise the breathing techniques he taught me, the ones he used to get me out of my panic attack. I want to be there for him, but I don't know what to say—disappointment is my middle name, after all. No one expects anything of me, they just hope and pray I don't screw it up.

Since I can't say anything helpful, I look for another way to let him know I care. My gaze falls on his fingers, splayed on the ridge next to mine. I hold my breath as I prepare to brush my fingertips against his. I don't think he'd even feel the touch, but the moment it happens, he opens his eyes, and his gaze locks with mine. I instantly look away and withdraw my fingers, cradling them in my other hand as if burnt. What am I doing here? Taking his hand as if... as if we were something we're not.

I feel his eyes on me, studying me quietly. When I keep looking ahead, he sighs. "Alright, enough about me. We're here to help you."

"Why?"

"Why what?"

"Why are you so invested in helping me?" It comes off a bit more petulant than I mean. I'm not mad at him for being kind to me. I just... *I don't trust him*, I realise with a start. People are never nice, so when they are, I can't trust them. I want to but internally I'm already preparing myself for when they inevitably reject me. And let's be honest, someone like Jin *will* reject me. "You don't have to, you know?"

"But I want to. What kind of teacher would I be if I didn't try to help?"

Before I can stop myself, I blurt out: "A normal one."

Jin's forehead creases. "You think it's *normal,*" he starts carefully, "that a teacher would ignore you?"

Time to rip the Band-Aid off, I suppose. "Look, I'm the opposite of a teacher's pet. If teachers could blacklist students, I'd be at the top." That should do it. He can keep his distance now.

But Jin has been taught kindness and empathy by his mother, so instead of backing out, he doubles down. "Well, in that case, let me be your first positive teaching experience."

I want to tell him it's me, not them. *I'm* the problem, the misfit, the troublemaker, the liar, the disturbance... but I can't. Turns out I'm not ready for him to detest me. So, instead, I press my lips together and stay silent.

Jin's hand lands on my knee. "You're doing it again."

I stare at his hand, painfully aware of its gentle pressure and warmth. "What do you mean?"

"Keeping everything inside. I think that's the problem," he continues before I can argue otherwise. "You're too guarded and because of that, you're shutting the wind in when you should let it out. Come on. Let's try something." He gets up, balancing precariously on the ridge, and reaches out his hand. "Stand up."

"That's dangerous," I say cautiously, because that's what sensible people are expected to say. Balancing on the ridge of a roof, no matter how wide, high enough for the wind to pull and push in the middle of winter, is one of those stupid things teenagers get themselves killed over.

However, sensibility has never been my strongest suit. My heart yearns to join him on the roof, to experience the raw power of the wind over Prague for myself. It reminds me of my dream and how I leant into the wind until it picked me up and I flew. But flying is limited to the world of dreams or maybe the Wyld Lands. Here, you don't fly, you fall.

The hand is still there. "It's safe, I promise." Who is this Jin who's so eager to take a risk and have me share in it? "I know it looks dangerous, but I'm actually controlling the wind right now." He raises his other hand in the air and lets it be buffeted from one side to the other, showing me how strong the wind is. Then he flicks his wrist and the hand stills. His whole figure might as well be made of stone.

Control. The reason he's so steady has nothing to do with formidable balance and all to do with his mastership of this element. I won't fall, because he won't let me.

Slowly, I let him pull me up. *Don't be too eager. Don't let the wind control you. You're the mage not the vessel.*

The wind blows into my face, trying to pick me off the roof, but just as it's about to bear down on me, it swerves and blows past. I feel its power and yet I'm completely safe. Though I repeat, "Don't get too excited" like a mantra, it only takes a second before I feel the rush of adrenaline flooding my veins, my lungs expanding, and I'm drunk off fresh air. "This is amazing," I have to shout, because this high up, the wind roars in my ears.

"Try seizing it," Jin shouts back. "Feel its movements in your hand, in your mind, and then push."

"Push what?"

"Push me!"

I swallow heavily when he suggests it. I have to tell myself he's so much better than me at this and there's no way he's going to fall. But

I've seen the destructive force of my power. What if it comes back? Is he strong enough to overcome me at my worst?

He leans in, his cheek almost touching mine. "Just a little. Try it." To demonstrate, he tightens his grip on my hand—my fingers tingle electrically—then throws the wind against me.

I stagger backwards, held upright only by his touch. Then the pressure is gone and a light breeze blows into my back.

"Now, your turn."

Flustered, I try to do what he told me in class, how I need to focus on the flow of the air travelling in and out of my body, on how it flows around me. Where is it coming from? Where is it going? Where does it pivot and do something completely unexpected? If I can understand all that, perfectly reading the wind, I can control it. The thing is I feel it all, but when I try to seize and push the wind, nothing happens.

For a moment, I hope he's simply masked the effect of my efforts to prevent an accident, but his face is still expectant. He's still waiting for me to do something. Anything

Frustrated, I do it again. The wind is here! Why is it refusing to talk to me? Why has it shunned me?

"Keep going," Jin says. He must've noticed I'm trying. Not because he felt something, but because it's been too long since he told me to.

With each try, I grow more and more agitated. One cannot control the wind. It's a wild, freedom-loving being you can't even grasp. Unlike the other elements, it's completely invisible. Cloudy or sunny, you can't tell it's windy until you've stepped outside and felt it on your skin or seen the trees bend under its strength. Jin's techniques have nothing in common with my experiences. I've never tried to tame the wind, I simply welcomed it and let it do its worst.

In our training sessions, Jin always grounded me with his breathing techniques. But this time, he doesn't intervene, he doesn't try to steer me away from a panic attack, after a while, he even does the opposite, shouting, "More! Give it more!"

Compelled, I give it everything I have. I channel my frustration and anger into a single-minded thought.

A gust sweeps under my right arm into Jin's chest. He falls backwards, surprise visible on his face, then the air flows put him upright again. "That's it. That's the one," he shouts, laughing excitedly, "I knew you had it in you!" He looks so proud it breaks my heart. He's too perfect for this world.

"Now, I want you to remember this feeling! I know it's not what I taught you but we can adapt. We can make it work." He sounds as if he *needs* to make it work. "Let's try this again."

We try again until night has completely fallen. And while I can't replicate that one perfect attempt, I'm actually feeling a shift. I start to get the pattern, get how it's supposed to work, even if the actual thing still eludes me.

When we finish, both our cheeks are red from the cold, the stars shining above us, mirrored by the streetlights below, and we can't stop grinning.

Jin is so proud of me, and I'm pretty sure I have a major crush on him.

15

To our surprise, Ms Martínková is waiting under the trapdoor when we come down. It's the first time I've seen her displeased. Her frown deepens when she recognises me, and my heart sinks.

Despite her initial reaction, it's Jin she addresses. "I don't think a private date is a proper use of your privileges, Mr Čermák."

Jin turns surprisingly red. "This wasn't... I..."

"He was trying to help me with my air flow problems. No date stuff included." If you disregard watching the sunset over Prague or sitting under the stars far above the world. But this wasn't a date, just Jin helping me get over my block.

"I'll take it from here," Ms Martínková says in a sharp tone that suggests I should pull in my head and follow her without protest. I do, because I don't want to get Jin into trouble after he went to such lengths for me.

As soon as we leave him behind—apparently he doesn't need to return to the dorms right away—Ms Martínková throws me a worried glance. "Don't take this the wrong way, but I would hate to see you get too attached to our Head Boy. I don't think you need that kind of distraction at the moment."

Now *my* cheeks are burning. She's read my thoughts perfectly. I've got a crush on Jin, an embarrassing, unrequited crush that'll get me nowhere. And Ms Martínková is right; I don't have time for dating or swooning over a boy. Midterms are coming up, and my wind powers are still woefully underdeveloped. Still, it's not exactly something I want to be called out on by Ms Martínková.

"I mean it," she says, with an uncomfortable persistence.

"It's only tutoring."

"Then I'd urge you to find another tutor."

Confused, I stare at her. "Why?" Is there a rule against dating—or potentially wishing to date—Year 13 students?

Ms Martínková sighs. "Just trust me on this. You've got enough other things to worry about than Mr Čermák."

I want to roll my eyes so hard. So far, Ms Martínková has been nurturing in every way my mother isn't, now she's showing a side that's a little more like my own: controlling what I should and shouldn't do. It grates on me and I feel my temper rising, but no wind. That part of me is lost, even after Jin's lesson. Instead, I swallow my anger and nod sharply. "Understood."

"You will," Ms Martínková whispers. "One day, you will."

We enter the dorms and I know my time is running out. There's something else I want to talk about, something I'd almost forgotten about in Jin's presence. "The elemental. What happened to it?"

"It was captured by the guardians and will be returned to the Wyld Lands in due time." There's no hesitation, a reply well practised.

"Is it okay?" I want to take it back the moment I ask—it strikes me as childish and uneducated. I might as well have asked whether the ocean is okay.

Empathy softens Ms Martínková's features as she regards me. "It will be once it's back where it belongs." We stop in front of my door. "Elementals can be scary, but they're not here to harm us. They simply wander into our world from time to time."

"Jin said someone let this one in."

Her features harden instantly. "If so, that's guardian business. You'd be well-advised to stay out of it until you've completed your education."

Again with the guarded response. Something else is going on here, but Ms Martínková is right, it's none of my business. After all, I've got enough on my plate.

"Don't worry. These kinds of interruptions don't happen very often. Now, I wish you a good night. Stay safe."

I can't quite tell whether the last bit is a stern reminder or a sign of worry. Either way, Ms Martínková leaves, and I brace myself to enter my room.

Inside, Pavlína is waiting. She's been working at her desk but throws me a disdainful look as soon as I enter. Her greeting is a derisive snort.

I'm rather tired after a long day and my patience has grown thin. "What?"

"Oh nothing!" she claims, only to launch right into a little tirade. "I thought you'd finally come to your senses and given up—believe me, you'd be doing yourself a kindness."

"Is that so?" I drop on my bed and flick my shoes off. I'm certainly not going anywhere right now.

Pavlína narrows her eyes. "You believe you can pass midterms?"

"I don't have to pass all of them."

I know I have very little chance of pulling off such a feat, but Ms Martínková has assured me it's not necessary. Surely, the headmistress knows more about such things than Pavlína.

She laughs. "Well, with that attitude you won't." She gives me a smile that cuts like a knife. "There's no way you'll get through the midterms, much less the end of year exams. You don't belong here. Your magic might as well be non-existent, and once the teachers have come to the same conclusion, they'll expel you."

I wish I could pretend her words don't phase me in the slightest. Somehow, I manage to raise my eyebrows and wait until she's finished to ask, "Are you done?" but inside, I feel like vomiting.

Sure, I can pass any subject where the test requires acquired knowledge, but there's no way to wing it when it comes to my magic. Already, my success during Jin's lesson is fading, and there's a tightness in my chest. Soon, they *will* find out I'm a fraud, and then this wonderful little adventure will come to an end.

Pavlína throws me another disdainful glance, then huffs and returns to her homework. I fall back on my bed and close my eyes, trying my best not to cry. Not here, not in front of her, not anywhere.

16

Though I'm woefully behind in Wyld Lands Geography, another magical subject, it's quickly becoming one of my favourites. It's not so much Geography as it is everything about the Wyld Lands. Since I arrived, we've talked about early exploration parties and the gruesome ends many of them came to. Their names don't mean anything to me, but there's something wildly romantic about risking your own life to explore a place no one ever has before.

Perhaps no human souls are supposed to be in the Wyld Lands—the result of explorations certainly suggest so—but ever since staring into the elemental being and feeling the wind from the open door, I can't stop thinking about going there. Is it stupid? Probably. Is the very thought of it exhilarating? Most definitely.

We've moved on from the explorers to charting their path on a map by using their old diaries, which were recovered by sole survivors or follow-up excursions. It's a group task between Ester, Jamila, me, and Lucio, the little Italian-wannabe macho I faced off against in air class. All it took was Jamila staring at him once for him to drop the whole act.

"'An ocean so vast we do not dare cross it'," Jamila reads, then comments, "well, that's helpful. We should be right about here." She runs her finger all along the coastline.

I have no idea about the dimensions of the Wyld Lands, but that excursion could be literally anywhere.

Ester shakes her head and repaints the line further out in the water. "The map was drawn fifty years after the Edmundsen excursion. The sea in the Wyld Lands is ravenous—it eats the coastline by dozens of metres each year."

Lucio buries his head in his arms. "This assignment is impossible to complete. How are we supposed to chart a path according to an out-of-date report?"

Meanwhile, I'm utterly fascinated. "Do the Wyld Lands really change that much?"

"They're in constant flux," Ester explains. "Like Earth, but in a time lapse."

Jamila continues to read, "'I told Flavia to climb the peak in the East to check which way is the safest from here on out. It's definitely not the one ahead'"—she pauses to turn the page—"'Ten-metre waves are the norm. We thought about sending a party to the beach, but it is crumbling away as I sit here and write'."

"There you have it," Lucio whines and pushes a finger on the map rather randomly. "We'll just mark this spot and mention the crumbling in the report, then call it a day."

"If we work backwards we can probably do a lot better than that," Ester protests, clearly not one for half-arsing homework.

I don't care either way—the task is good practice for what might be asked of us in the exam, but I'm too fascinated by the reports themselves. Jamila's deep voice draws me in, and I see myself standing at that coast, looking out at a beach that becomes less and less with each approach of the ocean. Cliffs crumble beneath my feet, waves crash over my head... I should be frightened, and yet, all I feel is awe; awe at nature's raw power.

"Do they still go on excursions?"

I'd never thought about what I might do after school—some kind of job that I can't ruin too easily, which doesn't leave me many options, at least according to my imagination. Now I'm filled with this need to follow in these brave mages' footsteps. I don't care about the risk, not when *I'm* the biggest risk. I want to feel the water sucking the soil out from under my feet and the wind whipping through my hair. And I want to fly.

"All the time," Jamila says, a curious look on their face. "It's vanity if you ask me, but mages have been dreaming of taking the Wyld Lands since time was young."

I don't want to take them, just experience them. The very thought that anyone could look at that raw beauty and only think about how to conquer and subdue it is beyond me. The Wyld Lands don't strike me as a place for humans to take, but then again, we're talking about elemental mages, people who can control the very elements that shape the Wyld Lands. It doesn't seem too far-fetched that they should feel challenged by its very existence or would be eager to grasp it in its entirety. If I feel this attracted after just a few weeks here, so many more must be.

"There's even school excursions," Lucio says, nibbling on his thumb. When I look at him, he quickly removes the finger and straightens his back. "The year 12 and 13 air students are going after midterms."

"Really?" After all this talk about the dangers of the Wyld Lands, it's the last thing I expected to hear—I'd thought they'd all think me crazy for wanting to venture there. "I thought it was dangerous."

"It is," Lucio says, and this time I notice he's wary. *He* doesn't want to go.

"Theoretically all of the Wyld Lands are," Ester explains. "In reality, many places are safe enough with the right preparation."

"On a short-term basis," Jamila adds. "Nobody can actually survive there permanently."

I'm experiencing whiplash listening to the three of them, while simultaneously trying to recalibrate what I know about the Wyld Lands so far.

"There is one," Lucio pipes up.

Ester pulls a face. "That's a rumour."

"What is?" I finally manage to get a question in.

"Rumour has it the infamous Stormwitch has been hiding out in the Wyld Lands ever since he fled the crime scene twelve... no, thirteen years ago," Jamila explains. "Or was it twelve? I can't math right now."

My head is swimming. "The Stormwitch? Who's that?"

"Sorry." Jamila pulls a face. "Sometimes I forget how new you are to this. His real name is Jarek Janda. He's the one who murdered Jin's father. No one's seen him since."

For some reason, the talk of crime seems to excite Lucio and he perks right back up. "That's because Janda is the one guy who could survive the Wyld Lands."

"For twelve years?" Ester asks doubtfully. "You can't even build a shelter there because the elements tear it down so fast, no matter the material."

"Maybe he doesn't need shelter." Lucio seems to have a very unhealthy hero complex considering we're talking about a murderous, magic-addicted witch.

Ester holds her ground. "Everybody needs shelter, especially when they try to live in a world as exposed to the elements as the Wyld Lands. There's more than enough places in our world where he could hide."

Neither option sounds terribly secure. "So, the killer of Jin's father is still running free?"

I wonder if Jin has ever considered vengeance—it'd be all I would think of. Then I remember how much he struggles with everybody's expectations. Hopefully, no one is *expecting* him to search for his father's murderer.

"Well, there's one other option," Jamila says in a light-hearted voice. "He could've gone hiding in the Wyld Lands and perished there. It's probably the most likely outcome."

Lucio pulls a face. "Likely but boring." He really worships this mad murderous witch.

Ester gasps at him. "Would you rather he come back and kill us?"

He finally seems to realise what he's said and raises his hands in deference. "I never said that. Just that someone as skilled as Jarek Janda can't just go off and die like that without anyone knowing, all alone, in secret. They say he could command entire storm fronts."

"There's no evidence of that." Ester seems determined to have the last word today, which is quite untypical of her. I remind myself never to get between her and facts.

I don't know about all this talk regarding Jarek Janda. It's a bit unsettling to think someone exists who can command the weather like that. I hope Jamila is right and he simply found his unceremonious end in the Wyld Lands, but then again, I hope he didn't, because that would put a serious damper on the crazy plan forming in my mind.

"What do I need to do to go to the Wyld Lands with you during term break?" I ask Jin when I meet him again for air class training. I know Ms Martínková told me to stay away, but I've never been particularly good at listening.

While he hasn't taken me back to the roof, Jin has been paying me a lot of attention during the classes. My progress is still pretty much baby steps, yet each success, no matter how small, excites him. In turn, his excitement is infectious. It makes me believe I might make it through the tests after all.

"Push again," he says, waiting until I've found my grip on the breeze he's summoned and start turning it against him. "Good. The camp's only for Year 12 and 13."

"I figured," I say, slightly annoyed. "Hence my question what I need to do to come along."

"Jump a year?" Jin jokes, pushing my feeble attempt back just enough to ruffle my hair.

It would be much easier to command the wind if I didn't enjoy its touch so much. Especially when that touch is initiated by Jin. *No, stop getting distracted.*

Jin relents. "Look, there's a good reason, we're not taking Year 11 students along. You guys have had less than a year of training at mastering your element; *you've* had even less than that. The Wyld Lands are a dangerous place."

"And yet, they let students in." I thought the whole place was locked up, barred to protect us all.

He laughs at my comeback, seeming to genuinely enjoy my company. "They do. And without supervision."

"Well, are they dangerous or not?" I'm starting to get a little cross, which lends me just enough power to push the wind back into his face.

"They are, but the place we're going to is pretty stable—the school has sent camps there for generations. Year 13 students are well-versed in monitoring elemental activity and know when to break camp if necessary. It's also not very far from the entrance, so evacuation is a matter of an hour at most. It's risky, but a very calculated risk. And one necessary to take."

"Why?"

"Because it's important to feel the strength of the Wyld Lands, to know what's out there, even if you're not planning to become a guardian." He blows a strand of black hair out of his eye, which I've managed to upset with my counter-attack. "Good job."

I can't prevent the blush in my cheeks at his appraisal. It's embarrassing. Anyone with half a brain can see how head over heels I am for him. Anyone but Jin, which is my only saving grace. Before he can notice, I ask cheekily, "Good enough to let me come to the Wyld Lands with you?"

He laughs, and I realise I love the sound of his laughter. It reminds me of what he was like on top of the roof—free of all the expectations that usually tie him to the ground.

"You've just started out," Jin repeats.

"I really want to go."

"Why?"

"Because it sounds amazing." Even I know that's not a good enough reason. They're not keeping the Year 11s away because they don't want us there. Time to play the only ace I possess instead. "Remember the open door?"

Jin's mirth is instantly replaced by concern. He glances around, as if worrying someone could hear us. "What about it?" he asks, sounding tense.

I suddenly realise why he'd be so on edge. "I didn't open it." His face relaxes ever so slightly. "I was just going to say that I felt the wind coming from the Wyld Lands. When I was breathing in that gust, my lungs felt capable of doing this—no asthma, no struggle, just clean fresh air."

"Full of dangerous promise," Jin says. He blinks as if he never meant to say that. His eyes land on my chest—not in a pervy way, but rather as if he's appraising my lung capacity. "You think going there would help you open up?" he asks at last.

"Something like that." I don't think that at all, I know it. Whatever it is that's holding me back here, it doesn't exist in the land behind the barred doors.

Jin sighs. "I wish..." He stops himself before he can disappoint my hopes. "Alright, I think there's a certain merit to it. It would be highly irresponsible of me, though, to permit you if you can't even pass a single level of air mastery." He raises his chin in a challenge. "I'll take you along *if* you pass the midterm."

17

Mindset is everything. So instead of worrying about how I could possibly pass the test when I'm still struggling so much with the basics, I pretend it's already a forgone conclusion that I'll pass and make the necessary arrangements.

Despite Ms Martínková's warning, I've joined Jin on the roof once more. Only this time, it's not for more practice—we'll do that later—but because I have to make a call, one where being able to breathe is absolutely vital.

Jin straddles the roof a few metres away, carefully watching me while I balance on the ridge, walking up and down slowly. I have no doubt his wind will catch me if I fall. Except, I won't.

"Are you going to make the call?" Jin asks after watching me for a while. "Maybe you should go home instead. Visit your parents—"

"Mum." I've got my phone in my hand but have yet to make the call.

Jin opens his mouth in surprise, likely about to ask me what happened to my dad, but I don't give him a chance to do so by finally pressing the call button and turning away.

The phone rings a couple of times before my mother finds it in herself to pick up. "I'm still at work."

"Sorry." I don't sound very sorry.

The exasperated sigh comes to no one's surprise. "What is it?"

I'm already done with the whole conversation. "I'm going to stay here for the holidays." My feet carry me to the end of the roof, and I stare into the abyss, not seeing any of Prague's beauty in this moment.

When I'd planned to call, I was expecting to make a plea to stay, but all my carefully laid-out arguments went out the window the moment my mother picked up the phone.

After a few shallow breaths, she asks carefully, yet still in a very judgmental manner, "I suppose it's going well, then?"

"Marvellous." It's not like my mother will be interested in any of my struggles. Really, this is as good for me as it is for her.

Another sigh. "Well, I'm glad you're keeping at it." Glad, but not proud. "Do they cover holidays?"

I didn't actually consider that. Swirling around, I ask Jin, "Can we stay at school during term break?"

He raises an eyebrow, probably wondering why I'm only asking now. "The ones during the school year, yeah. It's only two weeks."

"Who's that?" my mother asks. I doubt she heard much, as far away as Jin is from me.

"No one."

"Milena." A sharp note enters her voice. "Are you lying to me right now? Do I need to call the school to find out what you're really up to? You are *still* at school, aren't you?" The edge becomes even sharper.

It takes me a moment to realise she thinks I've skipped school and am trying to cover my tracks or something equally stupid. "I *am* at school," I reply, clamping down on my teeth to keep any choice words from spilling out.

The wind on the roof grows a little stronger, plucking at my clothes. Jin's frowning at me, so I turn back around again. "Call the school if you must."

"Milena, I'm trying to have a civil conversation here."

"Are you?" Probably shouldn't have said that.

We're on sigh number three. "I'll call the school."

"Whatever." Unless I seriously misjudged the situation, Ms Martínková will set her right. "Can I stay over the holidays now?" In my head, I repeat the words I don't dare to say aloud: *you don't want me home anyway. You don't want me home. You don't—*

"If that's okay with the school, sure."

"Thanks." Since you should always end things while you're on a high point, I end the call and almost throw my phone off the roof while I'm at it.

"Keep the phone," a soft voice says from behind.

I whirl around, nearly upsetting my balance. "Am I that easy to read?"

"Honestly, no." Jin's hands are raised slightly, and the wind buffets me from the direction I'm leaning into, setting me right again. "But that gesture was."

My arm is still raised in an unfinished throw. With a sigh of my own, I put the phone back in my pocket. I never want to call my mother again—at least not in the foreseeable future—but that doesn't mean I want to give up my phone.

"Do you want to talk about it?"

And unload all my crap and issues on one of the few good people in my life? As fleeting as this thing between us might be, I'm not going to be the one who ends it. *If* I can help it. "Not really."

I sit down and straddle the roof like he is, already feeling at home in this world in the sky.

Jin's frown deepens. He's probably used to all sorts of people coming to him with their problems. Well, I'm not going to be one of them. He's got enough on his plate. Unlike my mother, he lets me be. "Training then?"

"Yes, please."

The smile I get in response is exactly as distracting as Ms Martínková warned me about.

I spend every free minute either revising or practising with Jin. A day before midterms start, I still feel like there's only a fifty-fifty chance I'll pass. On the roof, the wind comes to me a lot easier, but unfortunately, the test will be on the ground—less chance of injury, and less chance for me to pass.

Luckily, Jin doesn't give up as easily as I do. As soon as he's happy with what we've achieved on the roof, he moves my training to the training facilities by the woods. It's a bit more shielded than the courtyard and allows us to train until the night bells ring, at which point we need to be in our respective dorms.

On this last day, my worries are getting the better of me. Instead of improving, I struggle breathing once again. Jin is relentless, though. He wants this as much as I do. We keep going at it until the sun starts to set and something else catches his attention.

"Pavlína."

Shit. How long has she been standing on the side near the shed where they keep the wooden sticks and other supplies in, watching us?

"You missed dinner," she tells Jin. "I wondered why." Her eyes flit towards me and I know I'm screwed. She's precious about him and won't allow me to have a piece of him, however small.

Jin runs a hand through his slightly sweaty hair. "Is it that late already?" He turns to me. "Sorry, I didn't want to keep you from nourishment."

"I'm good. The training is more important." My own words annoy me almost instantly, since they perfectly set up Pavlína's next barb.

Only, she doesn't go for it. Instead, she smiles agonisingly sweetly. "That's so kind of you, Jin, sacrificing your personal time to tutor absolute beginners."

I don't know if she meant for her comment to hit that way or not, but I suddenly feel bad. Jin has spent so much time with me, trying to get me through these exams. And like an idiot, I just accepted it without ever questioning his personal sacrifices. "Are *you* hungry?"

Jin frowns at Pavlína before shaking his head. "No, I'm okay. Did you actually bring us something or did you just come to inform us we missed dinner?"

Surprised, I stare at him. I didn't expect him to call her out like that.

Pavlína gasps audibly. "What do you mean? You didn't ask me to."

"I didn't ask you to come find me either."

Is there trouble in paradise? Jin sounds annoyed with her, as if he's tired of her bullshit, which honestly, I can easily get behind, but it strikes me as weird since they're supposedly such good friends.

"Excuse me?" There's the real Pavlína, the bitchiness returning to her voice. She swirls her finger in a circular motion to encompass Jin, me, and the training area. "Is this supposed to be a secret?"

"Secret" is such a loaded word. We haven't exactly told everyone about it, and we've tried to keep the rooftop excursions secret from Ms Martínková, but all that was a natural course of events—we never even discussed it. The way Pavlína puts it makes it sound as if we're sharing something just between the two of us.

"What do you really want?" Jin asks, again with the direct confrontation.

"I don't want anything!" Pavlína barks.

"Nah, you were curious." Jin presses his lips together, looking severely unimpressed. "Just had to come snooping and meddling."

Pavlína actually looks hurt. "What's going on? Do you not like me anymore?"

This all feels a little too personal, so I turn my back on them and practise my air magic. I can't exactly turn my ears off, though.

Jin lets out an angry huff. "Of course I *like* you. I'm just not sure, I should, because..."

"Because what?" Pavlína shouts. "Is it something *she* said? Is she spreading lies about me? That I'm some evil person because I tell the truth instead of lying to her like everybody else. Including you?"

I wish I could pretend this is about some other girl, but even the rising wind can't blow the doubts away.

"The truth?" Jin asks. "I'm curious. What's that?"

"She's not one of us."

I feel Pavlína's gesture in my back. Tears sting in my eyes. The humiliation in front of Jin is real.

"I've watched you two," Pavlína continues. "You can't possibly believe she's got what it takes. Ever." Her voice almost breaks under the vehemence of the word. "She'll never pass the first level, much less master air. Whatever got her here was clearly a fluke."

My entire body feels like lead and the wind escapes me despite it picking up. As glad as I am she's no longer putting up a fake front for Jin, I wish she wouldn't so casually tear me down. More importantly, I wish I had the confidence or thick skin to blow her off.

Jin doesn't reply. It's such an odd pause I can't resist and look over my shoulder. He's got his hand raised towards Pavlína's face while listening to something else. His eyes find mine, questioning but then dismissing me. Suddenly he moves into action.

"Get in here, both of you!" He opens the shed with his key and hurries us along.

Pavlína takes a step towards him, then pauses. "What's wrong?"

I haven't moved at all. You'd need at least six elephants to get me into a shed with Pavlína. Or a gust strong enough to throw me off my feet, which is exactly what Jin does. Unless the wind has increased its strength.

"Get in. Now!" Jin shouts. His words are picked up by the billowing wind and thrown into the air.

And then I hear it. The blaring alarm for an elemental attack. A second one, so soon, and this time it's an air one.

I taste the freedom on my tongue when another gust delivers me straight into Jin's arms. He pushes me into the shed before I can relish the feeling, then closes the door. "No wandering this time." A second later, he locks the door, leaving me alone in the dimness of the supply shed.

Only, I'm not alone.

Pavlína glares at me, standing as far away as possible as she can in the tight space. "This is all your fault."

I have no idea if she means the fight she just had with Jin, being stuck with me in a supply shed, or the terrifying storm that's building outside this very moment.

18

When we entered the shed, the small, dimmed window in the back was enough to let in some light. With the storm brewing outside, it's nearly pitch dark inside, save for the flashlight from Pavlína's phone, which she jealously guards. If there was a way to keep the light from me, she'd find it—she's that venomous.

"What did you tell him?" she spits from her side of the shed where she sits cross-legged on the ground.

I've found a place on a mud-crusted mattress cart, but the upper ground does little to make me feel superior. If anything, the closeness of the shrieking metal whenever the wind manages to get under the corrugated roof is making me flinch. I don't want to be stuck inside where things could fall on me, not if there's a storm outside that I could run in instead.

"I prefer not to waste too much energy on bullies," I say, before closing my eyes to listen to the wind. If it's not biting into the metal, it sounds different from our storms. Like a hauntingly beautiful melody. Oh, how I long to feel it on my skin.

Pavlína huffs loudly. "I'm not a bully."

"If you say so."

I meant what I said. My energy is too valuable to be wasted on fighting with her. If I actually open the bag of counter-arguments, there'll be a matching wind in here.

A gust hits the shed so forcefully the walls sound like they're caving in, and the practice staffs clatter in their holder. Pavlína shrieks. She's *shrieking*. The wind ebbs away again. I open my eyes. "You good?"

Pavlína breathes heavily, her face ghostly white in the flashlight. "Am I good? What kind of imbecile are you? Of course I'm not okay! We're in the middle of an elemental storm. Here! In Prague!"

"It's going to be fine. The guardians will do their thing, and then it'll be back to the Wyld Lands." And I won't have a chance to see it.

"You really are stupid, aren't you?" Pavlína gasps and holds onto the ground when another gust hits us. "I'm going to kill Jin." When it passes, her eyes find me again. "It's not normal to have two elemental breakouts in the same place so soon after each other."

"Well, how am I supposed to know?" The image of an open door flashes in front of my eyes. I want to go in so much my chest hurts.

"Exactly," Pavlína spits. "You don't know anything! You're nothing but an imposter, an intruder, a—" The rest of her list of insults gets lost in another scream as the whole shed shakes and rattles as if it's going to fall apart.

Somewhere, screws have come loose. Even when the wind has mercy on us once more, a metal pane keeps moving back and forth. Any more violent gusts, and the shed will be much less of a safe house and more a death trap.

"This can't be an elemental," Pavlína mutters, her voice shaky. "I bet it's the Stormwitch." Her breath shudders and she gulps. "He's come back to finish the job."

"You're on his list?" What's *her* connection to the infamous Stormwitch?

Pavlína finds it in herself to glare at me, gaining a bit of strength. "My mother is the Guardian Captain. Of course he'd come for me."

I can't help it. Her childish fears make me laugh. Granted, I don't know much about the Stormwitch beyond him being extremely powerful and having killed Jin's dad, but he's been gone for fifteen years or something. "You think he's going to kidnap you?"

"Or murder me." Her glare loses a lot of venom when the shed gets hit again by a lesser gust. "Stop laughing!"

I really shouldn't laugh. It's something about the promised danger in the wind and the ridiculous situation I've found myself in. But even though I hate Pavlína, I can tell how freaked out she is. Was she there when Jin's dad was murdered? Did she stand in his wind? Does her body remember even if her mind couldn't possibly? "I'm sorry."

Pavlína takes a shuddering breath, not launching straight into an attack for once. "Come down here."

"Why?"

She breathes several times, her eyes hollow in the pale light, before she can bring herself to whisper, "I don't want to be alone."

I kind of like my vantage point. There's less things to topple down on me, and I can feel the wind under the roof. There's electricity in the air that sets my nerves on fire in the most delicious way. Something I'll lose the moment my feet touch the ground. "Come up."

Pavlína violently shakes her head. "No way! That's dangerous. *You're* dangerous. I mean, you're in danger."

The last bit doesn't sound as convincing. Did I scare her when I dreamt of the Wyld Lands? Was she freaking out just as much then as she is now?

With a sigh, I swing my legs from the mat cart and drop to the floor. As expected, the earth grounds me, taking away all the exciting tension from the air. I plop opposite of her, mirroring her crossed legs. "And now?"

A gust hits the shed, more violently than before. The outside force translates to enough strength inside to send a racket full of kendo swords falling. Metal screams and one of the corners tears lose. It flaps violently in the ongoing wind, sending tumultuous air into the shed with each blow.

"Do something!" Pavlína screams.

"Me?" What does she expect me to do?

"You're the air mage!"

Only she was right before—I'm nothing but a fraud. The wind is so close. It's battering my face, whipping through my hair, but I can't establish a connection with it. Whenever I try, it slips through my fingers like water from a lake. "I can't."

With the most bone-chilling shriek, the rest of the wall is torn off, exposing us to the full force of the storm. Rackets move. Swords fall. Pavlína clutches my shoulders, using me as a shield, and I suddenly feel it—the wonder, the raw strength underneath. There's nothing but air, flimsy, invisible, and yet packed with so much potential.

The wind picks up the wall and flings it into the dark cloud. Somewhere nearby, lightning strikes, thunder splitting our eardrums only half a second later. By all that's true in the world, we should be dead or badly hurt, but we aren't.

I've got both feet planted on the ground, arms raised in front of me, moving on their own accord as they swipe away clattering sticks and falling shelves. I don't take from the wind, I breathe in and out and redirect, shielding me and Pavlína as if I've never done anything else, and all because I trust the wind like no other person in my life. It never hurts me, not intentionally, not directly, and if it does, it's because it's a force of nature, not because it hates me.

I don't know how long I stand there, flowing with the wind instead of pushing against it, but at long last, its force lessens. The guardians take control of the being and remove it from our world, which instantly feels lesser because of it. "It's gone."

Pavlína lets go of me, gingerly stepping over the clutter all around us. She throws me a wary glance before clearing her throat. "Looks like all those private lessons paid off."

It takes me a moment to realise she's complimenting me, and truly, it was the most in control I've ever felt. I was following the motions Jin endlessly drilled into me and they worked. Flawlessly. My first thought goes to the exams tomorrow. If I perform like that, there's no doubt I'll get to go to the Wyld Lands.

Okay, I need to try and not get ahead of myself. This could be a fluke, a glorious, wonderful fluke, but a fluke nonetheless. I haven't passed the exam yet and there's still Pavlína to deal with.

"You and Jin," I start. "You're in love with him, aren't you?"

She stares at me, then blinks. Her eyes grow wide, the usual derision entering her expression again. "Not like *that*."

"What do you mean?"

"I don't swing that way," she says, her tone implying I should know that, like so many other things. "But he's my oldest friend, and I won't let you take him away from me." The words are less of a threat than a promise to herself.

Just like in the storm, Pavlína is terrified. She may not love Jin in a romantic way, but he's dear to her. And the way he had a go at her before scared the living shit out of her.

"I'm not trying to take him away," I say, hugging myself, fearing it'll be her who takes him away from me. Only I don't have Jin. My bond with him is so much weaker than theirs. "He's just being nice."

Pavlína snorts. "I've seen the way he looks at you, like you're some revelation. You're not," she clarifies. "You're a lousy air mage, and a mess. It took me one glance to see it, but Jin... Gosh, he's such a pure-hearted soul. He sees a walking mess and falls in love with it."

My cheeks are burning. Jin is in love with me?

It can't be. I know in my heart she's wrong. The jealousy is real but her conclusions are wrong. Why would he? Who would fall in love with a mess? And Pavlína got that much right—I *am* a mess, even worse than she thinks I am. If Jin truly has feelings for me, it's because he doesn't know me, because he sees my helpless little self and feels obliged to assist, not knowing the destruction in my veins.

"You don't deserve him!" Pavlína says, tears in her eyes.

I agree. I don't.

Just then, we see him running, dust-covered and with a bleeding scratch on his cheek. His eyes fall on me, then Pavlína, and then the shed in shambles around us. "I'm sorry," he blurts out before he's even reached us, leaning heavily on his knees. "You're okay. Are you okay?" He sounds breathless and confused.

Pavlína and I share a glance, silently wondering which of us will go to him and relieve him of his worry. It's not going to be me, so I watch as Pavlína runs over, fusses about his injury, and tells him we're okay. She never mentions my contribution, and though part of me yearns for him to know his teaching wasn't in vain, I can't deal with his reaction.

He doesn't know me, and I can't tell him. And thus, we're caught in between—too scared of the truth, too guilty of the lie, not worthy of either.

19

Contrary to Pavlína's belief, there was no human hand in the storm, just another elemental that broke free from the Wyld Lands. I don't get the chance to ask Jin whether the door was opened yet again, but I notice a guardian is permanently posted to the portal when I cross the courtyard.

The courtyard's in surprisingly good shape, but then I already knew the metal of the supply shed made it sound worse than it was. A few remaining branches and shingles are scattered on the ground, the rest already swept up by air mages and cleared aside. I see at least two broken windows and personal items carried away from their original place. The statues are all fine, and so are the people. Mages are a resilient bunch.

And I'd better get resilient fast, because the next week is murderous. The teachers claim they've spread out the exams, but that's still resulted in days with at least two but often three exams. I've tried my best preparing for them all, though my focus was clearly on the practical.

Elemental History leaves me physically drained when I hand in my papers at the ring of the bell. I tried to catch up but I'm not sure I got a single date or name correct and jumbled up most of the context. Hopefully it'll be just enough to keep me alive for another term.

I completely botch the non-magic History as well, having paid almost no attention to the even less interesting events of World War I. On the other hand, Chemistry goes well, and Maths leaves me on a high note, with the rest of the subjects landing somewhere in the middle. And while Wyld Lands Geography was the most enjoyable exam—we had to do a version of the group project with added context questions—I'm not sure I actually did well. I hope so, but we'll have to see once the results are posted.

Neither of those exams matter in the end, because the only test I truly care about is the air magic one. The good news is I haven't had any breathing problems throughout the week; the bad news is my stomach is cramping terribly, and not just because I'm on my period—I can't get the thought out of my head that I won't get to go to the Wyld Lands if I don't pass my first level. The matter's made worse by the entire school being present for the tests. We've got fire and water in the morning, then earth and air in the afternoon, and of course, the first level attempts are going last. I have to sit through every single student's test first before I get to mine.

Most students do well—Ester does an amazing job at her water level, splitting the fountain's water neatly as if she were Moses, then demonstrating how she can command the water to jump into her hand. The older students can produce orbs of water but her attempt is still admirable. She doesn't even get her skin wet.

The same can't be said for another student who ends up splashing both himself and the two people next to him. I ache deeply for him, fearing exactly the same outcome.

I hadn't yet seen the fire mages in action, but I'm mesmerised by the higher-level presentations. A Year 13 boy with dark hair and eyes and deep-brown skin juggles the fire so masterfully he creates circular patterns and thrilling fake misses. If his other job aspirations don't work out, he can always try for the circus.

Jamila struggles a bit with making their flame hop from the set up micro-pyres. At first, it doesn't want to move at all, and then they set the entire column beneath on fire. The last hop is picture perfect though, and they show no problem when walking through literal fire. I'm impressed.

After lunch, we move on to the earth students, who I find the most boring, since it's all just strength and brute force. Every time the earth shakes underneath me, I want to throw up. To my dismay, Pavlína goes straight for level two and passes with flying colours. There aren't many who shoot above where they're supposed to be, so everyone claps wildly when she's awarded her level.

Generally, the elemental tests have a great vibe, if only I could bring myself to enjoy them. Those who are already done are turning it into some kind of party, cheering loudly for their classmates and welcoming each finished student with claps—or hugs in the few cases when a level isn't awarded.

Jin gets the loudest roars when he first passes his level six water test and then follows it up with a level *seven* air test. Since you need only level six to graduate, the accolades are entirely deserved. I'm stunned by his display of picking up three different-coloured feathers, mixing them, and then separating them out again to gently deposit them in the dead centre of their respective columns.

For a moment, I forget all about my own test and clap as wildly as everybody else. Jin's gaze finds me, a grin stretching across his entire face. He nods as if to say I can do that, too—someday. I'm not so sure about that, but I'm definitely inspired.

"We're so screwed," Lucio mutters next to me.

"You're going to be fine," I whisper, though I quietly agree. "Our task is much easier."

Just a week ago even our test seemed impossible, though comparably, it's really easy. All we need to do is show three things: one, push objects off three podiums with increasing distance; two, lift an object off the ground and deposit it a few metres away as gently as possible; and three, balance on a beam while the wind buffets you to show your understanding of air currents.

My classmates are all doing all right. Everyone topples the first and second target, with some struggling to reach the third in the allotted number of attempts. The object lifting is a bit shakier, but since no precision is required, most pass that one, too. The balance beam serves for a few laughs from the audience, but it seems to be the least important task. Judging by its continued occurrence in future level tests, no one expects a Year II student to withstand the wind for too long.

I'm starting to curse my last name, which has me almost at the end of the entire test run, forced to watch each triumph and failure as my stomach gets progressively worse.

"You've got this," a voice whispers, suddenly at my side.

Startling, I turn and find Jin crouching next to me. He's still wearing that stupid grin, and it does entirely different things to my already upset stomach. "Just remember the training and you'll be fine." He gives my shoulders a quick squeeze, somehow drawing some of that nervous energy out of my stomach and transferring it to my head instead.

Lightheaded, I get to my feet and walk over to the starting point to face the three columns. Mr Vávra looks a lot less encouraging and more like he's steeling himself for my inevitable failure. He gives me a nod. "Give it your best, Milena."

I close my eyes, trying to tune out the crowd who can't keep quiet despite some enthusiastic hushes. My stomach grows tighter and tighter, and I know if I don't seize the wind now, it'll burst from me. I raise my arms, following Jin's instructions.

Just like in the shed, the wind comes to my immediate attention. I direct it outward, and it blows not just past the first, but the second and third column as well, wiping all three objects off in one fell swoop. If there'd been a fourth column, I would've reached that one, too.

The crowd falls quiet at once, as if collectively holding their breath. Mr Vávra makes a surprised little sound, suddenly smiling, before making a note on his tablet. "Task two please, with a little more control."

I'm not good at the control thing, not today, when I can hardly contain the joyous wind that's bursting out of me. I pick up the box with ease, whirling it through the air before nearly flattening it upon impact. Not the gentle landing I was aiming for, causing both me and Mr Vávra to wince, but it landed smack down in the middle of the target area. I hope that counts more than the impact.

By the time I move onto the third task, I feel buoyant with my unexpected success. I've finally moved past my weird block and can feel the wind again. When I step onto the balance beam, I feel like I'm on the roof above the school with only Jin's eyes on me.

Gusts buffet me from all sides as I twirl and dance across the beam, unable to stay still as a statue. I'm a butterfly in the wind, free, light, and always changing, not a tree rooted to the ground that breaks before it bends. Not once do I miss my step, and when I lean, it's because the air holds me there. I can't fall. Not today. Not when I'm on top of the world.

When the wind lessens after a while, I feel bereft.

"I think that was long enough. We've got a few more students to get through," Mr Vávra says, the amusement palpable in his voice. "That was quite impressive, Milena, though I want you to work on your control next term."

Suddenly, the nervousness is back. "Did I pass?"

He laughs. "Yes. Yes, you passed."

With a little squeal, I run back to my previous spot and straight into Jin's arms.

"I knew it!" he shouts loud enough for way too many people to hear, then whirls me around. It's almost as if I'm back on the beam, only this time, he's the wind to my butterfly wings.

Someone clears their throat nearby, and Jin sets me down with an adorable blush gracing his cheeks. "Sorry," he mutters, still fighting the grin on his face without much success.

The person who pulled us back to the ground was Grisha, who seems more amused than anything. "Favouritism." They click their tongue in mocking derision.

"Teacher's pride," Jin says with a cough, and I can't help but giggle. In that moment, I see exactly what Pavlína saw. I might even believe it.

A sudden thought crosses Jin's face and he slaps my shoulder. As if he needed to get my attention. "Hey, that means you're coming to the Wyld Lands with us!"

"Yes!" I can practically feel my eyes glowing, a grin of my own stretching my face. "I can't wait!"

"I'll better tell Martínková right away, then." Jin winks at me before pushing through the crowd, expertly fielding questions to our relationship status with nothing more than a smile or shrug.

"The Wyld Lands?" Grisha asks. "You're gonna come with us?"

I shrug cheekily. "It's my reward."

They laugh and I giggle along while the last of my classmates passes her test. Then my eyes catch Pavlína who's standing not too far away, staring at me as if I've broken an important promise. Abruptly, she turns on her heels and hurries away.

Chalk it up to my high point, but I run after her, catching up just before she reaches the dorms. "Wait, please."

Pavlína whirls around. "What was *that?*"

"You have to be a bit more specific."

She laughs hollowly. "You practically acing that test. Jin. The *Wyld Lands!* Why do *you* get to go? Why do you even *want* to go? To be alone with Jin? To have him all to yourself?"

As tantalising as the thought is, I doubt there's going to be much alone time. "It's a big class trip."

"Of Year 12s and 13s! You've just started out!" Once again, she's got nothing but vitriol for me.

I cross my arms, refusing to be stripped of my joy because of her miserable black heart. "It was a deal I made with Jin. He thought it'd help me with my breathing problems."

"Breathing problems, ha!" Pavlína waves a hand at the testing ground. "I didn't see any breathing problems there."

"I had a good day," I say, a little flustered now. Obviously, I still want to go to the Wyld Lands. I earned it.

Pavlína narrows her eyes before mirroring my stance. "I don't like you."

"Never would've guessed."

"You're a nothing, and yet, everyone blows sugar up your ass. You get to join late, skip out on homework, get tons of private lessons from our Head Boy, and now you're telling me you get to go on a Wyld Lands trip a whole year early. It's not fair."

I know so little about the workings here at the Wyld Lands Academy, I never considered how that might feel to anybody else. Pavlína is right, but only in that regard. Because all the other things she mentioned… "I worked my ass off to make up for all the stuff I missed. I didn't choose to start late."

"Then why did you?" she demands.

Broken glass, screams, a lab in ruins. I can't tell her that. I can't tell anyone. "Because not everyone can be as lucky as you and born into this."

"You think I'm lucky?"

"You *are* lucky, Princess."

Pavlína glares at me. "Fine. Enjoy your spoils. I hope the Wyld Lands teaches you a valuable lesson, because there's no way you're ready."

"We'll see."

Only we don't, because when I wake up the next morning, I can't breathe.

20

As the winter holidays begin, I find myself in the Infirmary Wing, hooked up to an oxygen machine. Even with the extra help, my asthma's playing up so much every single breath is an act of labour. All I can do is sit propped up with pillows and breathe—everything else is way too strenuous.

My mother's been texting me non-stop—she gave up on talking when I took ages to scrape together enough energy for a reply. She's at a conference but she's ready to drop it all to hurry to my side and bring me home to recuperate. I don't want that. All I want is for this episode to pass so I don't miss the air camp in the Wyld Lands. I've worked too hard to have it taken from me by my stupid asthma.

Unfortunately, Ms Martínková doesn't think it's a good idea. She's here to take a look at me after Jin went to her on my behalf. He's hovering near the door, fluctuating between anxiety and encouragement. If I know anything about him, he'll be blaming himself for my state.

"I'm sorry, I don't see how this is going to work." Ms Martínková seems confused by our request to let me go, despite my health issues.

Jin jumps in to save me from having to talk too much. "Because exposure to the Wyld Lands could help. As I understand it, her breathing problems started when she came to the school. I suspect too much exposure to earth magic."

"Earth magic is steadying for air mages. They balance each other," Ms Martínková says in a tense voice.

"But she's not in balance," Jin points out, "she's struggling to breathe. It only gets better off the ground or near the Wyld Lands." He searches my face to confirm his theory. "As soon as the door closed the first time, her breathing got worse. It improved dramatically when she spent nearly an hour in a wyld storm."

Put like that, it makes a lot of sense. I like this explanation much more than that there's something wrong with my lungs.

"And it got worse again, much worse," Ms Martínková points out.

"Because she spent half an afternoon exposed to earth magic." Jin throws his hands up in the air. "I know it doesn't make sense, magic doesn't work like that, but it does for her."

Both the director and I frown at him. He's starting to make a lot less sense.

"When you say we balance each other, it means we take just enough off each other's edge to enter an equilibrium. I can control my airflow better when paired with an earth mage, but I also lose power. What if..." He suddenly sucks in his lips and rolls them out without saying anything.

"What are you insinuating, Mr Čermák?" Ms Martínková's voice has taken on a dangerous tone.

Jin looks as if he's about to faint. He swallows. "Nothing. Just that something knocked her out of equilibrium, and going to the Wyld Lands might be just what she needs." He pulls up his shoulders. "I just have this feeling."

"Please," I whisper, hoping it'll tip the scale.

Ms Martínková takes a long look at Jin and then me before shaking her head. "I'm sorry, my dear, but I don't think that would be wise. If Jin is right, the Wyld Lands could be deadly for you, in more than one way."

"The Wyld Lands are always deadly," Jin mutters.

"And you're willing to risk her?" Ms Martínková snaps. "You're making me wonder whether you truly have your fellow student's best interest at heart or if this is something more personal."

Jin stares at her in confusion. Then his cheeks redden considerably. "I promised to take her if she passed the exams, and she passed her air test with flying colours. Did you see?"

"I was watching, yes." Ms Martínková sounds less than impressed. "I saw a lot of brute force and little control." She turns to me and pats my hand, as if it makes her assessment any easier to swallow. "You did a good job in what little time you've had here, but as I told you, we need to work on your control. You don't want to accidentally hurt anybody, right?"

Fear floods me, filling my veins with ice and causing a coughing spell. *Please don't tell Jin all about my shortcomings. I can't deal with that now.* All I manage to croak is, "Please don't..."

Her gaze softens. "My dear, even if Jin is right, the Wyld Lands could be the worst place to send you. The winds are stronger, yes, but so are the powers of the earth. You might forget how to breathe altogether."

I can't imagine it after the few tastes I've had. But then again, no earth elementals have escaped the Wyld Lands while I've been here.

"And even if that doesn't affect you, you can't even stand right now. All students must be prepared to quickly evacuate at a moment's notice—that requires a minimum level of physical fitness. You aren't in any shape for that."

She strokes my cheek when she notices my eyes filling with tears. "Right now you need to focus on getting better. There'll be plenty of opportunities to visit the Wyld Lands later, I promise." She sounds like she really means it.

It's not good enough. "What if I never get better?" I whisper in true teenage drama fashion. I suck in a rattling breath. "I want to feel that wind just once."

Ms Martínková closes her eyes with a shudder. "It's too much of a risk," she says when she opens them again. With a swift motion, she gets up. "Rest now."

She sweeps out of the room, leaving me to bite back tears. *I won't cry. I won't cry.* It costs me more than I can give right now, but I manage to keep my emotions at bay.

"Milena?" Jin asks tenderly.

"I'd like to sleep now." I wish someone else could take over breathing for me; it's too much of a hassle right now.

"Of course." He reaches out to me but curls his fingers before they get anywhere. "I hope you're better soon."

There's such a heavy weight on my lungs, I don't think I'll ever be better again.

Later that day, after a granny nap, I'm visited by Ester and Jamila. Since it's the holidays, they're not wearing their school uniform. Ester's natural style is very cosy with a knitted dress over thick tights and what looks like a hand-made pullover. In contrast, Jamila prefers tight-fitted jeans and a leather jacket that hugs their curves and leaves nothing for the wind to catch. They're also wearing a shirt with a band logo I immediately recognise. Most importantly, they brought a selection of snacks. They take a seat on my bed either side of my feet.

"How are you feeling?" Ester asks.

"Sorry for myself," I admit, which makes Jamila grin. "I should be packing for the Wyld Lands camp now, not laying around in a hospital bed doing nothing." At least, my breathing has improved enough to allow me to speak full sentences.

Jamila grasps my hand, gingerly avoiding the line they put in so they can pump me full of cortisol and steroids. "There's still one and a half weeks of break. We'll do lots of other cool things."

I've never had friends so I have no idea what these kinds of things might be. The only thing I know is they're not the Wyld Lands.

"Yes!" Ester chimes in. "We can explore Prague, eat palacinky, go ice-skating... It'll be fun."

Jamila clasps my fingers with a wistful smile. "And Jin will be back before you know it—camp's only for two days. You'll have plenty of time to snuggle up with him or whatever you guys do."

I need to catch my breath and not for medical reasons. "What?"

"He's your boyfriend, isn't he?" Jamila asks. "Lucio says he is, and everyone saw you at the tests. Fair warning: the whole school's talking about it."

I think I'm going to be sick, sicker than I already am. "The whole school is talking about me?"

Though she's far away, I feel Pavlína's hate waver around me. I tried to talk to her after the test but she'll hate me for all the public attention

I drew, and surely, everyone else will be able to see what Jin apparently can't: that I'm not good enough for him. Just a little Year 11 girl with a big crush.

Ester watches me curiously. "Are you okay?"

"We're not..." I take another deep breath. "He was just doing his job, trying to whip me into shape."

"Oh, too much information," Jamila jokes, pretending to be aghast.

"Not funny."

Ester exchanges a glance with Jamila before forcing a smile at me. "People are just very excited. Everyone loves him."

Yeah, and they're going to hate me. Probably do already. "So, break plans," I say, trying to move away from the hurtful topic. I don't want to make alternative break plans, I just want to be magically better and go with the other air mages.

"Yes, we could take the train to Kutna Hora and visit the Church of Bones," Ester suggests, her eyes shining.

"Isn't it always full of tourists?" Jamila asks, not sounding very keen.

Ester pouts. Apparently, she's really interested in this creepy church. "Not in winter. What do you want to do?"

The two continue making plans for enough days to last the entire break and all upcoming weekends. It's not going to happen—they're just being nice because I'm hurt. We'll do one or two things and then I'll be abandoned for other friends... or private dates, since I've got a front seat to so many glances, accidental touches, and insider jokes.

"Well, we'll leave you alone for now," Jamila announces after an hour. "Fingers crossed you're much better soon."

"Oh." Ester's reminded of something and pulls a book out of her bag. "You'll probably like the first Spirit Seeker book. It has a massive storm in it." Ester deposits the book on my nightstand—I recognise the blue-haired girl on the cover.

They open the door, almost running into Jin. The Head Boy takes a step back while Jamila throws me a knowing glance.

Once they're gone, he steps in, fighting a grin on his face. "Good news."

"Really?"

"Really. I managed to convince Martínková to let me take you. We're going."

Now this *is* good news. A smile blooms on my face almost immediately, my chest feeling lighter already. Who is this wonderful boy and how did he pull off this miracle?

"You excited?"

Hell yeah, I'm excited!

21

My stats improve enough overnight that I feel almost hopeful. My chest is still tight and I can't shake the wheezing when I breathe, but I can stand on my own two feet and I'm strong-willed enough not to let my body take this from me.

Unsurprisingly, I'm the youngest in the group. Everybody else knows each other, and of course, they all know Jin, horsing around with him while I lean against the wall, trying to preserve my energy. The nurse gave me a bag full of inhalers and adrenaline in case of emergency. She's not happy to see me go, but Ms Martínková overruled her professional opinion.

By the time the doors are finally opened, I'm already exhausted. Maybe I won't be going all the way to the camp, a step into the Wyld Lands might suffice to make me better. Who am I kidding? It'll never be enough until I reach the peak of my dreams.

Ms Martínková tells Jin to take care before she steps in to activate the portal. I'm the last one to file into the building. The doors are closed behind me to guard against elemental beings, leaving us in a space too tight and dark for my taste. But then something wonderful happens. A fresh breeze whips through the building, bringing air from another world. I see light swirling ahead, and then a picture appears just like the paintings outside Ms Martínková's office. A hum beckons me from ahead and my chest rises in response.

As silly as it may sound, I feel like I belong there, like I was ripped from this world before I could remember and finally found my way back. Maybe it's a mage-thing, hence their inability to leave this world alone. The Year 12s, who've never been here before, are certainly astonished.

"Control your power while you're with the others," Ms Martínková tells me when it's just the two of us. "Remember that."

A reminder of what a loose cannon I am. I give her a sharp nod, then step into the wild world behind the portal. The wind welcomes me with a gust strong enough to keep me from taking another step. It's like an overeager puppy that forgets how big and strong it is. I love it.

The portal closes behind me, sort of vanishing from sight. One second it's like a cut in the world, the next, the cut has healed, no scar remaining. It's wondrous, but not as much as the world in front of me.

First off, there's no winter here: the air is warmer and everything's green, perhaps even a little too green. Mountains rise all around me to breathtaking heights, their peaks shrouded in clouds. Their flanks are covered with trees, growing thick enough to form a jungle, before giving way to coarser growth and snow. Lightning and thunder roar across one range, and in the distance an avalanche thunders down the mountain side. Nearby water rushes down a cliff I can't see, while steam rises from the bottom of a valley. Beautiful lakes glisten in the sun, beckoning with unknown depths. The grass I'm standing in is so long it tickles my thighs as it sways in the wind. Clouds bulge and are torn apart within seconds, the fragments racing each other across the sky, until once more lightning splits the heavens. My hair flies free and tangles before I can take two breaths. Someone stupidly brought a hat. It brushes my cheek before whirling out of reach.

"Let's get to camp," Jin shouts, his voice barely loud enough to reach over the wind.

The group moves as one. The experienced air mages create a tunnel for us to walk through, shielding us from the more violent gusts. Everyone seems to be in good spirits and prepared for a little hike.

I'm completely in love with this world, but I realise Ms Martínková was right to worry within minutes. I don't have the stamina to keep pace, soon trailing behind everyone else. As much as I love the wind, it makes it even harder to make my way through the high grass. If this world is allowing me to breathe easier, I wouldn't know it since the exertion steals every breath I make.

"Hey." Suddenly Jin's at my side, forcing the wind to blow around us. "Sorry I left you alone. Come on, I'll carry you."

"Carry me?" I gasp for air.

"Yeah, come on." He nods towards his back. "It's the least I can do when you're still sick."

It's embarrassing but the alternative is he'll walk me back, and I'll have to admit to Ms Martínková she was right and that the Wyld Lands aren't the long-lost home I imagined them to be.

As I climb onto Jin's back, he huffs. Not a good sign. "Am I too heavy?"

"No!" Jin sounds horrified. "Uhm, it's not you. You just feel... Gosh, how do I say this without sounding like a complete ass?"

"Just say 'you're too heavy. Get off of me'."

His hands dig deeper into my thighs as he readjusts his grip. "You stay right where you are."

To be honest, I feel heavy. Heavy and unwieldy. Jin might be biting down on his complaints, but I hear the increased strain in his breathing. Bravely, he forges on, carrying me nearly all the way to the campsite.

The site is located at the bottom of a canyon with striking tones of red, yellow, and even purple creating twisted, dreamlike shapes that beg to be painted. The path we're on is so narrow I need to walk by myself, but Jin's wind presses me against the cliff side, never allowing me to lose my footing. When we arrive at the bottom, the others have already set up the tents in surprisingly well-carved hollows and are out playing with the wind.

A group of students are climbing the side of the canyon only to jump from various heights. When I see the first one fall, my heart stops, but he does a flip in the air before catching a breeze and landing perfectly on his feet. Others jump from even higher, not a parachute in sight.

"They're flying."

Jin grins at me. "You want to give it a try?"

I remember how I flew in my dreams—they're just jumping from the cliffs like divers. The wind cushions their fall, but it never stops them fully, and they're still more graceful than I'd ever be. "Not at the moment."

"Okay."

I feel bad for keeping him from having fun with his friends, so I claim I need to recover in the tent Grisha set up for me, then proceed to spend the entire time until dinner feeling sorry for myself. I'd hoped the Wyld Lands would magically heal me, that my dreams would become reality. Instead, I feel like a stone thrown into a deep lake. Everyone else is swimming while I sink to the bottom, unable to enjoy light and air.

Dinner looks fun from afar. Everyone's chipping in, preparing food to roast over a fire guarded by at least three air mages until everyone gathers around to eat. No one tries to engage with me since none of them actually know who I am. I'm the intruder, observing when everyone else is participating. It reminds me of every time I entered a new school; the eternal outsider.

The only one who takes any notice of me is Jin, and his attention is in constant demand from everybody else. It isn't until dinner finishes and the fire's burning higher he manages to cut himself loose to crouch next to me. "Are you finished?" he asks softly.

"Yeah. I'll probably go to sleep and—"

"No." He sounds surprisingly adamant. "Come on, there's something I want to check out."

He doesn't leave me any choice as he drags me up to my feet and leads me away from the camp. Further and further we go into the canyons. When I look back, the fire's gone, and we're alone. Somewhere ahead, I see a mighty rockfall, and my heart sinks as I think about the canyon walls collapsing around us.

"What did you want to show me?"

Jin points upwards. Darkness is falling quickly but in the sky stars bloom. Way more stars than I've ever seen before. The milky way is a thick band bursting with light, and there are nebulas. Real, colourful nebulas.

"Wow."

"It's pretty amazing, isn't it?"

Jin puts his hands on my shoulders, the touch feeling as if water is running under my shirt. The sensation makes my stomach flutter, but I keep my mouth shut, not wanting Jin to stop touching me.

I keep staring up until he whispers, "How do you feel?"

"Good," I answer promptly.

He lets his hands fall with a sigh. "No, you don't."

I turn to him, raising an eyebrow. "Why did you ask if you know better?"

"Because it's the polite thing to do?" He gives a little shrug before pressing his lips together. "I didn't want the standard answer," he admits, "the one you give to everybody."

"But I'm good," I protest. "I'm not in pain and I can breathe. There's nothing wrong, so I'm good."

He sighs heavily, reminding me of my mother. But instead of pushing, he sits on a boulder and pats the place next to him. "I'm sorry."

"For what?" I ask cautiously before I sit next to him, instantly pulling up a leg to bed my head on.

"For not taking the hint and leaving you alone."

I swallow. "Who says I want to be left alone?"

He throws me a long glance, as if somehow every cell of my body is screaming the truth at him. Suddenly self-conscious, I lower my leg and sit up straight.

"You never tell me anything about yourself. Not even how you really are."

If I could be wound any tighter, my organs would burst. "Obviously," I start slowly, "I'm not fine. I mean, it's no fun being unable to breathe."

"You're still having problems?"

Now that he's asking, I realise I don't actually have breathing problems. My lungs feel bigger than they did just moments before. Do I dare take a deep breath? No, the disappointment's lurking too close.

"You don't let anyone in, do you?" Jin asks softly. When I don't know how to reply, he probes a little deeper. "When was the last time you let loose?"

I can't keep myself from grimacing, instantly recalling the wreckage of a lab I left behind.

"That bad?" he whispers. "Look, you don't have to tell me anything if you don't want to, it's not my place to demand anything of you. I just…" He gives me a half-smile. "I just want to get to know you better."

A sigh escapes my lips, and my shoulders deflate. "I don't…" I swallow, unable to speak the words out aloud.

"What?" Jin raises his hand and gently brushes a strand of hair from my cheek. "What is it?"

He's so kind and adorable. How can I possibly keep him in my life after telling him who I am? "I don't want you to hate me," I whisper at last.

His eyes widen. "Hate you? I could never do that."

I moan in frustration. "You can't say things like that."

"Why?" He turns to face me, crossing his legs under him. "Come on, what makes you think I could possibly hate you?"

"Everyone does," I blurt out. Before he can protest, I hurry to say, "And you're perfect, the golden boy, beloved by everybody. You shouldn't be hanging out with someone like me." I wave behind me in the direction of where we came from. "There's a party waiting for you. Why are you wasting your time with me?" I manage to laugh but the sound is hollow. Tears spring to my eyes.

Instead of leaving me, Jin grabs my hands. "Tell me. Tell me everything. Let it all out." There's an urgency in his voice I can't resist.

"You want to know everything?"

He nods.

"All my dark shameful secrets?"

Jin chuckles, then smiles. "All of it. Come on." He pulls me to my feet. Standing on the boulder, we're two metres above the ground. "Tell it to the wind. Throw it all out there."

I don't know what the point of all this is, but I'm too tired to hold back. "Okay, fine. I'm not like you."

"That's a good thing in my opinion," he jokes.

"Not in mine," I retort. "This is my eighth school in four years. I was expelled from every single one."

He didn't expect that. No one ever does. "What for?"

"Destruction of school property. Violent behaviour. More destruction. Last time, I almost killed somebody." Phew, I've never said that one out loud.

Jin squeezes my hands. "Go on. Tell me what happened."

"The wind happened. It always does." Right now, it's blowing through the canyon, howling as it hits the crevices in the stone. "When I get upset, my magic gets loose and I can't stop it." I bite my lips then force myself to say it anyway, "I don't want to stop myself."

"What got you upset?"

"That's the question you want to ask?"

He shrugs. "You can tell me whatever you want."

"I didn't want to tell you anything." But now I can't seem to stop myself. If he wants to know it all, he'll have it all. "At my last school, there was a couple—the *it* couple of the school or whatever shit they called themselves." Just thinking of it makes me want to puke. "I didn't know that when I joined the class, and I thought he was flirting with me. Very nice guy, almost like you."

Jin gives me a sceptical look, as if he's already decided he doesn't want to be compared.

"He kept being nice and I kept being stupid. When he asked me to meet him in the lab, I said yes." How stupidly nervous I'd been, checking my face in my phone every single minute, as if that would've made a difference. "He comes, lays it on thick, and then he leans in to kiss me, but instead of kissing me, I hear the shutter sound of a phone camera."

The tears are threatening to flow over. The memory still cuts as deep as the real thing did back then when I was in the lab. I force them back in, taking a deep breath through my nose.

"His girlfriend took the pictures and promised to show everybody what a wanton slut I was. Then they laughed about how stupid I was because I couldn't hold back my tears. And then the wind came."

"I'm sorry," Jin says in a horrified whisper.

"Sorry?" I laugh, though all I want to do is cry. "You don't need to feel sorry for me. I called the wind and it whipped through the lab until I stood in a maelstrom of broken glass and furniture. I almost cut them to pieces; she nearly lost an eye. So, there. That's the kind of freak I am."

"You're not a freak," Jin says, though his voice can't quite hide his shock. "You didn't know how to control your magic then."

"I can't control it now either," I snap. "Look at me." I tear myself free from his grip and hop off the boulder, landing on my two feet like the stone I am. "You don't see me whirling through the air. No one has ever seen someone suck as much at the basics as me. *You* had to work with me every waking hour to get me into shape for the exam."

"Which you passed," Jin protests, climbing off the boulder. "And of course you can't ride the wind yet—you've been at our school for less than two months, and you're not a legacy student like most."

"Ha!" I raise my finger at him, triumphant. "According to Ms Martínková, my father was an air mage. But he left when I was four. He knew I was hopeless; more trouble than I'm worth."

Jin shakes his head, dumbfounded. "I don't believe that. Whatever made your father leave had nothing to do with you. You were only a child."

"A terrible, wilful child who had the worst tantrums."

"Every child has tantrums."

"Not every child destroys the room they're in," I shoot back. The wind blows the tears out of my eyes before they can fall. Forcefully, I pull back from the edge and soften my voice. "Look, I don't need you to make me feel better about myself. I know what I am and what I'm not. You did well. You're really kind."

Jin winces as if I've stuck a dagger in his heart. "You weren't some kind of task for me to complete."

"Oh, please. You saw a younger student struggling and came to help. And I'm grateful for it," I assure him, "I truly am."

He shakes his head. "You never needed my help."

"What are you talking about? I could do *nothing* before you stepped in."

Jin takes a step closer and points at my chest. "That's because you keep everything so closed up inside there. Even now."

Shaking my head, I take a step back. "I don't understand."

He follows me, not willing to back down. "You open the door and then you get scared and talk yourself out of it, forcing it shut. You want to cry but you push the tears back. And you do that all the time. When you talk to your mum or to Ms Martínková, and every single time I ask you a question."

"I don't want to be a burden."

"Why? Because that makes you more real? Tangible? Or because it makes you challenging? A person with edges for others to rub against?"

The stupid tears are back. I blink wildly. "I don't want…" I don't even know what I don't want.

But Jin does. "Hurt. You don't want to get hurt," he repeats. "So, instead you build your walls sky-high and keep all that wonderful chaos deep inside."

"How do you know it's not awful?" I burst into tears, gasping in the strong wind that's blowing through the canyon.

"Why don't we find out? Together." He grabs my hands and pulls me closer. "I promise I won't run away. I'm not tricking you or just doing my job. I want to know you, Milena, like I've never wanted to know anyone before."

I can't think straight. What does he mean? What more does he want from me?

"Tell me how you feel." Jin steps closer, touching our hands to his chest. "Really feel."

For several heartbeats, I stare into his light eyes as the wind continues to beat the rock around us while the stars shine above. How do I really feel? Confused? Overwhelmed? "Lonely. I feel lonely."

He closes his eyes, relieved I finally gave him something true. "Tell me more," he begs. "Let it all out."

"I don't belong here," I admit. "I don't belong anywhere." The wind blows my cheeks dry, but more tears follow now I'm no longer trying so hard to keep them locked inside. "It's always the same. I go to a new school—sometimes, they're nice, sometimes, they already know and are all little assholes, but it doesn't matter because sooner or later, I screw it all up. Again, and again, and again!"

I shake my head violently as a wave of frustration rolls over me. "No matter how hard I try, I'm always the problem. I don't know if my dad left because of me, but why else would he? If it weren't for me and all the problems I cause, my mum and dad would still be together. They would have other children. Easier children.

"My mum's really trying her best, but she's had to deal with me for the last sixteen years. She hates me, and I can't even blame her. I would hate myself if I were her." No, that isn't right. "What I mean is that I *do* hate myself. Because I can't ever get it right."

"Milena," Jin says softly, but it's too late now.

"She's at the ends of her wits with me. I'm at the end of my wits with me. I want to be good. I really, really want to be good, but I can't. It's all too hard and I never fit in, not even here, where people don't think I'm crazy because I can call the wind."

The wind mirrors my turmoil. It hasn't been a wind for a long time, but a grown storm that's ricocheting between the walls of the canyon. Dark clouds have swallowed the stars, dipping us in near complete darkness. The lack of sight emphasises the roar of the gusts as they whip past us, sending pebbles flying.

"Ms Martínková says I need to learn to control myself, but I can't, it's impossible. Pavlína has it right: I don't belong here, and I don't deserve all the good things that happen to me."

"Yes, you do," Jin insists, agitated in his own right. "Please calm—"

"I don't!" I shout in his face, while trying to tear my hands free. "Didn't you listen to anything I said? I'm not worthy of your kindness. You'd be far better off without me. Anybody would. Really."

He grimaces. "Who told you all this?"

"I don't know."

My mother's exasperated sighs. My father's absence. My classmates' look of horror and disgust. My teachers' disappointment. Myself. In the mirror. Late in bed. Every single time something feels a little too good.

The tears stream freely now, though the wind won't allow them to fall on the ground. "I just want one place to stay in." My voice starts to falter, straining to be heard in the cacophony around us. "One place to belong. One person to—"

Suddenly, the air to speak is robbed from me when Jin's lips press against mine.

22

One minute, there's a storm inside of me, bursting from the seams, tearing down every wall I've ever built; the next, silence envelops me as Jin steals the breath from my lips. That point of touch between us becomes my sole point of focus.

I have no idea what I was even talking about before. Jin is kissing me, and his lips feel so soft and warm. His breath mingles with mine until I no longer know where I end and he begins. He lets go of my hands only to wrap his arms around my body and pull me tight. As the space between us vanishes, my hands wander up his chest and neck until they somehow sink into the soft hair on top of his head.

My fingers dig deep as his tighten around my waist. His tongue slips between my lips and finds mine, eager to play. I've never done this with a boy, leaving me completely unprepared for how the soft touch sends full-body shivers through my veins. I suddenly want more of him. Even though our bodies are already pressed against each other, I want to be closer.

My greed makes us stumble, and with a laugh, Jin breaks off the kiss. I gasp for air, only now realising how long I must've gone without it. The storm has ceased and the stars are shining above us once more. In their light, I see Jin's eyes glisten with unabashed lust. A smile tugs on his lips, a wild, free thing that can't be contained. It mirrors the one on my face.

An intoxicating mix of excitement, embarrassment, confusion, and desire fills me, making my head swim. "Wow."

"Sorry."

"Sorry?" I laugh at him. "For what?"

He can't stop grinning either. "I should've asked. I..." He closes his eyes, taking a few deep breaths. "I didn't know what else to do to make you stop."

Confusion wins out. "Make me stop?"

Jin opens his eyes again. They watch me full of warmth. "The wind was responding to you."

"Oh." That's not quite what I expected. "Is that bad?"

"No! No, no, it's..." He takes another deep breath. "It was exactly what I'd hoped for. I just didn't expect it to be this strong. For you to be this strong." The look he gives me does something dark and delicious to my stomach. "You're... Wow."

I'm still confused, unsure of whether he diffused the bomb or whether I blew him completely away. "So, was it a real kiss?"

His eyes widen. "Oh, it was real." He nods eagerly. "I mean, I've wanted to do that ever since I saw you... Ever since I saw the wind in your hair."

"You did?" His confession leaves me speechless. I don't know when he saw the wind in my hair—in the courtyard or on the roof, most likely. Either is so much longer ago than I expected. "I thought you only—"

Jin pulls me closer, resting his forehead on mine to look deep into my eyes. "There is no *only* in how I feel about you. This isn't just some fleeting emotion because I don't know you better. I'm not going to turn my back on you."

My knees feel weak as he reminds me of all the self-doubt that plagues me.

"You can trust me," Jin whispers.

I wish I could. I wish I could just let myself believe his feelings for me are as true as he claims them to be. I want to believe him. Just once, I want someone to love me despite all I am.

He must've felt my doubts and lack of trust, because he turns his head to the side and kisses my cheek, then again, and again until his lips touch the corner of my mouth. With bated breath, I wait for him to plant the next kiss. When it comes, I fall straight into it. At least two dozen more follow, as if the multitude could somehow make me forget how inadequate I feel. To be honest, it's a valiant attempt. I'm positively swooning when he lets go of me again and takes my hand instead.

"Shall we go back?" he whispers.

I don't want to go back. I want to stay here in some abandoned canyon in the Wyld Lands where only the two of us exist, and kiss until every breath has left my body. But since I've retained at least one functioning brain cell, I nod. "Sure."

My answer earns me another delicious kiss. "I hope you can breathe easier now."

Chuckling, I intertwine my fingers with his. "A little."

Jin rolls his eyes while grinning at the same time. "Fine, I'll keep kissing you until the end of time."

I laugh out loud. "The end of time? I'm going to hold you to that now! That'll take a lot of stamina."

He grins. "What can I say? I'm an overachiever."

The laughter is almost as good as the kissing, it makes me feel light as a feather. In fact, I haven't felt this good in a long time. It might've been Jin's plan all along, but airing out all the things I kept inside has lifted a weight off my shoulders, and an even bigger one off my chest; weight I'd grown accustomed to because the alternative has always been destruction. I'd been scared of the feelings dwelling inside of me: the loneliness, the hurt, the intense hate that sometimes burrows deep into my stomach. They're still there, but they're no longer secret and thus as hurtful.

"Oh, fuck," Jin murmurs when we walk around the corner, reaching the campsite.

I stop and stare, a familiar feeling rising in my stomach. The camp is in literal pieces. Destruction has blown through it, not a single stone left unturned. People are going through the remnants, trying to salvage the scraps, while others take care of those who were wounded.

"Was that me?" I whisper, horrified.

Jin gives me a long look and I see him swallowing. "No, that's just the Wyld Lands for you. Beautiful one second, terrifying the next." He squeezes my hand. "It's not *your* fault."

He hides it well behind pretty words but his body betrays him. This is my fault. When I was airing all those grievances, the storm responded to my plight. It grew so strong Jin had to literally kiss the air from my lungs to stop it.

Control, Milena. You need to learn to control yourself.

I'd completely forgotten Ms Martínková's warning. It'd been too hard, too impossible. I passed my exam, but I didn't learn anything. It's either all or nothing for me and the wind.

No one else thinks it's my fault. They welcome Jin and immediately tell him about the wild storm that blew through camp. We were lucky to miss it, and there's some knowing looks exchanged. For a group that's just been assaulted by powerful winds, they're in surprisingly good spirits. But their jokes and laughter can't hide the wariness underneath.

I have no idea what this place looked like just half an hour ago, but it must've scared the shit out of them. And here I am, feeling sorry I missed it, that I didn't feel the strength of that wind against my body. I'm seriously deranged.

Jin squeezes my hand once more before he helps with the clean-up. "We've got to leave," is what I hear throughout the camp.

Leave. We've barely arrived. I haven't even had the chance to explore the Wyld Lands yet, to experience the elements in this place. I've only just managed to breathe freely, and now it'll be taken from me.

A girl's watching me. When I notice her staring, she quickly averts her eyes. No one else pays me any attention, so her gaze stays with me. She alone seems to see through Jin's pretence and know who's really to blame.

Guilt and passion battle inside of me. It's the Wyld Lands, Jin says, and maybe so. But I called that wind. I became that wind. Or maybe I'm giving myself too much credit—the wind may have come to me, but it has a life of its own. It doesn't care for me, it just blows and blows, tearing through the countryside, picking at everything not fixed in the stone.

I still haven't flown. I know in my heart I won't be able to do so back at the school. I can only discover my full potential here.

"Do we have to leave?" I ask Jin as he tightens the straps on his backpack. Not much was salvageable, but he's taken it upon himself to carry as much out of this dimension as he can.

"I'm afraid so. We don't have shelter for the night and people are hurt. We need to get them to the infirmary."

It all makes sense, and still, I feel the resistance in me grow. *Go on without me,* I want to say, but I'm not that stupid—the Wyld Lands will tear me apart. I don't have the experience to survive on my own out here.

"Do people ever try to live here?" I ask as we climb the canyon wall, the mountains in the distance rising under the carpet of stars.

Jin throws me a doubtful glance, weirded out by my question. "Who'd want that?"

It leaves me some things to mull over. His reply makes it sound as if he'd think anyone who'd ever consider it crazy. And rightly so, because that much force is terrifying. I guess I must be crazy, because when I look at this land, I feel an immense love for it. I want to drink in the stars, dance in the wind, and swim in the ocean.

Yep, I'm crazy.

Control, I think. *Control yourself. Don't let the wild tendencies win.*

It's not a life I relish living, but that's probably something every sullen teenager said ever. It's time to grow up and embrace the structures that keep us all safe; cut down the poppies, so the meadow can bloom.

23

We reach the portal in the early hours of morning. Everyone is exhausted since none of us had had any sleep, a boy is whimpering because of his leg, hit by a rock in the storm, and bothering him more and more with each step, and Jin and two others have been lugging our rubbish with them. They drop it in front of the portal with exhaustion and a bunch of others collapse right next to it, moaning and groaning about the strenuous trip. No one's laughing anymore.

I'm the only one still full of energy—I feel better than I have in weeks. On the way down, I had to be carried, but now I could keep going until the sun rises. I want to climb one of those peaks and look for the ocean, to jump a cliff and see if the wind catches me or tumble into the pool at the bottom. Most importantly, I want to stay.

There's no chance of that, though, so I trot through the portal at the end of the line, throwing one last glance at this wondrous world before it's taken from me yet again. I steel myself against the inevitable loss and wait for my breathing problems to return, but they don't come—I can still breathe fine when the portal is closed and we're exiting the building, a sorry bunch.

The teachers have already been alerted. The injured are ushered off to the infirmary, while the others are sent to their dorms.

Jin gives Ms Martínková a short report, claiming full responsibility. "I didn't see the storm coming. I should've read the air flows, but I was distracted and let them get away from me."

I had no idea about all the tasks he was supposed to fulfil. "It wasn't his fault," I chime in, "the wind came up suddenly."

Ms Martínková throws me a long glance before nodding at Jin. "That's right. There's always the risk of that in the Wyld Lands—they're not called wild for no reason. From what I can see, you made the right call and brought everyone home safely. Now, go, get some rest. You look absolutely shattered." I want to go with him, but Ms Martínková calls me back. "How are you feeling?" she asks, concerned. "Has your condition worsened?"

"On the contrary. I feel completely fine, like I could run a marathon." I have *never* run a marathon. I don't even participate in athletics events if I can help it.

Ms Martínková smiles. "That's good to hear. I'm glad the Wyld Lands helped in that regard."

"Can I go back?" I have no idea where that came from, but I feel so light and airy, the words just bubble from my lips.

She laughs. "No. I don't think that would be wise."

"Not now, but some other time? When's the next camp or excursion? Is there anything I can sign up for?"

"You can sign up for your bed right now," Ms Martínková says sternly but not without warmth. "It seems to me you're feeling a bit high. Caught a good wind?"

High? I've never taken drugs, though I have to agree, letting the wind blow through me always makes me feel amazing. "I didn't get the chance to fly."

Her smile is tinged with something sad. Regret, perhaps? "You will, Milena. One day, you'll fly unlike anyone before. Now, off to bed. Don't make me tie you down."

I want to hear more about my future flying potential but she shoos me towards the dorms. It's so early, Pavlína's still asleep. I don't think I'll ever drop off, but the moment my head touches the pillow, I fall through the veil into the Wyld Lands, and this time I get my chance.

I'm woken by agitated noises outside my room. The clock tells me it's about ten thirty in the morning. I feel groggy, as if I had too much to drink last night. Slightly disoriented, I sit up and let my eyes roam the room. Pavlína's gone. Then I realise one of the voices in the corridor is hers.

"I had to protect myself!" she hisses. "Your girlfriend's out of control."

"Protect yourself?" That's Jin. "You nearly killed her." He's furious.

Confused, I swing my legs out of bed and probe my ability to stand. Still a bit groggy but passable.

"Stop being so dramatic," Pavlína says. "A little earth magic's never killed anyone."

"She couldn't breathe! It always helped you."

Wait, stop. Obviously, they're talking about me, but what's this thing about killing me with *earth magic?* I thought my breathing problems were self-made, or maybe because of how much general earth magic is around—like in my room. Did Pavlína do something specifically?

"That's because she's also being dramatic. That girl has never had basic lessons, yet they put her into my room. And then I have to deal with her lousy control and late-night attacks. She called the damn wind in her *dreams*." Pavlína's voice settles. She's probably crossing her arms. "I did what I had to do to protect myself and my stuff. It always worked on you, remember?"

"I'm not—" Jin doesn't say what he's not. Instead, he continues in another direction. "Then you should've told a teacher, got proper help—they could've given her a single room. You had no right to coat her in earth magic."

She did *what?*

"You put so much earth in her, you landed her in the infirmary."

Okay, that's enough, I need to know what's happening here. I pull the door open, startling both of them. "You did what?"

Pavlína rolls her eyes. "Awesome, the prodigy arises. Now you can both blow me away with your righteous winds of change or whatever."

Jin breathes heavily, clearly fighting for his composure. "Pavlína used her magic on you, without your *consent*." He stresses the last word specifically for her benefit. "It's the reason you were struggling so much in class."

"Or you're just bad."

"And with your breathing. I washed the remnants away when we were in the Wyld Lands." That weird sensation of water running down my spine comes to mind.

"'When we were in the Wyld Lands'," Pavlína mocks him. "Gosh, you two make me sick."

I stare at her, bewildered. "If I understand correctly, you *actually* made me sick."

I've been bullied before—many, many times actually. But no one ever physically hurt me, much less sent me to hospital. These weeks of utter misery... She must've removed her spell in the shed when she wanted me to protect her, and then doubled down on it after witnessing my triumph at the exam. While I *slept*.

"You're such a bitch," I say to her face. Then I whirl around and start packing.

"Agreed," Jin murmurs.

Instantly, Pavlína lashes out. "You're such a hypocrite! When I told you about her dream winds, you told me I was overreacting. She destroyed half the room. Why are you on her side? Why do you look at that whirlwind of destruction and shrug it off? If I hadn't done what I did, she would've torn the whole school down by now."

Gee, and she's calling us dramatic.

"So, you went ahead and loaded her with earth until she *literally* stopped breathing?" Jin's still furious. "You know, I looked away every time anyone complained about you. I thought, oh, that's just Pavlína. She's a bit abrasive, but there's a good heart underneath. Just give her a chance. Well, look who's the fool now. I can't believe you'd do something like this."

As good as it feels to have Jin defend me, I don't want to be the reason his lifelong friendship with Pavlína comes to an end. Fortunately, I'm all packed up, so I grab my bag and my pillow and push through the two of them.

"Where are you going?" Pavlína screeches.

"Somewhere safe."

All I hear is "Well, can you blame her?" before I exit the corridor. It only occurs to me once I've left, but I haven't actually made a plan; I only knew I had to get out of there.

Reason tells me I should go to Ms Martínková and request a formal room change, but she'd only put me up with another earth mage, and I've had quite enough of them. Instead, my feet lead me to the room Ester and Jamila share. Fortunately, both are home.

"Milena!" Ester greets, surprised. "You're out of the infirmary."

Was it only yesterday I was in there? "Oh, you're behind the times," I say. "I spent most of the last day with Jin in the Wyld Lands."

"They let you go?" Jamila asks. They sit up cross-legged, suddenly alert. "Okay, you need to tell us everything."

"I will, if... Actually, I'm here because it turns out Pavlína's a little psychopath."

Jamila shrugs. "What's new?"

"She's the reason I couldn't breathe—and I don't mean that figuratively. Can I sit?"

I want to ask whether I can stay, but I'm not sure our friendship is quite there yet. In fact, after what just happened with Pavlína, it might not be the best idea to move in with somebody else.

They move aside to make some space for me. Jamila nods at my backpack. "What's with all your stuff? Are you planning on going somewhere? Moving back to the Wyld Lands?" they joke.

"God, I wish," I admit. That would be the dream. At least for the few hours it'd take getting killed.

Ester shudders on my other side. "Surely, Pavlína isn't that bad."

"I'd take the Wyld Lands over that bitch anytime." I'd rather die on my own terms, free and unbound, than be bogged down by the weight of earth. "She used her earth magic on me while I was sleeping. According to Jin, she put so much in me, I couldn't breathe. She's the reason I was struggling so much—just because I entered her holy space and upset her perfect little world. And now she's mad because I stole Jin away."

"Did you?" Jamila asks, earning a groan from Ester.

"Well, let's put it this way: right now, Jin's tearing Pavlína a new one. He's really mad. And as for us: we kissed."

I bite my lip. What if they take this information and do something bad with it? It'd be so easy for them to stir up shit for me. So far, people seem supportive of the relationship I'm forging with Jin, but the danger remains. It could all be a ploy to bring me down later. They say you always fly highest before you fall.

Ester gasps, her eyes widening, while Jamila squeals. "Oh my gosh, Milena! Why didn't you lead with that?"

Fake, fake, fake. I need to turn the little voice off before it destroys everything. Not everyone is a Pavlína. Or a Lída. Most people are kind. At first.

"You've got to tell us everything," Jamila doubles down. "How did it happen?"

I tell them what went down in the Wyld Lands, one crumb at a time, always gauging their reaction. By the end, I'm almost convinced they're truly happy for me. "He just did it to stop the storm." I play it down at the last minute. "But he kept going afterwards."

"The storm?" Ester asks. "How does a kiss stop a storm?"

"It's the Wyld Lands," I explain. "They're a bit more responsive to my wind magic."

I suppose this is the big thing. Whenever I've told people about the wind, they laughed or accused me of lying. It's different here—people know about the elements. Technically, we've all gone through the same thing.

Jamila narrows her eyes a little before asking, "Why was there a storm in the first place?"

I blush. "I may have talked myself into a rage. Really, it was Jin's fault, he kept telling me to let it all go. In his opinion, I keep too much to myself and then I explode." I try to laugh it off, but the sound sticks when I notice Jamila's furrowed brow. "Listen... I can't stay with Pavlína after what she's done. Could I—"

"Oh, you can sleep here," Ester says, before I even finish the sentence. "We've got a couch you can use." She jumps up and starts clearing off books and clothes.

"Thanks." Nervously, I check with Jamila, "Is that okay with you, too?"

Jamila takes an extra second before releasing whatever doubts they're having and nodding. "Absolutely. You can't go back to that earth bitch."

"You guys don't..." How do I put this? "You don't use your magic on each other, right?"

There's another set of exchanged glances, then they both burst out laughing. "No," Ester promises. "We practise sometimes—Jamila's fire helps me let off some steam."

"And Ester's water smothers the flames."

Which is how it's supposed to be. Taking the edge off each other, providing balance. Not hamstringing your roommate and trying to kill them.

"Awesome."

It would be so nice to trust these two. I really hope I'm not making another mistake.

24

Once I've settled into Ester's and Jamila's room, I search for Jin. He's not hard to find since I know his secret hideout. When I open the roof latch and stick out my head, I find him sitting on the roof, glaring down at Prague. He doesn't move until after I've seated myself next to him.

"How are you?"

I love how his first order of concern is me. "I'm okay."

He raises his eyebrows, staring, and I laugh.

"Look, I already knew Pavlína was unhinged. I always thought she might push me down the stairs to get her room back, but I guess I'm just not familiar with how magical bullies work."

"It's worse than bullying," Jin says, his voice thick with pain. "She doesn't understand so I want to cut her some slack, but... what she did was..."

I raise my eyebrows. He's going to cut her some *slack?* "She did this while I was *sleeping.*"

Dismay washes over his face. "I know. What I mean is..." He takes my hand and squeezes it. "Pavlína was there for me throughout my childhood. She knows about my panic attacks. That's when she came up with the technique. When I lashed out, unable to control myself, she steadied me with earth. And I appreciate her for that, it *helped* me, but that's because I'm an air mage."

"It didn't help me," I remind him.

Jin looks so pained I want to take him in my arms and hold him tight. "I know," he whispers. "Earth magic steadies air mages. Earth magic in a wind *witch* is like binding a stone around a bird's neck. It's cruel."

Wait, what? I must have misheard. "What are you saying?"

He turns towards me and starts painting shapes on my wrist. "Mages and witches draw magic differently from the air. Mages have a talent, an affinity they can build on with lots of practice. We learn to read our element: the way the air flows through the sky, the vibrations of the earth. Teaming up with an opposing elemental mage can greatly enhance our control over the element. It serves as a lifeline, a stabilising force, but it also takes a little from us, because it's too hard to fly when your feet are stuck on the ground."

My wrist tingles from his movements.

"Witches are different—they don't *use* the element, they're from the same cut. Their soul is tied to the element, and when you use opposing elemental magic on them... Well, it's how you fight them, because it's like a stone around your neck. It weighs you down, smothers you, grounds you, when all you want to do is soar."

I blink once. Twice. "But I'm not a witch."

Jin winces again, the agony on his face cutting deep into my skin. "Oh, you definitely are. I've had my suspicions for quite some time. When Pavlína told me about the dream you had, it was my first thought. But I didn't want to believe it. And then you were struggling so much, it couldn't possibly be. Witches are known for their vast potential, and you showed so little of it."

"Ouch."

"I don't mean it badly. Deep inside, I knew it was there. When you balanced on this roof, so completely at ease with the height and the wind…"

"That was because you were there to catch me. I trusted *you*."

Jin gifts me with a wistful smile. "But you don't trust anybody. You certainly didn't trust me then; you trusted the wind."

I bite my lip, not wanting to admit how right his answer feels.

"And then your exam. You surpassed my wildest dreams."

"You were happy for me," I accuse.

"And I still am," Jin assures, then proceeds to plant a kiss on my wrist. "But you were so good, unleashed, and then… nothing. That's when I knew something was wrong, and I had this suspicion, knowing what Pavlína was capable of. And sure enough, when I took you to the Wyld Lands, I saw all that earth magic clinging to you."

I still don't get how that makes me a witch. "She overdid it. She was jealous because of you, and because I got to go to the Wyld Lands. So, she put way too much magic on me. That's why it felt so bad."

He nods carefully. "There's no doubt about that, but if you were a mage all it would've done would've been to block you from the wind. You would've been unable to do magic, but you'd be fine otherwise. Instead, you needed medical attention just to allow you to breathe. And when I washed it away… I never should've goaded you on. It felt right in the moment but I was in way over my head. Your anguish whipped up that storm."

"I'm not a witch." Something ugly seizes my chest. Jin can't possibly be right.

"It's getting windier," he points out.

"We're on a roof," I snap.

Jin smiles sadly. "Look, it's not a bad thing."

"Oh, isn't it?" I tear my hand from his grip and back up. "Witches are evil. They're addicted to magic. They're terrorists." Every lesson I've had about witches said the same thing.

Again, pain flashes over Jin's face. He lost his father to a witch, a wind witch, the same thing he claims I am.

"How can you even stand being near me?" *He doesn't love me*, a voice sings in my head. *He can't possibly love me now.* I was wrong. I was wrong to trust anyone could.

His gaze turns more serious. "Call me stupid or naive, but I like to think not all witches are like that. My mother taught me not to judge others, and witches are humans. Right? I mean, they're born with their magic, much like us, just a little different. But they're not bad people, per se. That never made sense to me."

That mother of his deserves a bloody award. If my husband was murdered by a witch, I don't think I'd be so forgiving.

Jin reaches for my hand again. Reluctantly, I give in. "You might be a witch, Milena, but you're not a bad person."

I laugh at him, the action cutting into my own chest. "That's not what everybody else says." *No, no, don't accept this. Stop it from making sense. It's not allowed to make sense.*

"Then everybody else is wrong," Jin says, sounding almost angry. "Don't listen to the Pavlínas of the world. I can't fathom how hard it must've been to be born with a force inside of you which you can't control; of being a child like that. I believe you tried your best every single day of your life, and I know you're going to continue doing that."

Once again, I can only laugh, though the edges are fraying quickly. "Oh, yeah, because I've had such great success with that. Did you listen to anything I said? The wind always got me in trouble. You were there!" I accuse him. "You just said yourself you shouldn't have encouraged me to let loose. I let loose and it took out the entire camp. How is that me trying my best?"

He won't let go this time, though he throws a worried glance at the sky where a storm's building. It's becoming a bit dangerous to be out here in the open and it's all my fault.

"What?" I prompt. "Are you going to kiss me again to stop the disaster? Is that your masterplan? Kissing me until the end of my life?" Wasn't it romantic when he said it back in the Wyld Lands? Now it just feels like another stone bound around my neck.

"Don't be angry with me," Jin begs. "I'm trying my best, too."

"Why?" I still don't get why he doesn't just run the other way or tell people what I am. He could just let Pavlína finish the job.

Jin lets go of my hand but only to wrap his arms around me. "Because I believe in you. You're here now. You've never had the right training. But I'll help you. I'll help you learn to control it, and you're going to prove to everyone, and most importantly to yourself, that you're not a bad person. That you deserve just as much happiness and love as everybody else."

Then he kisses me. I can't make myself believe it. You don't tell somebody they're the magical equivalent of a psychopath but it'll all be good if they just let you love them. I don't deserve his love. Worse, it feels more like a burden now, a promise I need to keep. There's too much to prove, the consequences too dire. I don't want to be tied to him—not like this. Not with this Damocles' sword hanging over my head.

"We're going to get through this," Jin lets go then kisses my nose. "Together."

I manage to cobble together a smile but it's like butter. It slips off my face before it fully takes shape.

"I believe in you," he whispers, kissing me on the forehead.

Pavlína was wrong to use earth magic to tie me down—Jin's words are so much more effective than her magic could ever be. They tie in neatly with my mother's expectations. I know I'm going to disappoint him, just as I've disappointed everybody else in my life.

Including myself.

25

My thoughts are going haywire as I lie on the couch in Ester's and Jamila's bedroom that night. I can't believe I'd never thought of it myself. A witch. Most of Elemental History deals with the rise and fall of witches who've wreaked havoc on our world one way or another. I was so busy cramming dates and events I never stopped to ask myself what made a witch a witch.

It seems so obvious now: my lack of control, my vast potential for destruction, and my utter need to be in the Wyld Lands, close to the source of my magic. It's everything we've been warned about. People are literally training at this school to identify and neutralise people like me.

Am I doomed to become the next big headline? Did I paint a target on my back with my performance at the exam? Does Ms Martínková suspect? She must have some inkling or she wouldn't constantly be telling me to control myself. Control myself. Keep my emotions in check. Bury all the pain, the hurt, and the loneliness.

In the darkness of the room, the wind howls outside the window. It's calling me. It can't be contained, so how I could I hope to contain myself? Without anyone finding out?

I sit up straight on the couch, suddenly awash with fear. Jin is too kind. He wants to help me, but what if someone else finds out what I am? Someone like Pavlína? She won't hesitate before ratting me out to the guardians. And then what? What do they do with witches these days?

All I remember is how they drowned those fire witches in London. Surely, we've moved past those barbaric measures. But what if we haven't? *There's no death penalty in Czechia,* I tell myself, but I'm not so sure when it comes to elemental mages. They're not known to the general populace, even my mother had no idea what kind of school she was enrolling me in. What if Jin realises I can't be saved and hands me over to the guardians? What if they whisk me out of here and to some secret place which I'll never leave again?

The wind outside gains in strength as I struggle to control my breathing. I know I've messed up and likely will mess up again, but I don't want to die just because of what I am.

Hastily, I make a decision. Once again, I pack my stuff, this time only going for the essentials. I can't carry too much around with me.

But where should I go? Back to my mum? No, they know where she lives and will find me immediately. Even if I told her all about elemental magic, she wouldn't believe me. She'd hand me over, believing it's in my best interest. I don't have any friends—the only one I ever had has long since moved on. And I don't have much money to make my way alone.

The wind calls for me, and then I know where I could go. It's absolutely ridiculous, and yet the moment I think of it, I feel a calm settling over me. I'm a witch. I belong in the Wyld Lands with the elements. If I die there, at least I'll die free.

"Milena?" A whisper rings through the night when I try to sneak to the door. Ester.

"Just going to the toilet." She puts her head down again, and I slip out and hurry down the corridor.

As quietly as I can, I head outside. A cool breeze welcomes me and I feel a weight lift from my shoulders. This is the right thing to do. I won't hurt anybody this way, and I get to go to the land of absolute freedom; my soul's home.

I hurry towards the portal building, sticking to the shadows. It's not until I reach it I hit a snag in my plan: I don't have any keys. Despite the thought, I try to lift the bar, but it won't move beyond a few millimetres.

Frustrated, I stare at the lock. Who could have the keys? Ms Martínková, for sure, but that only brings up the next problem: how would I break into her office.

"Looking for something?"

A voice from the side scares the living shit out of me. It's followed by a flash of a flame. It crackles to life to illuminate the face of a boy I vaguely remember seeing at the tests. He's got dark unruly hair and a pair of heavy eyebrows but brilliant white teeth. His eyes are almost black out here.

Internally, I could hit myself for forgetting about the guardian they placed here after the last elemental escaped. Way to go.

"I..." I'm pressed against the door with my back. "No, I was just... strolling. I mean, I needed to get fresh air."

"You're Milena Šimková, aren't you? The air mage who came late?"

There's no reason to deny it, so I nod. "And you are?"

"Ravi."

"Just Ravi?"

He gives me a ghostly grin. "Ravi Kumar. Year 13."

The same year as Jin. Was he at the table with him? No, Jin doesn't hang out with fire mages very often. All I know is he can't be one of the guardians, not yet. That means, he shouldn't be out here either.

The best defence is often attack, so I ask, "What brings you out tonight?"

"Nice try, but I don't trust you."

I feel like I've been smacked in the face. "Okay."

"Don't take it the wrong way but rumour has it you've got the hots for Čermák, our famed Head Boy." His flames burn higher as he spits it out.

I don't like the way he talks to me, so full of disdain. "That's none of your business."

"Then stay out of mine."

"What business?" Until just now, I didn't even know he existed. "I was minding mine until you assaulted me."

"You call that an assault?" he asks.

I raise my chin. "You startled me."

Ravi huffs. "You don't think you startled me, slinking around outside the portal building like that? I thought you were a guardian."

Wait a minute. He thought I was guarding the portal? Why would he worry about that in the first place? "You were trying to break in."

"No, *you* were." When I give him a long look, he grins. "I've got a key. You can't break in with a key."

I don't care how this Year 13 student got a key—I want it. "Will you let me in?"

Surprised, Ravi cocks his head. "Why?"

"Why would anyone go inside? To step through the portal, of course."

"Like that?" He gives me a once over. "You won't survive a day in there."

I think I'd do better than that but he's reminded me the Wyld Lands aren't kind to humans, not even to witches. "What is it to you?"

He chuckles. "What are you running from? Has Čermák rejected you?" He makes it sound as if I should've expected it. "Let me guess, he's not the perfect gentleman everyone claims he is."

"He is," I snap. It's not Jin who's the problem, it's me. "This has nothing to do with Jin, I just want to go to the Wyld Lands. So, are you gonna let me go or not?"

With a haughty huff, he crosses his arms. The flames flicker around his arms, softening slightly. If anyone looks outside, they'll see us straight away; he's like a damn beacon. "Give me a reason."

Oh my god, he's on some kind of mage power trip. "Forget it!" The wind rises to the tone of my voice and blows the flames into his face.

Sparks singe his eyebrows, but he only blinks and coughs. "Now that's interesting. Looks like the other rumours are true, too."

Fear grips my stomach tight. "What other rumours?"

Ravi leans forward. "That you're a..." He pauses dramatically, grinning wildly. "Witch."

The word makes my back crawl. How many people have figured out what I am? "That's ridiculous." My voice is so shaky I might as well have confessed.

"Is it?" Without warning, a lick of flame shoots at my face.

I shriek and bat it away with my hand. It's a fool-hardy reflex, but it works—a gust blows the fire against the door instead. Before it touches the wood, Ravi closes his hand, and the flame extinguishes.

"Can't have a trace," he says, sounding nervous for the first time. "But that confirms it."

"Confirms what? That I'm a witch? I only defended myself." Surely air mages can do such a thing. If not, what are they learning here?

Ravi shakes his head in amusement. "Defended yourself? You're a Year ii and you've only been here a hot minute. Besides, you made the wrong movements for proper defence. The air mages do it like this." He imitates a smooth hand gesture that has nothing in common with my panicked slap. "So, you're a witch."

"I'm going to bed." My voice hitches slightly, but my march gets the point across.

"See you tomorrow, little witch," Ravi calls after me.

I will definitely not see that guy tomorrow. Especially not if he keeps calling me a witch in public.

It's not until I reach Ester's and Jamila's room again I notice he never sounded scared or threatened—excited for a minute and amused, but not horrified like Jin was, despite all his pretty words.

He stopped my flight today, but now I know where I can find a key to the Wyld Lands. I just have to figure out how to get on Ravi's good side.

26

I don't need to wait long to find out what Ravi is all about. The next day, he kidnaps me at lunch time and drags me towards a table at the very back of the room. To my surprise, Jamila's there, and so is the girl from air camp who was staring when I came back with Jin. Jamila watches me with wide eyes.

"Sit!" Ravi more or less shoves me into a chair. Then he puts his foot up on it and leans over me. "I did my research on you."

I give him a side eye. "That couldn't have taken long."

Ravi grins, takes his foot off, and sits in the chair next to me like a normal person. "Loulou told me about your stunt in the Wyld Lands." He nods at the girl from air camp.

She bristles at the affectionate nickname. "You're so lucky it happened over there, where all these stupid mages can't tell a wild storm from a witch storm."

Are people talking witch business as if it's no big deal now? "Stupid mages?" I ask carefully, then search Jamila's eyes. They're the only person I know at the table, which has three more boys and another girl gathered around.

Jamila clears her throat. "You can't tell anyone about this. Not even Ester."

"And especially not Čermák," Ravi adds with a pleased little smile. "Since you're all kissy-kissy."

"I don't know why you're inviting her to sit with us at all," a boy complains. He looks nervous, and I notice the water in his glass rising and falling. "She's going to out us to him."

"It's good to have someone on the inside," Ravi muses.

I exchange another confused look with Jamila. "On the inside?"

"Well, you know, Čermák is all geared up to join the guardians the minute he leaves school. He'll follow his daddy's path and start hunting witches within the next five years. They'll probably promote him before he finishes basic training—they can't wait to dig their claws into him. And good little soldier that he is, he'll excel at that, too."

The thought of Jin hunting witches makes me uncomfortable. He's too sweet and soft-hearted to hunt people down like animals. Heck, he doesn't even believe in this whole witch-mage narrative.

Slowly, I'm starting to add things up, though. Ravi thinks I'm a witch, and he can't stand Jin who he believes will take his father's place after school. Can it be?

"You're a witch," I say to Ravi, then let my gaze rove the assembled students around the table. "You all are."

How is this possible? How can there be so many witches right here at the school? Sure, there are many more mages, but this is more than a handful. If that's the usual ratio, why haven't I heard about more witches in history? Mr Reisz made it sound as if a witch comes by once in half a century, not a whole bunch with each generation.

"Guilty as charged," Ravi says with a wide grin. "Though you'll do us all a favour by keeping quiet about it."

The boy who spoke up before winces and shakes his head. "Why would you trust her when she's Čermák's girlfriend? If he finds out she's a witch, she'll lead him right to us."

"I want to see him try," Ravi says, his eyes gleaming slightly.

Jamila comes to my defence. "I trust Milena. She's like us, just looking for a place to belong. And you might think Jin's some great evil, but he actually likes her."

"Yeah, until he finds out she's a witch," the boy mutters.

"He already knows," I say softly.

There are several glances around the table, some surprised, some fearful. The boy who spoke whimpers and his glass flows over in response. Jamila reaches over, turning the liquid into steam before it can spread. I'm amazed.

"Really?" Ravi asks, his eyes narrowing. "How did that come about?"

"How did…? Oh, look you don't need to worry about him." The least I can do is repay Jin's kindness and improve his standing with this group. "Contrary to your belief, he doesn't hate me. If I had to guess, he's wary, but he figured it out himself and he seems convinced that if I learn how to control my air magic, there won't be a problem. That's possible, right? Controlling it?"

"Not in the same way mages do," Jamila says softly. "But yes, it is possible."

"I want to learn how," I say, suddenly eager to stay. When Jin told me what I was, I thought the only future was a life on the run—or a glorious death in the Wyld Lands. But now there's another way. All these witches can't be persecuted. "What do I need to do?"

"Oh, it's simple," Ravi says, making it sound anything but simple. "You just have to keep your emotions in check: always, every time. Keep them locked tight and learn to forgive." His jaw tightens. "Forgive them all their shit. Turn the other cheek and smile."

I get now why he might think it's rather impossible. The whole thing doesn't sound very pleasant, and my hope evaporates again.

"Meditation helps," Jamila says. "Just learning how to stay calm. I can show you some breathing techniques."

"That's the way?" I ask, dismayed. "I just need to make myself dead inside, and then everyone will be safe from me?"

Jamila rolls her eyes a little. "Finding balance within yourself is not the same as being dead inside."

Ravi raises a hand to stop them from speaking. "No, no, Milena is right. That's the whole problem. While everyone gets to enjoy themselves and mess up, we always need to keep ourselves in check."

"Don't drink," the boy whose name I still don't know adds helpfully. "Sleep a lot and work out."

"Some drugs help," Loulou muses. "I take some for anxiety. They help me relax."

"That sounds horrible," I whisper. Nothing against medication, but I don't want to bury this part of myself so deep I don't recognise myself.

"No, what's horrible is all of this doesn't matter when you slip up," Ravi explains. "When the guardians catch you, that's it, game over."

I'm almost too afraid to ask. "What will they do?"

Ravi gives me another of his toothy grins. "Now, that's the big question. When I was in Year 11, they found a witch during the exams. She did marvellously—jumped four levels, and so the guardians took her in. We were told she graduated early, but when you look into it, no mention of her anywhere. She's gone."

"My brother vanished similarly," Loulou said. "He graduated but failed to come home for Christmas. Instead, we moved, changed our name. I never saw him again."

"My family have changed their name four times," the water boy moans. He looks exhausted.

"Basically, it's a big shit fest," Ravi announces cheerfully. "Either you mask yourself successfully or you're done for." He challenges each witch around the table to protest, but they all cast their eyes downward, even Jamila.

Ravi turns to me, and for once, his fake cheeriness makes way for concerned earnestness. "That's why I brought you here, despite the whole Čermák thing. No one else is looking out for us, so, we have to look out for each other. The goal is to graduate, learn what we can to manage a life in peace and stay out of sight of guardians. You've already ruffled a few feathers from what I've heard, so it's high time we taught you some tricks."

"With meditation and drugs?"

"Beats ending up dead," Ravi says with a shrug. "Look, we all know it sucks, but that's the reality of our lives. The good thing is we're all in this together. We look out for each other. And if you really want to go the other extreme, I always have that key to the Wyld Lands."

That's right. He's got the key to my escape. "How did you get your hands on that?"

"Hand-me-down." He grins again. "We witches have a long history of sticking up for each other."

"You're one of us now," Jamila says, smiling. "Welcome to the world's shittiest club."

"Hear, hear," water boy mutters, while Loulou smiles.

As horrible as it all sounds, it can't keep the warmth from spreading inside me. After all these years, it looks like I've finally found my people.

27

After lunch, Jamila takes me to the park. There, at the edge, is a graffiti-covered stone area that's still a bit wet from the melting snow.

"It was an open-air theatre back in the day," they explain. "Now we use it as a meeting place and to practise." She shows me blackened stains from a fire long gone. "You need to be careful. Sometimes couples come out here for some privacy. Don't want to give them a nasty surprise, so always check first."

They make a quick round around the decrepit space before settling in the centre. "Join me for some yoga."

They look over their shoulder, then send out a heat wave that makes the water dry up, leaving the place almost cosy. I'm deeply impressed. My mother used to do yoga for a while. She claimed it calmed her, but she gave up after a few months, so I'm a bit sceptical of its success rate. Nevertheless, I follow Jamila's movements, trying my best to copy.

"So, is everyone in your family a witch?" I ask.

Jamila glances around before nodding. "We've managed to stay under cover for generations by always guarding our feelings."

"But not all feelings, right?"

"It's better this way," is the only answer I get. "We barely use our magic at all."

"Really?" I look at her, aghast. "Is that the big plan? Not using it at all?"

Jamila shrugs, not feeling my horror. "Fire's hard to control. When it slips out of your fingers it almost always hurts others. It's not like Egon who gets everything wet when he's upset. You can dry things, you can't unburn them." Egon is the boy who couldn't control his water.

"I'm sorry." Sounds like their element is even worse than mine. Still, I couldn't fathom closing myself off completely from the wind. "Don't you miss it, though?"

"That's why I'm here. I get to play with my element and hopefully figure out a way to do it safely. I won't ever make top student but that's okay. The attention is bad anyway; better to stay in the middle of the pack."

I pull my knees to my chest and sling my arms around them. *The middle of the pack. No attention. Fade into obscurity. Keep your head down. Hide what you are.* "It's not fair." You can't tell me I've got a gift for air magic and then tell me I'm not allowed to use it.

"The world isn't fair," Jamila says, sounding unperturbed. "You do what you have to do to survive."

"But did no one ever try to stop it? Speak up against it?"

"We haven't got to that part of history yet, though I'm not sure if it gets taught. Or if... Whether it gets taught in any meaningful way. There have been several movements throughout history pushing witch rights from either side of the line, but usually disaster strikes and the whole thing gets framed as a terror attack. Mages are notorious for pushing that narrative."

"Why?"

I mean there's a pretty obvious reason when I look at all the terrible disasters by witch hand in the past, but now I know a handful of witches—and have realised I'm one myself—I can't just stupidly believe what we're told. Like Jin said, we're humans, too.

Jamila gives me another shrug. They've really got the nonchalance down. "Because they're scared."

That tracks, I suppose. "Because we wreak havoc wherever we go?"

"Because we're so much more powerful than them." Jamila gives me a dangerous smile. "Our connection to the Wyld Lands is stronger than theirs. They play with the elements, we are the elements. If we banded together..." For a moment, their voice had become more agitated, but now they take a moment to re-adjust their stance, breathe in and smile. "I've been listening to Ravi too much."

"What's his deal?"

He seems to have his fire well in check despite acting sort of erratic in the short time I've been around him. On the other hand, he's had almost three years of schooling. It should give me hope he can still have feelings and not burn down the whole school at the same time.

Jamila switches to another pose. "He's restless this year. At least that's what Louise said. He used to be quite relaxed, but this year he's feeling the pressure. I suppose when everyone around you starts making plans for afterwards and you're stumped on what to do, it adds to your anxiety. I mean, there aren't that many jobs where you can successfully mask what you are."

I'm starting to feel sorry for Ravi. Maybe that's why he despises Jin so much. Jin has his future laid out for him, and while he definitely feels the pressure of following in his father's footsteps, he probably has all different kinds of doors open to him without even trying. And Jin is trying so very hard. He's a mage dream-come-true.

"Does Ester know you're a witch?"

Jamila raises her eyebrows. "No, and you can't tell her. She'd freak out. Remember what we're taught at school. Ester's new to our world but she's already scared of witches."

"Did you try to talk to her about that?"

A head shake. "No, it's perfect. Ester's lack of knowledge is what keeps me safe. Her presence covers me, just as Pavlína would've covered you if she weren't such a bitch."

"Yeah, that didn't work out well." I take a deep breath, settling in the new pose. "So, we keep Ester in the dark."

Jamila nods. "Yes, and you're going to be a perfectly unremarkable student who writes great mage-coloured essays on evil witches. Don't let anyone doubt where your loyalties lie."

I don't like this masking, this internalised witch-phobia I'm supposed to double down on. It might be what I have to do to survive, but that doesn't mean I have to like it.

"So, your family. You're first generation?" Jamila asks after a while.

How much can I trust them? Our witch blood puts us on the same side, but how tight can a tie made out of necessity be? Jamila just admitted their family are masters at hiding between mages; they'll protect themselves before standing up for me. And yet, if I can't trust a fellow witch, who can I?

"My mother is definitely neither witch nor mage. She doesn't even know what kind of school this is, and whenever I told her about the wind, she accused me of lying, so nope."

"And your father?"

I know from Ms Martínková he went to school here, but not whether he's a witch or mage. "He left us when I was four."

"I'm sorry," Jamila says reflexively, then ponders it some more. "Are you still in contact with him?"

"No, he's gone-gone."

The wind rises in response to my inner turmoil. It's not enough to be noticeable but I know better now I know what to look out for. With a deliberate breath, I let go of my hold on it.

Jamila stops her yoga and bites their lip. "I might just be making shit up. Obviously, I don't know you or your family situation well enough to make an educated guess, but if he was a witch, he might not have left voluntarily."

"You mean he was caught?"

I don't know what to do with this theory. It would explain why I never heard about my father again, why, out of the blue, he simply upped and left. Or why he would leave a witch child all alone in her oblivious mother's care.

Then again, what if he was a mage and realised he'd fathered a witch? What if he couldn't bear to be associated with me—or, if I want to be more favourable to him, didn't want to be in a position where he had to report me?

Fact is, I'll never know. Whether my father hated or loved me is irrelevant, just as whether he was a mage or witch. He's gone and has no place in my life. "It doesn't matter. It's not going to make me feel better." If anything, knowing he was killed rather than just up and left would be worse.

Jamila winces slightly but nods. "You're right. You've been fine without him for the last twelve years, you'll be fine without him for the next."

I don't know about that but I nod anyway.

Together, we make our way back. As so often, mages are training in the courtyard, among them Jin. He's laughing with his friends while showing superb control over his two elements. My heart aches as I watch him.

Jamila bumps my shoulder. "I still think this is a good relationship for you. No one will suspect Jin's girlfriend to be one of us, and if he's really supportive, he'll keep you safe."

Their comment sours the relationship for me. I'm not just with Jin because he makes a perfect front; I don't think he'd appreciate that either.

He turns and catches me watching him. An easy grin spreads across his face and he waves. Instead of butterflies, there's a nest of venomous snakes in my stomach. It sucks. Why can't I have a good thing and actually enjoy it?

28

Now that I've popped up on his radar, Ravi is drawn to me like a bee to nectar. He's always calling me over to their table until I finally give up, joining them voluntarily, and sometimes walks me back to the dorms while regaling me with history facts I'm sure I won't find in any of the schoolbooks.

"How do you know all this?" I ask after he tells me the Carrington sisters blamed for the Great Fire of London were framed. The fire started in a bakery, and they tried to contain it but failed, and hence were publicly blamed for starting the whole thing.

"My mother's great grandmother was a Carrington," he claims. "Her family came to India to get away from the English guardians. We—" He stops when another student passes us. "Our history isn't well-recorded. If it was, you can bet your ass some overzealous guardian would burn it down. All we have is oral history."

"Is that why you're passing it on to me?"

Ravi gives me one of his signature grins. "Just making sure you get all the facts. Besides, you're the only one who's not already dead inside."

"Only for lack of knowledge."

He starts laughing, and I feel something move inside me. There's something dangerous about his laugh, a temptation I need to resist. "Right. I'll stop talking then. Wouldn't want you to lose that spunk."

"Isn't that the whole point, though?"

With a glance over his shoulder, he pulls me behind one of the big cupboards, effectively trapping me between wood and plaster. I'm not *not* liking it.

"Listen," he says, his voice suddenly much lower. "I would hate for that to be the point. It makes my skin crawl just imagining it. What kind of life would that be?"

I'm glad someone's said it out loud. "Not a very desirable one."

His eyes light up. "*Exactly.*" He glances over his shoulder again and leans in closer, nearly whispering into my ear. "I want to change things."

"How?"

"That's the big question. I tried it the gentle way, starting discussions in history to see if I could question the status quo. All that got me was a bad grade from Reisz and a warning from Martínková."

Somehow that doesn't surprise me. If there really is a war on witches in this world, it only makes sense the school would try suppress any uprising. I can't help but admire Ravi for the courage it must've taken to speak up against the pushed narrative, knowing full well they'd investigate him if they ever got suspicious.

"So, my next step is a bit more... radical."

I should be alarmed. Instead, the word sends a thrill down my veins. "Radical?"

"You'll see," he says with a wink, then pulls back.

I'm a little frustrated he's leaving me hanging like that, but I guess I have to earn his trust before he confides anything incriminating in me.

I stop myself short when I realise what I'm thinking. This is dangerous. It's literally a life and death matter. I should heed Jamila's advice and keep my head down, not get all excited at the thought of overthrowing the system.

As we step out of the corner, we cross path with a group of other boys, Jin among them. He sees me and stops, telling the others to go on without him.

"Čermák," Ravi greets with mocking grin.

Jin's eyes narrow. "Kumar."

The tension in the air could be cut with a knife. It makes me wonder what their history is. Is it really just the very different fates life dropped in their laps?

Ravi never loses that smile. He gives me another wink and walks past Jin, almost shouldering him in the process. Jin watches him leave, glancing over his shoulder before he thinks of checking on me. "Since when did you start hanging out with him?"

I hear the hurt in his voice, instantly filling me with guilt. "Jamila introduced us." That's not technically true but I won't rat out a fellow witch. Not even to my surprisingly witch-tolerant boyfriend.

"Why?"

"Why what?"

He visibly attempts to smooth his features but can't shake his discomfort. "Why did they introduce the two of you? Do they not know you're... I guess we've never talked about it." Suddenly, he seems a little nervous.

I'm still not quite sure what he's getting at. My head's too full of witches to make sense of it. "About what?"

A blush appears on Jin's cheeks. "About us."

"Oh." Oh! I see how it might've looked between Ravi and me just now. The two of us huddled into a dark corner, looking guilty when caught. "I wasn't making out with Ravi, if that's what you're worried about."

The blush intensifies. "I wasn't..." He drops his shoulders. "Fine. I was."

I try to fight it but a goofy smile appears on my face. "You're jealous."

"Are we...?" He's too nervous to say it out loud.

My heart goes out to him and I decide to let him off the hook. "I'm not interested in kissing anybody else."

The relief is imminent. Jin's face relaxes and he takes a step toward me. "I don't want to kiss anybody else either." He takes my hands in his. "So..."

"So?"

"Will you be my girlfriend?"

I have to be careful not to squeal. This will be my first official relationship, and it's with one of the coolest and kindest guys at school. Surely, life can't be that bad if I get to have a teenage romance. "Yes."

Jin's smile widens disproportionately. He picks me up and whirls me through the air once before stumbling into the cupboard with me and pressing his lips on mine. I sling my arms around his neck, all thoughts of witches wiped away from the moment.

Life is beautiful, and I won't let Ravi or anyone else take this away from me.

29

Without Pavlína's earth magic weighing me down, my air classes are going much better than during first semester. I can hold my own against the others now, surprising Lucio with my sudden skills.

"Whoa, slow down, Šimková!" he calls out when I push him with enough strength to topple his sorry ass.

I laugh, not because I'm mean, but because it feels so very good to have my wind back. All that training with Jin has helped me call it when I need it, and I feel pretty good about my control.

"That was good work, Milena," Mr Vávra says with an appreciative nod. "Glad to see the exam wasn't just a happy fluke."

He's a patient teacher and I see where Jin gets his skills from. I glance across the courtyard to where Jin's working on his feather trick with even more feathers. It must be incredibly hard to separate the different air streams into so many strands and keep control of all of them. And if everything I've learned about witches is right, I'll never be able to replicate it.

Fortunately, I don't have to, as Year 11 is more about controlling one flow of air and trying to redirect it. From direct confrontations, we move on to sideways movements. It's a lot of fun since most of us are absolutely shit at it, exerting either too much force or too little, which results in constant by-blows that knock the wrong people around.

Afterwards, it's not just me who's out of breath and feeling a bit heady. I volunteer to tidy up the targets, carrying them to the repaired shed at the edge. Once I've stored them and tidied up some of the mess my classmates left behind, I close up behind me...

...and get knocked into the wall when the ground gives way beneath me.

Startled, I turn around and find myself opposite Pavlína. The earth mage is glaring. "You seem to be enjoying yourself a lot."

I haven't seen her since I moved out of our room, and while I can't say I've missed her, the same doesn't seem to be true for her. "Is that not allowed?"

Pavlína grimaces. "I would've thought you'd be a bit more careful about showing off." She leans in closer, then hisses, "I know what you are, witch."

It's as if the sun's suddenly stopped shining. My veins turn to ice, and I'm reminded of how I froze in the lab while Lída gleefully told me what she was going to do with the pictures she'd obtained of me and her boyfriend. *Don't call the wind, don't prove her right.* "A witch?" I try for a mocking voice. "Are you kidding me?"

Her eyes narrow further. "I know my witches. You have no control over your powers and you reacted badly to my earth magic."

"You mean when you literally coated me with your magic without my consent?" Pavlína cannot be left to believe that I'm a witch. Jin might not care because he's the most amazing human being on earth, but Pavlína is a different matter. "I wonder what the teachers will have to say about that."

"I wonder what they'll have to say about you being a witch."

My breath hitches in my throat. The two threats aren't even remotely on the same level. I can get her into trouble; she can get me killed. "Only I'm not a witch. I doubt they'll take lightly to baseless accusations either." Please let the teachers be reasonable about this and dismiss Pavlína's claims as the jealousy they clearly are.

Pavlína inhales sharply. "I'll find proof and expose you for what you are in front of everybody. And then Jin will see I was always right about you."

"Really? You're doing this for a boy you don't even love?"

"I love Jin," she says with utter conviction. "He's my best friend, my big brother, but he's also an idealist who always sees the good in people, and I won't let you take advantage of him, witch." Somehow she manages to make the word sound even more malicious than before.

"Oh my god, you're so delusional. Instead of accusing me of some perceived wrongdoing, how about taking a good long look at yourself in the mirror?" I force myself to give her the once-over, though I'm quivering with fear. "Seems to me like Jin finally realises what a witch *you* are. I don't think trying to throw me under the bus will earn you any brownie points."

Her eyes narrow so much I wonder if she can even see. "Guess we'll find out." She gives the earth one more push, slamming me into the door before she turns around and walks off in a huff.

I give myself a minute to recover my breathing and shake off the disgusting feel of her earth magic before taking myself to the nearest bathroom. My head over the toilet, I wait for the sickness to leave. I have no idea whether my bluff was successful or how determined Pavlína is about getting me out of her way. Will anyone follow up her claims if she rats me out?

When I feel like I can be trusted on my own two legs again, I flush the toilet and wash my hands in the sink. Even though I never touched her magic, I feel dirty, and no amount of scrubbing changes that. What if she gives me breathing problems again? *Then you go to Jin. He knows what to do.*

With a plan in place, I feel strong enough to drag myself to lunch before time runs out. Unfortunately, Jin has already left, and the witch table is empty as well, but I find Ester and Jamila still eating.

I grab a plate and a sandwich plus drink, then falter right at the table. Ester can't know about our witch genes. "Hey," I start carefully. "Can I talk to you, Jamila? Alone," I add belatedly, feeling terrible about how exclusionary that is.

As expected, Ester lowers her eyes. "I'm finished anyway." And with that she grabs her tray and hurries away.

"She doesn't have a birthday soon, does she, so I can make it up to her?" I ask warily.

Jamila smiles. "I'll talk to her later, make up something." A look of worry passes over their face. "What's the matter?"

I sit hastily, glancing around to check if I can see anybody else. "Pavlína accused me of being a witch."

Jamila's cheeks turn ashen. "How did she find out?"

"It's an educated guess." I quickly tell them what happened on my first night here and how she retaliated by using her earth magic on me.

"What a bitch!" Jamila exclaims a little too loudly, then proceeds to bite their lip. "But this is bad, really bad. You know who her mother is, don't you?"

I nod. "The Guardian Captain." That's right. I don't have to worry about Pavlína telling the teachers, she can just go straight to her mother. Surely, Captain Sokolová will believe her own daughter without a doubt. Or if not without a doubt then enough to test me. "I'm screwed."

"Can't you make up with her?" Jamila asks. "I know you two have had your difficulties, but maybe if you apologised." Even as they say it they scrunch their nose in distaste

"For what? I've never done anything to her." Minus one dream wind, but surely that doesn't warrant such hatred.

Unless it's not hatred I need to worry about. I'm suddenly reminded of how frightened she was during the storm. What if my night wind frightened her just the same? If fear is her biggest motivator... There's exactly two ways to deal with fear: show her that she's got nothing to worry about or scare her well enough to keep her away.

I have no idea how to do either.

"She's friends with Jin, isn't she?" Jamila asks. "You could—"

They break off when a teacher I don't know makes her way to our table. Jamila lowers their head but the teacher is definitely coming for us. My heart beats a million miles an hour and a breeze blows through the dining hall.

Not now. Not this soon.

"Milena Šimková?" the teacher asks.

"Yes?" I want to say, but it comes out as some kind of meek squeak. Embarrassed, I clear my throat and repeat myself, trying my best to send the wind away.

"It has come to my attention," the teacher starts, "you have taken it upon yourself to change your dorm assignment."

I let out a sudden sigh of relief, realising this isn't about me being a witch. "Uhm... I was having trouble with my roommate."

She looks at me with great disappointment. "If you have a problem with your roommate you would've been welcome to talk to your dorm adviser, which is me, not take matters into your own hands. Our assignments are done with great care, and we can't have three people in a dorm designed for two. So, if you would please return to your room and handle all future altercations like an adult, that would be great. Understood?"

"Yes." I bite my tongue to prevent myself from saying anything else. Like how Pavlína attacked me and that I don't feel safe. She's there, of course, lurking behind the teacher to watch me get scolded. It's a warning shot. If I'd hoped Pavlína would be too proud to get adults involved, I now know better. "It won't happen again."

"Good. I expect the move to be completed by the end of the day." And with that, the teacher turns sharply and leaves the hall, sending Pavlína scurrying to the side.

My heart rate calms and with it the wind that's been rising in the hall. It was mild enough no one questioned its presence. No one but Pavlína, who points two fingers at her eyes and then at me, before she gifts me with a sinister smile.

Next to me, Jamila looks disconcerted. "You need to make peace with her ASAP."

"What happened to her being all bark no bite?" What drew me to Jamila in the first place was how they didn't care about high school bullies.

"That was before she found out you were a witch," Jamila whispers. Then they straighten their back and take a deep breath. "No, you're right. We can't let her get away with this. Here's my take: Pavlína doesn't know shit. If she did, the guardians would've already taken you away. She's trying to get a rise out of you. You can't let her."

Because if I do, I'll give myself away. Why is the only thing you can do about bullies ignore them? That's what my mother used to say, too: *just ignore them. If you stop reacting, they'll get bored and find someone else.* Safe to say I haven't had the greatest track record using that method.

"I'll try."

After all, it's the witches' only way of survival. Swallow the pain and turn the other cheek, then hope you fade into obscurity.

30

Of course, getting a teacher involved was only the first step in Pavlína's plan. That day, I move my things back into my room, only to find them soiled with earth the next morning. As I scrub at least one set of clothes clean to wear for the day, the wind howls outside. I refuse to acknowledge it, building wall over wall around my anger, and while I'm keeping my cool at the moment, the walls aren't made to last.

Meanwhile, History's becoming a real drag. Ever since I learnt I'm a witch, along with many others, the narrative about "good mages versus deranged witches" has become tiresome. You'd think Elemental History would be more about how humans started to use elemental magic, but apparently, I missed that part and now we're at the "how humans shouldn't use elemental magic" stage.

The current unit is all about the guardians: how they were founded and what challenges they faced in their early years; said challenges are witches, naturally.

"Within their first decade, the guardians attended to thirty-four witch attacks, six of which were aimed at the organisation itself," Mr Reisz explains. "One, which we're going to look at it in more detail, nearly brought down the guardians. It was led by a water witch named Zelda Aranida who managed to infiltrate the guardians and made herself a vital part of the organisation for nearly five years, upon which she staged a coup."

He turns to his slides on the smartboard and pulls up a portrait. It's a horrible shot—she has her nose upturned and frowns. Either she's got a lazy eye or the photographer took the shot when she blinked, but the result gives her an unsettling look, which I'm sure is exactly what they were going for.

"Let's have a look at what the early requirement for guardians were and how it became possible for Zelda Aranida to pass them."

The following examination is unbelievably boring and I find myself drifting away and watching the storm outside instead. The swirling snow helps regulate my feelings, and since there's no wind in the classroom, I assume the storm isn't my fault.

For five years, Zelda Aranida was an exemplary member of the early guardians, responsible for at least seven arrests, when suddenly letters were found that pointed to her leaking information to well-known witch terrorists. With a small group of supporters, she tried to fight against the accusations, but in doing so revealed herself and caused a flood in the headquarters.

We read through snippets of her defence and have to work out where the hints were, which feels a lot like nitpicking to me, but of course, I keep my head down and make a half-arsed attempt of it. In the following discussion, I completely withdraw. Contrary to me, Ester participates with a fervour that makes me sick.

I try not to hold it against her, but when she starts pointing out the manipulative language—"Without my strength, the guardians wouldn't have been half as successful"—I start to bite so hard on my lip I taste blood.

Thunder cracks outside as slurry—half snow, half rain—slams against the windows. It's a glorious storm, mirroring my mood perfectly, but I'm stuck inside, forced to listen to more mage-washing of history.

Of course, I have no idea whether my sympathies are misplaced. I could be the one with a bias, interpreting everything I hear in the least favourable way for mages. Perhaps Zelda Aranida truly was a mastermind who tried to bring down the guardians from within, but in my imagination she was framed. Was she even a witch?

I raise my hand to ask how they could be absolutely sure of her witch status but lower it before Mr Reisz sees me, digging my fingers into my arms instead. Starting a discussion in class is a surefire way to get myself riled up and bring that storm outside in.

When the class is finally done, Jamila and Ester find me. "Are you okay?" Jamila asks, an edge to their voice. "You look a bit pale."

I breathe in and out a few times before forcing a smile. "Just my period. I'm okay." I've noticed it's always a bit harder to control the wind when I have to deal with cramps on top of everything.

Ester instantly commiserates. "Do you want some painkillers? I can't get through mine without."

"No, it's not that bad." I wish there were painkillers for my brain after that lesson.

"Do you guys want to do homework after lunch? Elemental class is cancelled in this weather," Ester asks. "Though I've heard Jin and a couple others are offering dry classes in the gym." She gives me a pointed look, as if it's a forgone conclusion I'll join my boyfriend.

And she's absolutely right in her assumption, because there's no way I can stomach the homework—a summary about Zelda Aranida's coup and subsequent arrest. "Training for me."

Ester laughs. "I thought you'd say that. How about you?" she asks Jamila.

Jamila shrugs. "Sure, why not? The sooner we get it done with, the better." There's that, of course.

"You know what made me wonder, though?" Ester says as we follow the stream of students towards the dining hall. "It's comparably easy for witches to blend in. How can we be sure they're not living among us already? At this school, for example."

Personally, I don't find it easy to blend in at all, but of course, I don't say that. Instead, I tell myself again and again that Ester doesn't know any better and is only parroting what she's heard in class. Fortunately, I've got my period excuse already out there, so I've got my obvious wincing covered.

I leave it to Jamila to engage. "I don't think you've got anything to fear at school. The teachers are most certainly onto it."

"But what if one of *them* is a witch?" Ester insists.

"Do you have someone specific in mind?" Jamila asks.

Ester pauses to think about it. "Well, no, but that's the point, right? No one thought Zelda Aranida was a witch, either, until they found the evidence. She only exploded afterwards. So, technically—"

"Stop!" I can't take this anymore.

Jamila throws me a warning glance which I answer with a glare before managing to take a deep breath and slap on a smile. Or what I think passes as a smile.

"What's wrong?" Ester asks, so wonderfully innocent.

How can I put this without giving myself away? "Well, I don't think the lesson was meant to make us suspicious of each other." It totally was. "How would *you* feel if someone accused you of being a witch based on a failed water exercise because you weren't focusing enough."

Ester pales, and I love her for that. "Oh, you're right. I guess I got a bit carried away. The last thing we need is a witch hunt."

"The very last thing," I agree.

Jamila throws me a grateful look before pointing ahead. "Oh, look. There's koláče today." They have them every other week, but they're yummy poppy-seed-filled sweet dumplings, so I'm not complaining about the fake enthusiasm.

We load our trays with plenty of dessert and some proper lunch before turning to find a table, when I suddenly stumble on a raised floor panel. With the tray in my hands, I fail to catch myself, crashing dramatically and sending my food flying.

Deadly silence spreads through the hall as everyone turns to look for the cause of the sudden noise. My elbows hurt viciously. Then the laughter and chatter sets in, the mocking tones worming themselves into my body. One voice rises above the others, leading the chorus of laughter: Pavlína.

Just then, a window's thrown open and wind and rain cause a distraction. While everyone is busy screaming about their food, someone bends down and helps me up.

"What a hellish storm," Ravi says good-naturedly as he pats my shoulders, miraculously turning me towards the exit, away from prying eyes. I'm still stunned, when he leans in. "There was a rock. Amazing how they just suddenly appear, right?"

Of course, there was a rock. Just as there's a gust blowing through the hall.

"Smile, Millie, you can't kill them all."

Even he sounds a bit strained, but it's a good reminder I need to get my emotions in check. I won't let Pavlína win.

Once he's successfully led me out of the hall, he sits me down on a bench near the windows and produces a pack of tissues from his backpack. "Show me your elbows."

I do as I'm told and watch him dab away blood from where I lost skin from the impact. "She knows, Ravi," I whisper.

"No, she doesn't," he says. Apparently, Jamila told him about Pavlína's obsession. "If she did, she wouldn't pull those kinds of stunts. Just ig—"

"Ignore her," I finish, with a groan. "I'm not particularly known for my endurance as a punching bag."

He gives me a lopsided smile. "Yeah, I've heard about your tumultuous past." When I look down in shame, he tips my chin back up with his fingers. "We've all had one. Look, if you want me to set a little fire to her stuff, I'm game."

I appreciate that, finding myself smiling despite what just happened. "You'd do that?"

"For you, anytime."

He says it with such cheesy delivery, I burst into giggles. Ravi grins, making me giggle even more. In the meantime, Ester and Jamila appear, carrying another tray for me.

"Mind if we join you? It got a bit uncomfortable in there," Jamila says with a wink.

"Are you okay?" Ester asks, fussing over the state of my elbows.

"I'm good."

My anger's gone, replaced by something else instead. It takes a moment to realise it's happiness; happiness because despite something terrible happening to me, I instantly had friends at my side. I'm not alone this time. And that keeps me sane.

31

"I saw you laughing with Ravi yesterday," Jin greets me when we meet on the roof the next day. The storm has blown past, taking the rain with it and leaving us with a rather warm late-winter day. "You two have been spending a lot of time together lately."

As opposed to the two of us, I assume. I raise an eyebrow. "What's your problem with him, anyway?"

"You mean apart from him being suddenly interested in my girlfriend?" He sounds a little hurt. With a glance at the city beneath us, he sighs. "He's a troublemaker. Always has been."

A troublemaker. "So, like me." I didn't plan for it to come out that confrontational, but his choice of words makes it impossible for me to stay calm.

Jin moves his hands to calm the sudden cold breeze blowing above us. "No, not like you at all." He clicks his tongue. "He's extremely confrontational in class. There's not a teacher who hasn't reprimanded him and won't be happy to see the back of him after graduation. He constantly stirs up trouble and challenges... any kind of authority."

For good reason, but I can't tell Jin that. Instead, I try to dissect his words. "You mean, he challenges *your* authority?"

He grimaces, so I must have hit gold. "Among all the teachers', yes. He breaks curfew, smokes on school grounds, and mocks me and others near-constantly."

So, Ravi is one of the few people who's not in love with Jin. "He's your Pavlína."

Jin's not impressed, which tells me he doesn't feel bullied but annoyed. Nothing can touch the golden boy, certainly not some fiery troublemaker. "What's she done now?" he asks, sounding tired.

I calm myself, knowing full well talking about her will stir up feelings. "What hasn't she done? Let me see." I raise a hand for a visual count. "Dirt on all my clothes, unstable ground under my feet, rocks in my shoes, nasty comments all day long. Oh, and she's got it in her head I'm a witch."

"You *are* a witch," he says with a glance to the sky, which is responding to me despite my attempts to keep calm.

"Yeah, but she can't know that." When he doesn't seem to get it, I get a bit blunter. "Jin, she's not like you. Once she's a hundred per cent sure I'm a witch, she's going to deliver me to the guardians on a silver tray."

"No, she won't," he says with utter conviction, as if Pavlína couldn't possibly mean what she said.

I gasp. "Of course, she will."

Jin takes my hands, rubbing his thumbs into them. "Breathe in. And out. Come on. In." He inhales. "And out." And he exhales.

"What are you doing?" I tear my fingers from his grip.

"You need to calm down," he tells me, making me aware of how much stronger the wind has grown on the roof. It's picking up my hair. "Come on, we'll work on it together."

I stare at him as if he's grown an extra head. "Really?"

"Milena, please. It's important."

A huff escapes me. "Is it?"

"You need to learn how to control yourself."

"Why does it sound an awful lot like *you* want to control me?"

Jin's eyes widen. "What? I don't want to control you."

"Sure." I don't care that the wind increases in strength. As I stand on the rim, it grips me with its full strength, whipping my hair and skirt around. I'm not going to avoid this conversation just because I'm a witch. "You don't want me hanging out with Ravi, you don't want me fighting with Pavlína, and all you care about is that I keep calm. Well, I'm not calm; I'm upset."

His gaze full of caution, Jin looks up at me. "I can see that. But please—"

"I'm allowed to have feelings!"

The wind keeps him from following my example. Instead, he wraps his hands around the ridge, whether to keep himself from falling or from using magic to counter my storm, I don't know.

"Of course, you're allowed to have feelings. I just want you to be safe."

"Safe and under control."

A look of pain passes over his face. "That's not true." He raises his shoulders only to drop them again. "I know this is incredibly hard for you."

"No, you don't." And how could he? Frustrated, I take a step back without looking and sit again, never once faltering. "You're not a witch. You have no idea how it is."

Jin nods sadly. "I'm sorry. I didn't mean to... *control* you. That's not what this is about."

"It isn't?" Jin's all about control. He's a master at it, having displayed his skills again and again.

He shakes his head. "I love you, Milena. I just can't bear the thought of seeing you get hurt."

The wind around me comes to a complete rest. Did he just say he *loves* me? I don't know when I last heard someone say they loved me. When did my mother say it? I can't remember. Has it ever happened?

"I'm sorry I don't have this under control yet," I mutter, and to my surprise, two tears run down my cheeks.

Jin's face softens immediately. He finally dares move again, slipping close to take me into his arms. "Of course you don't, you've only just started your training. But I'm here for you. If you need to blow me off the roof from time to time, I guess I'll just have to let you."

Despite myself, I laugh at his awful offer. "I don't want to blow you off the roof."

"And that's what tells me you're gonna make it." He seals his words with a kiss on my forehead. "You can do this, and I'll support you all the way. And I promise not to freak out about Ravi, though I really don't like him," he grumbles.

I sling my arms around his neck. "You don't need to worry about him. You're the only one I care about."

His arms around my waist tighten as he pulls me into him and kisses me. With a happy little giggle, I return his kiss, his words only really sinking in now. He *loves* me. Somebody actually loves me.

32

"The coast's clear," Jin calls before helping me down the ladder.

I climb down, squealing when he lifts me off the last step. We kiss again, and I couldn't be happier. "Being the Head Boy definitely has its perks," I tease.

Jin grins and stores the ladder away. "It does. Will I see you later? Let's grab dinner and eat outside."

"I'd love that." I throw a glance at my watch and curse. "Damn, Geography starts in three minutes."

"Sorry," he calls after me.

Flustered, I run down the corridor. Just as I'm about to wheel into the stairwell, I slam into somebody. They catch my momentum, holding me by the shoulders, and manage to keep us both upright. "Sorry about—*You.*" It's Pavlína. "What are you doing here?"

"The real question is what are *you* doing here?" She glances down the corridor where Jin is walking away in the opposite direction. "Had a little lunchtime date, I see."

"It's none of your business." I don't have time for this. Annoyed, I shake her hands off and turn away. Only, I can't turn away.

My legs have turned to stone or feel as though they have. I can't move a single step, nearly unbalancing myself when I try. "This shit again?" I ask, grunting in frustration.

"You seem tense, sweetie. How about you take a little breather?" And then she walks off.

"Pavlína!" Of course, she doesn't listen to me. She'll be late for Geography as well, but not as late as I'll be if I can't figure out how to get myself out of this.

Jin's already gone and there seems to be no one else in this part of the building. Pavlína must've followed us from lunch. I should probably commend her on her commitment to the cause, but all I want to do is to drag her by her hair and throw her off the roof.

As my frustration rises, I hear the witch mantra in my head: *take a breath. Don't rise to it. Let it go.*

Turns out none of that shit will get me out of this blasted rock. I pull until my calves hurt and summon my wind powers to try and blow the earth magic away. The latter throws me on my bum, causing more pain to my legs.

With tears in my eyes, I start to chip away at the rock. It takes literal hours, and by the end of it, my nails are chipped and bleeding. I've missed Geography, Maths, and Music, and don't need to bother turning up to air class anymore.

Instead, my feet carry me to the arena at the side of the courtyard where the earth mages are training. By the looks of it, they're raising spires from the earth as high as they can before they topple. Naturally, Pavlína excels at the exercise, leading her posse.

Time to change that. Without thinking, I call the wind to me and blow her beautiful little spire over. Since I'm not particularly good at precision, it blows her over, too.

It's so satisfying to see her topple and hear her scream, but it's only the start. Before she can get back up, I throw myself on top of her and push her face into the dust. "You love eating dirt, don't you?"

Pavlína grunts and swipes a hand, causing the remnants of her spire to launch themselves at me. I wince under the impact, while she uses my movement to throw me off and crawl away, sputtering and coughing.

"You dumb w—" she starts, but I stuff my wind into her face, making it impossible for her to speak. Before she can recover, I'm on her again. If she thought I was going to roll over and let her step all over me, she's got another thing coming.

Pavlína screams, this time fuelled by anger rather than pain. She digs her nails into my arms and throws me onto the ground. The hard impact drives the air out of me, or perhaps she's using her powers on me again. The thought makes me furious, and I push. With a loud shriek, Pavlína's picked up by a gust and thrown at least two metres in the air.

I scramble to my feet and wipe a bunch of loose strands of hair out of my face, breathing heavily. Just as I'm ready to attack again, my wind turns on me, pushing me away from Pavlína, then a pair of arms sling around my chest, physically pulling me back. At the same time, a stream of water hits Pavlína, turning her counterattack into ineffective mud.

"Let me go!" I screech and kick at my new assailant. "You don't know what she did!"

The arms strain against me, almost cutting off my circulation in the process. The wind is howling in my ears, which is why it takes me a couple of moments to understand they're talking to me.

"Stop! This is madness. Milena!" It's Jin who's got me in his grip.

On the other side, Grisha is holding back an equally enraged Pavlína. The other students have formed a circle around us, looking somewhere between amused and terrified. Not a single rock has remained standing. Above us, a storm is blowing. *My* storm.

"Let it go. Let her go!" Jin shouts into my ear.

With a cry of anguish, I relinquish my hold on the wind. Hot tears burn in my eyes as I inhale one ragged breath after the other. Pavlína deserves this. It's not fair she gets to use her magic on me while I have to control myself.

"Don't let her win," Jin cautions, softer now. "You're better than this."

I don't want to be the bigger person. I want to scream and shout and make her hurt as much as she hurts me. But I'll be the one who has to deal with the consequences, and Jin is right, I don't want her to win this fight. Slowly, I manage to calm myself.

It's only then I notice the earth teacher, who happens to be the same woman who oversees the dorms, has stepped in. "Never... Never in all my years of teaching have I seen such a shameful display of magic misuse. Do you have any idea the damage you could've caused with your mindless element slinging?"

Silver lining is she's angry at both of us; the problem is we're in trouble. A lot of trouble. "I'm sending you to Principal Martínková. Off you go. The rest, please tidy up the arena."

"It's going to be okay," Jin whispers as he lets go of me.

But he doesn't know that. He doesn't know a chat with the principal is the beginning of the end. I blew it. Literally. My mother will be delighted to hear about my latest digression. And Pavlína will get her wish and finally see me expelled. If not worse.

33

Mrs Svobodová, the earth magic teacher, marched us straight to Ms Martínková. Now, Pavlína and I are sitting outside the office while the principal gets a rundown of what transpired in class. We both look absolutely deranged, our uniforms dirty and torn, hair out of order, faces smeared with dirt.

"You're going to pay for this," Pavlína finally hisses after seething in silence all the way here.

She only gets a snort from me, and I'm damn proud of that.

"If my mother learns about this, you'll be in so much trouble," she continues.

"Aww, cute. You're going to run to Mummy."

Pavlína whips around and hisses, "I'm doing no such thing."

Looks like I've found her weak spot. "You literally just said it. Must be nice to be the Guardian Captain's little princess."

Her eyes narrow dangerously. "You have no idea what it's like."

Eager to drill deeper, I change targets. "What happened to your dad? Did he run from the two of you?"

Yep, another weak spot. Pavlína gasps audibly, then pushes me. "Is that what yours did?"

I nearly topple out of my chair. The legs scrape loudly across the floor. I'm just about to push back with my wind when the door opens and a loud huff interrupts me. "You're still going at it?" Mrs Svobodová regards us appalled. "Your parents will not be happy."

She leaves us with another huff, stalking down the corridor. In her stead, Ms Martínková appears. She looks tired. "Come on in."

Disgruntled, we settle in front of Ms Martínková's desk. I cross my arms, trying to keep the wind wanting to burst out of me in. My life depends on my ability to mask my affinity now.

"You're not going to tell our parents, right?" Pavlína asks. She must really fear her mother if that's her first concern. "Because it's all her fault."

Ms Martínková hasn't even managed to take her seat yet. She makes a point of sitting calmly before she replies, "Is it?"

"Oh, yes. I was in class when she came at me, screaming like a banshee. She made a spectacle of the both of us and tried to beat me up."

Tried? I want to say but bite my lip instead. Calm, I have to exude calm. "I'm sorry, Ms Martínková," I try to say, as maturely as I can muster. "I wasn't thinking straight. You see, Pavlína made me miss four of my classes after abandoning me in an empty corridor trapped in stone casing." To prove my story, I show her my fingers. "I had to literally claw myself out of there. And it's not the first time she's used her magic on me."

"I was only defending myself," Pavlína interrupts before I can get to her breath-inhibiting spells. "It all started when Milena destroyed all my belongings."

All her belongings? "Dramatic much? Besides, that was an accident. I was dreaming." Shit, I shouldn't have said that. Mages probably don't use magic in their sleep. Quickly, I try to distract Ms Martínková. "Do you want to know what she did to *protect* herself? Her earth magic is the reason I was having trouble breathing."

"Who's dramatic now?"

"Enough, you two," Ms Martínková's voice cuts through our squabble like a knife. She frowns, regarding us with visible displeasure.

I know that look so well, and it's not fair. Tears of frustration sting in my eyes. "I was trying to make up, but—"

"Yeah, when?" Pavlína bickers.

"I said *enough*." It's even sharper the second time.

Shivering, I force myself to lean back in the chair and await my fate with a remnant of poise. Next to me, Pavlína fidgets.

Ms Martínková sighs. "I'm disappointed by the behaviour you displayed today. Both of you! Attacking another student is unacceptable. Pavlína, you are more experienced than Milena. I would've expected a bit more support instead of this incomprehensible rivalry the two of you have going. You will write an essay about the beneficial effects of an earth-air relationship."

"Will you tell my mum?" Pavlína asks again.

She gets a smile from Ms Martínková. "I don't see the necessity if you can convince me you've learned your lesson. Now, off you go, get yourself cleaned up. I expect the essay by the end of the weekend." She turns to me with a much more severe expression. "Now, Milena. As you're probably well aware, we have a strict anti-violence policy at this school."

As Pavlína gets out of her chair, she smirks at me. She's in no hurry to leave, though she doesn't dare linger.

"Your behaviour today is unacceptable," Ms Martínková continues as the door closes behind Pavlína.

Aghast, I struggle for words. "She started it."

"That doesn't matter."

How? How can it not matter? "Pavlína's had it out for me ever since I arrived. She's responsible for my problems in first semester, and she sent me to hospital. She's been tormenting me all week long, and all you give her is a freaking essay?" My voice hitches at the end.

"I need you to calm down."

Sniffing, I let my head hang. *Calm down.* How I've come to hate these words, but she's right. There's already a wind in the office, upsetting the plants. For my own sake, I need to calm down.

With shaky breaths, I manage to assume some of that elusive calm. "I'm sorry, but it's not fair. You can't expel me just because I tried to defend myself."

"Nobody's talking about expelling you." Ms Martínková's voice softens. She gets up from her desk and walks towards the door, throwing a glance outside, then puts her hand on the wood and activates some kind of silvery shield. "And I'm sorry for what you experienced at Pavlína's hands."

I swallow, confused by her actions and words. "Then why did you let her off so easily?"

When Ms Martínková returns to her desk, she takes Pavlína's abandoned chair instead. "Because the last thing I want is for that girl to call her mother and report you."

A chill runs down my spine and I swallow my tears. Even in my emotional state, the hidden meaning doesn't escape me. "You know."

"That you're a witch?" Ms Martínková asks. She laughs softly. "I've known since the moment you walked in here. Even before that."

"I don't understand. Witches are... I thought they were persecuted."

She nods, the laughter already gone. "They are. But I'm hoping to change that."

"By inviting a witch to your school?" I don't think I could take on that responsibility.

"By allowing witch children to learn about their element in a safe environment and equipping them with the skills they need to deal with destructive tendencies. I want to prove to the world that witches can be taught, and that not all of us are dangerous and need to be subdued." She smiles sadly.

Her words have a much more soothing effect on me than my feeble attempts to breathe mindfully. "All of *us*?"

Her smile widens. "Yes, darling. I'm a witch, too. And as you can see, I'm a fully-functioning adult who isn't constantly setting fires all over the place."

I stare at her, slowly digesting her words. When I first met her, she practically told me she used to struggle with her element. Ms Martínková, too, had hurt someone. Because she's a witch. Like me.

"It's possible, Milena. We just need to give our youth a chance, something that hasn't been done before."

Do Ravi and the others know about this? Did Jamila's parents send them to this school because they knew a friend would watch over their child? But the only question that suddenly matters is this one: "Was my father a witch, too?"

"Yes." Sadness returns to her eyes. "Unfortunately, he was forced into hiding all those years ago. But not before he managed to hide *you*."

Is that what happened? Did my dad leave his family to protect me? Tears well up again. The words, "I didn't know," come out as a pitiful whisper-sob.

Ms Martínková lays a hand on my cheek. "I'm sorry. You deserved to grow up with a father, with a whole community." She takes a deep breath. "That's why I need you to help me here. We need to change the world together."

I let out a choked-up laugh. "How? I'm a mess. You heard what happened with Pavlína." Speaking of Pavlína... "Why would you put the two of us together?" It strikes me as incredibly dangerous to expose a witch to the Guardian Captain's daughter.

"Because sometimes I let my idealism get the better of me," she says bitterly. It sounds like something someone else had said to her before. My father, perhaps? Ms Martínková wrings her fingers, fighting for that smile again. "I thought that in putting you two together, I could create a strong bond. A friendship that would transcend the differences between witches and mages, so when it was revealed witches had learned alongside mages for all these years, your friendship would've been proof of the concept. A pillar in my *idealistic* world." She rolls her eyes in self-depreciation.

It's a beautiful dream, but it shattered against Pavlína's rock-hard exterior. "I'm in a relationship with Jin, though," I offer. He's a much better choice for that little experiment in my opinion. Someone who's already tolerant and open towards witches. "He knows about me."

Ms Martínková frowns at that. "Did you tell him?"

"He told *me.*"

She's biting her lip, not looking half as happy as I hoped she'd be. "Milena, I have to be honest with you: it worries me how close you are to Jin. I made him Head Boy because he's the perfect candidate for it and it makes the mages happy, but I don't trust him. The guardians already have their talons in him."

"That's not true." She obviously has the wrong impression, something I'm happy to rectify. "He told me he believes witches are humans, too. He wants the same things as you... us."

"I'm glad to hear he allows us some humanity." The sarcasm isn't very well hidden.

"That came out wrong," I insist, not willing to let Jin take the fall when he's been nothing but supportive. "He's an ally. Or at least, he could be."

Ms Martínková puts a hand on mine and smiles warmly. "If that's true, it would be wonderful news. It shows there's hope yet for us. Maybe your generation can truly change the world."

It sounds a bit better this time around. "I hope so."

In my mind, I already see it. We'll overcome our differences and find out we're not that different after all. Jin might become a guardian after school, but he'll never engage in witch hunts. If someone can change the world, it's him.

Now, if we can only change the Pavlínas of the world first. I take a deep breath and bring up the topic again. "What am I supposed to do with Pavlína? She hates my guts and she's got it in her head that I'm a witch. She doesn't have proof, but she's riling me up on purpose, so I'll lose my cool and expose myself."

Ms Martínková gives me a long glance.

I sigh. "I need to learn how not to lose my cool."

She laughs softly. "Yes, but I'll see if I can arrange an *official* room change. You shouldn't have to live in fear. Not at my school."

A warm and fuzzy feeling spreads in my stomach, and I very nearly jump up and hug Ms Martínková. Luckily, I remember she's my teacher before I embarrass myself. "Thank you."

"And next time she does *anything*, you come straight to me. Remember what I said: my door is always open. Now," she pats my hand, "let's get you cleaned up and ready to get back out there."

I get up, steeling myself for the looks I'll most definitely garner from my fellow students. "Do I have to write an essay?"

"No. But don't tell Pavlína that," she says with a wink, making me giggle.

For the first time since I found out I was a witch, I see a future for myself. I'll fight tooth and nail for Ms Martínková's dream.

34

As soon as I show my face outside, I'm swarmed by my fellow witches.

"Are you okay?" Jamila asks, protectively putting an arm around my shoulders.

"That was one hell of a cat fight," Ravi announces cheerfully, which earns him a thump from Louise. He raises his hands. "It's just what I've heard."

Somewhere in the crowd I see Jin, but he only looks at me unhappily and doesn't try to whisk me away, seeing as I'm already well cared for. I can't shake the feeling he's not pleased with me, but at least he's not with Pavlína.

I don't see her face anywhere, and I don't get a chance to look for her as my friends lead me to the hideout Jamila showed me earlier. Egon and another boy have procured food for us, ordering pizza instead of whatever's on offer in the dining hall tonight. Someone puts on music, and fires are burning, transforming the park into a cool little outdoor party, no mages allowed.

With Egon's help, I wash Pavlína's dirt from my face then join my fellow witch students. Between bites of hot cheese, rich tomato sauce, and crispy dough, I recount my latest altercation with Pavlína and how she's been tormenting me.

"And she got away with an essay?" Louise asks, shuddering at the thought. "That's straight-up bullying."

"Yes, but we all know who her mother is," Ravi says with a dangerous smile. He gives me a nod. "I'm so glad you made her eat dirt for once. I bet the little princess didn't know what hit her."

Next to him, Egon scowls. "Of course, she didn't. According to reports, you unleashed a full-blown storm on her and everyone around you. You're lucky they let *you* off with a slap on the wrist."

"So what?" Ravi protests before I get the chance. "She's supposed to take the abuse? That's bullshit. Milena's the victim here."

"She'll be an even bigger victim if the guardians catch her," Egon mutters.

"Don't listen to him," Ravi says with a sweeping motion. "The coward way is exactly what got us into this situation. All this hiding what we are only made them forget we exist."

He has a point there. By masking who we truly are, the mages never get the chance to see us as normal human beings—they only realise what we are in our worst moments. For Ms Martínková's plan to work, she'll have to make everyone aware of us at some point. I know she won't do that unless she's absolutely sure there'll be a positive reception, but that might be years from now.

"They most definitely haven't forgotten we exist," Louise says. "And if you keep ranting like that, you're going to catch fire."

"So?" Ravi asks, sharply. "Are you afraid of a little heat?"

I have no idea what their relationship is, but it sounds to me like they've been at it for a while, constantly going back and forth with these two lines of thought.

Louise purses her lips in response. "I don't want to get burnt just because you have an urge to play with fire."

Ravi laughs good-naturedly. "Oh, honey, and I thought you were going to blow on my boo-boos." When he catches me watching, he winks.

I blush and return my attention to my pizza instead. Louise and Ravi continue bickering until there's a strong wind blowing through the theatre and sparks fly from Ravi's hands. No one bats an eye at the magic swirling around us, though I see Egon casually playing with water between his hands, as if preparing himself for firefighting duties. And then I realise why everyone is so much more relaxed here: we're together. Witches from all four elements are present, ready to step in if anything gets out of control. And in those precious moments we're able to let go of all our inhibitions.

"It just annoys me so much," Ravi rants. "If it went before a court, Pavlína's actions would be seen as despicable, but no one's going to suggest that maybe *she's* dangerous and needs to be subdued. But if one of us gets caught? Straight to never-to-be-seen-again. It's so..." He grunts, having run out of words. "You know what? Sometimes, I really just want to see it all burn."

"We know," Louise says with an eye roll, making everyone burst out laughing.

I'm still trying to get a feel for the group dynamics, unsure about where my place is in all this. I understand Ravi's frustration: it's not fair. It's not even pretending to be. Part of me still can't believe that people vanish in secret in our time. Then again, my father *did* vanish, so I'd better believe all the horror stories. And that makes me want to believe in Ms Martínková's vision. Things need to change. And of course they will. Jamila and I might be keeping this from Ester at the moment, but I can't think for a moment Ester wouldn't immediately drop her anti-witch stance if she knew the truth.

Slowly, I begin to form a plan on how to break it to her. She's new to this world, and at the moment, she's only seen one side. Of course she'd believe what we're taught. Which student wouldn't?

My thoughts wander from Ester to Pavlína. Ms Martínková hoped I could build something with her. Pavlína might not have given me a chance, but I never really tried to look past that, either. Fired up by a new purpose, I vow to go back to Ms Martínková's original plan until I can be sure it's in vain.

When we return to the dorms at nightfall, I go straight to my room. Unsurprisingly, Pavlína is already there, working through her homework.

"Good, you're here," she greets. "You can take your trash out now." She points to a spot next to me.

My stuff has been gathered and thrown into a pile near the door, a piece of paper on top, while she reclaimed my bed. The paper informs me of my new room assignment.

"You can't wait to get rid of me, can you?" I keep my tone light, but she's already trying me.

She narrows her eyes. "Are you surprised?"

It doesn't even take a second to think about it. "No." I take a deep breath. "But I was thinking."

Pavlína yawns.

"We kind of started off on the wrong foot..."

"Oh, please!" Pavlína groans and rolls her eyes. "I don't need your apologies, witch. I need you gone."

I'm impressed I don't raise a wind when she throws my attempt at reconciliation back in my face. "Wow, you're quite the piece of work." Diplomacy is officially over. "Who's going to be left after you finished pushing everyone away?"

Pavlína gets out of her chair and walks over in a leisurely stroll. "I'll tell you who's going to be left: I am."

"All alone and—"

She scoffs before I can get any further. "Spare me your fake sympathies. You don't care about me. You just want to get back into Ms Martínková's good graces. She probably set you up to this." She oozes contempt with every uttered syllable. "Well, I'm not interested in your fake apology. It wouldn't be worth anything, anyway. You may have survived today but you won't manage another week. Soon, they'll all know what you are, and then it's bye-bye." To make sure her words really stick, she gives a cute little wave.

"Wow, you really are your mother's daughter, aren't you?"

I already knew her mother was her weak spot but it's still frightening how quickly her entire face changes until she's visibly seething with fury. If Pavlína were a witch, an earthquake would be shaking the walls of the room.

"You know nothing about my mum," she hisses.

I look down on her, raising an eyebrow to show her how little her tantrum has impressed me. "And you know nothing about me, and yet here you are, *judging* me."

"Because you're a *witch*." Pavlína pulls a face, trying hard to show off her contempt for my kind. "You should be locked up in a cell."

"For what? Existing?"

She snorts. "Oh, please. You're just a disaster waiting to happen. I saw your records."

"You what?" Those are confidential.

"You're an absolute delinquent. The only reason you're not sitting in jail is there's no proof. Yet." The word cracks like a whip. "I don't know why Ms Martínková allows you to stay at this school. I assume she thinks you could be rehabilitated, but that's never worked, and it definitely won't work in your case. And if I have to prove that to everyone, I will. And now,"—she throws a contemptuous glance at my pile—"leave."

Before I can find enough breath for a proper response, she opens the door and kicks my pile into the corridor. Apparently, it's not good enough for her hands anymore.

"Stop that! You're gonna break something." I cry out when her foot connects with my flying squirrel, and a gust blows through the door.

Instantly, Pavlína stumbles back. Her face pales a little, but she recovers quickly. "Call back your wind or I'll give you some real breathing problems."

Thing is, it's no longer an empty threat. She's already landed me in hospital once, and that was before she was convinced I was a witch. With an indignant look, I gather the rest of my belongings and carry them outside.

I've barely left the room when the door slams shut. The wind plays with my hair, its unnatural presence in the corridor soothing me. I take a couple of shaky breaths, afraid to feel my lungs seizing up again. For now, it seems as if Pavlína held back her magic. A mistake, I'm sure, that she'll rectify before the week's out.

Dread freezes my veins, the fear nearly overwhelming me. How am I supposed to survive this week, much less a whole year? I've already exploded once today, and I'm feeling like I'm keeping too much inside myself again.

I want this to work. I really do, but with Pavlína's threat hanging over me, I don't know if I can pull it off.

Shuddering, I lean against the door and take a couple of deep breaths. It's obvious I have no chance of reaching Pavlína. For some reason, she's had it out for me the moment I arrived. I don't know what's holding her back from calling her mother—mummy issues unrelated to me, I assume—but time is running out. I don't believe it'll take that much more for her to take that final step.

If I want to protect myself and Ms Martínková's vision, I need to pull out the big guns. And find someone Pavlína will listen to.

35

After what happened tonight, it doesn't surprise me to find Jin brooding on the roof. He doesn't look at me as I climb onto the tiles and make my way to the ridge. Instead, he takes several deep breaths. Something's off.

"Are you okay?"

He throws me a glance. "It was quite the day."

"Tell me about it." I swing my legs over the ridge and look out at the beautiful city. In the darkness, there's no hint of the red roofs, but the lights are just as pretty. "I just tried talking to Pavlína, but there's no getting through to her."

"You apologised?" Why does it surprise him so much?

"I tried, but she blocked me off."

Jin sighs. "Well, can you blame her?"

What did he just say? I stare at him, dumbfounded, trying to work through the accusation. How did Pavlína come out on top after everything that transpired today? I'm just about to give him a piece of mind when I realise he might not know what happened yet. No one apart from the witches know what Pavlína did to warrant such an extreme reaction.

"Okay," I say, more to calm myself than him. "Before you say something really dumb"—okay that didn't go so well—"let me tell you what she did *before* I threw myself at her."

Jin turns to me with a clamped jaw, giving off the impression he really needs to square himself to face me. "I'm listening."

Looks like I'm on trial here. It makes me angry but I fight the urge down yet again. "After we came down from the roof, I ran into Pavlína on my way to class. She'd followed us and told me yet again how she was going to get me expelled. And then she stuck my feet into rock, rooting me to the ground, and left. I spent nearly four hours trying to free myself." I show him my screwed-up fingers as proof. "She made me miss half a day of school." My voice starts shaking. "Can you imagine now why I would be furious?"

His face softens. He closes his eyes and takes a deep breath. "I'm sorry."

"It's not your fault she's a horrible human being." When he opens his mouth, I raise a finger. "Don't tell me she's not. I know she's got mummy issues, but most importantly, she has a witch issue. She's told me again and again and again she wants me gone. That's why she's doing this. She's bullying me until I snap and give myself away."

"You came damn close to that today. People have started whispering about witches. Grisha and I did a lot of a work shutting down those rumours."

He was defending me while I was busy talking to Ms Martínková and hanging out with the other witches.

"I appreciate that. I really do. Can you talk to Pavlína while you're at it? I'm afraid after today she'll report me to her mother."

Jin grimaces and shakes his head. "That won't happen."

"Why? Her mother's the Guardian Captain and she thinks I'm a witch."

"Pavlína's trying very hard not to involve her mother." He really seems to struggle with comprehending the gravity of the situation. "And as for Vanda... I highly doubt she'd run to the school because Pavlína can't handle her roommate."

Is that because Pavlína's mother—who Jin is on a *first* name basis with—doesn't care enough for her daughter or because the guardians need more substantial proof before they act? "Not even for a witch?"

"You haven't done anything wrong. I mean, sure you went off like crazy today, but apart from that, you're not a criminal."

"Yet," I say sharply, parroting Pavlína.

Jin frowns. "What's that supposed to mean?"

"How long do you think my innocence will last when word gets out? You just spent energy and time quenching those rumours," I point out. Why would he do that if he didn't understand the severity of the accusation?

"Because students can be a bit irrational. I don't want anyone to bully you because they think you deserve it."

"Then talk to Pavlína."

"I will," Jin promises, though he rolls his eyes at the same time. "I'll sit down with her and see what's really going on. The way she's treating you is unacceptable, witch or not."

I find it hard to breathe as he dismisses my experience so casually. Almost as if witches *do* deserve that kind of treatment—at least a little.

"In the meantime, can you promise me you won't flip every time someone makes you upset? I can't convince her you're not a danger when you literally prove me wrong the next day."

Once again, I can only stare. "Did you...? Do...?" I scratch my head, still trying to unpack his request. "Are you blaming *me*?" My chest tightens, much like it did when I was weighted down with earth magic. He's been so supportive until now, I feel blindsided.

Jin sighs gravely. "I'm not *blaming* you. You're just very emotional."

"I get literally bullied every single day by your bestie, and you say I'm *emotional*?" In my opinion, I've earned every right to be as emotional as I want to be.

His jaw works overtime as he tries to find a different angle. Instead, he throws a hand in the air. "Just notice how the wind responds to you. I can't even have a conversation with you without having to keep an eye on the air currents."

"Wow." I push myself backwards, suddenly eager to put distance between us. "Wow," I repeat, before finding other words. "I thought you were supportive."

"I *am*!" Look, who's emotional now. "I like you and I believe you're better than this, that you can rise above Pavlína's stupid meddling and be the bigger person."

Tears sting in my eyes. "In other words, keep my head down. Swallow all my feelings and keep myself in check."

He was the one who told me to open up, who told me I was too wound up and had to let loose. Looks like he didn't know what he'd unleash when he said it. I opened myself up to him, and once again, I'm too much to handle for those who claim to love me.

"No, that's not what I said. I just want you to practise some restraint." Something Jin's apparently grappling with today. "Do you have any idea how crazy you looked today? How completely out of control you were? You *hurt* Pavlína. And you could've hurt so many more. I had to physically restrain you just to make you stop."

Once again, he leaves me speechless. Horrified, I can only sit and watch as he plunges dagger after dagger into me. This isn't the Jin I know. I came here for solace, not a battering.

"She hurt me first."

"But she's not a *witch!*" Jin snaps, making me choke on his words. "*You* need to be more careful. Your powers require restraint. Do you need to *kill* somebody to realise that?" His jaw is shaking, the muscles straining under the bitterness of his words. One deep breath after another, Jin pulls himself away from the edge to say in a disgustingly calm manner, "My father was killed because a witch like you lost control over their power."

Tears are streaming down my face as I swallow each of his words, inscribing them deep into my brain. How did I screw this up so badly so fast that he's putting me on the same step as his father's murderer?

He seems to realise what he's said only a minute later. "Milena..."

I can't. I can't listen to anything else he might sling at me. Not when the wind's already slamming against the roof. Blinded by tears, I scramble down the roof, nearly sliding off it as I aim for the hatch.

"Milena, wait."

Unable to heed his call, I squeeze through. I'm in such a hurry I miss the lower rungs, nearly pulling my shoulders out of their sockets and knocking my shins against the metal bars. I drop to the floor and hurry down the ladder before Jin can catch up, fighting the urge to let go of this pain with every fibre of my being so I won't hurt *him* in the end.

36

Why, oh why, did I let him in? Why did I believe it'd be any different this time? That *I* would be any different? I'm still the same old me, screwing up everything remotely good in my life.

I can't believe how stupid I was, thinking embracing the wind which has caused me so much trouble already was the way to go. The moment I heard I was one of those terrible out-of-control terrorist witches, I should've run the other way.

Gasping, I claw at the door frame, struggling to hold myself up. I need to stop myself, to calm down before it all gets worse; so much worse.

In this very moment, I hate everything about myself. I tried but I failed spectacularly, yet again. Mum will be delighted.

So, what now? What's next for a walking mess like me? I can't do what the other witches do, this complete denial of what I am. It doesn't work, I'm too *emotional*, too much. It pains me physically to think of restraining all of me for the rest of my life. It feels impossible.

Slowly, I set one foot in front of the other. The paths of my future appear in front of me, all of them terribly winding and steep, impossible to walk. I can't go back to my mum, because this was my last chance.

With what I know about my ability and the world hidden right here in Prague, the thought of returning to a normal life is unbearable.

I can't follow Jamila's example and swallow all my feelings, constantly controlling the wind that feels so attuned to me. It's my only true friend. I wish I was strong enough to fulfil Ms Martínková's vision, but she chose poorly. I can never be what she and Jin need me to be.

As the possibilities dwindle, a new path emerges, one that feels right. It's fairly simple, really. I'm too much for this world, but I could be never too much for the other.

The pull of the Wyld Lands becomes unbearably intense within seconds. I know what I need to do now, where I can truly be myself without having to worry about hurting anyone, friend or foe. I can cry and rage and not have to worry about the consequences. Plus, there won't be anyone to disappoint.

Quickly, I cross the courtyard. Hopefully Ravi is still at the old theatre with the others. I'll get the key from him and make my escape before anyone can stop me. Yes, that sounds like a plan I can live with.

My heart soars when I see the flicker of a fire in the decrepit structure. "You're still here."

It's just Ravi and his fire. None of the others have stayed back. Behind the flames, his face looks ghostly. "Milena." His lips curl into a smile. "Should've known that wind was you."

It doesn't flatter me today. Instead, shame floods me. "Sorry."

"Never apologise," Ravi shoots back instantly. "Don't apologise for being yourself."

I wince. "Not today, please."

He picks up on the tone of my voice. "What happened? You didn't go back to that earth bitch, did you?"

"Well, yes, but..." I find it too hard to continue speaking. Tears are rolling down my cheeks once again. And here I'd thought I'd spent them all already. "Please, I just need the key."

"The key?"

"To the Wyld Lands." Hopefully, he still has it.

Ravi looks intrigued. "What are you planning?"

Isn't that obvious? "Running away," I say, sullenly.

"Oh." It sounds as if he expected something else.

"Wait, what did you think I was going to do?" My brain works faster than my mouth. I remember when I first met Ravi, slinking around after dark. And now again, all alone with his fire. The excitement in his question. "The elementals... You opened the portal."

Ravi gifts me with his beautiful wild smile. "I did."

"Why?"

"Because I'm fed up with their shit. I've had it to here!" He swipes his hand across his throat. "They think they can handle the elements? Well, let them handle them."

I take a step back, confused and horrified by this revelation. "I don't understand."

"It's not rocket science."

"But don't we want to show people we *aren't* the monsters of their stories? That we're good?"

Ravi cocks his head. "Who's *we?*"

That's probably a good question. I want to say "us witches", but everyone's approach seems to be different. "I just don't understand what you're trying to achieve. You're just going to make them hate us more."

He snorts. "Oh, Millie. You're so young and naïve." As if he's so much older. "They already hate us—it doesn't matter what we do. Ever heard of 'only a dead witch is a good witch'?"

I can't say I have, but it'd definitely fit the curriculum. "They're not really going to kill us, are they?"

"What? You think they're going to serve us cake and coffee? When our people vanish, they vanish for good—everyone knows that, but nobody cares. Nobody ever fucking cares!" The fire burns higher so suddenly, I stumble back another step.

"Ravi..."

He shakes his head, the ever-present smile looking tortured and ghastly. "Everything they tell you is a lie. Day in and day out, they tell you how horrible witches attacked the good people of this earth. The most favourable attitude towards us out there is that we're unable to control our talents, like a wild animal."

I swallow hard, reminded of how many times I was told to control myself by Jin and even Ms Martínková. It's always the same mantra: you're born with a ticking time bomb in your chest and it's your fault when it explodes.

"Funnily, they never tell you the other side. They never tell you about the students who mysteriously quit school in the middle of the year, then change their phone number and everything else. They don't tell you about the witches they hunt relentlessly, the ones they frame, and those they straight up assassinate. Did you know that accidents happen an awful lot more to witches? So *random*." The sarcasm pours from his lips. "Oh, and then there's the children." He laughs coldly. "You thought surely the children would be safe, right? Well, there's a reason, little Millie, why you had no idea you actually possessed magic until coming here. I'd bet my *ass* your parents hid and shielded you to avoid detection. Witches don't just start using their powers after puberty hits—we're born with it.

"'Oh, there was a fire at the daycare?'" Ravi's voice takes on a higher note as he impersonates some random person. "'Well, there's child protective services. What do you mean you want to contact your child? You can't'."

I'm feeling incredibly sick, as if I'm going to pass out any moment. My breaths come hard and fast. "Are you saying...?"

Ravi doesn't wait for me to finish the sentence. "They're killing children, yes."

An involuntary whimper escapes my throat.

"You're lucky you've made it this far. But don't worry, they'll catch onto you soon."

"Stop it!" I screech, unable to take any more.

Ravi throws out his arms. "I can't!" Flames shoot along his arms, hugging him tight without singeing a single hair. "They'll never stop hunting us. They won't be satisfied until every witch is dead."

Horrified, I shake my head and walk backwards. I stumble over a low wall and land on my backside, unable to get up again. "There's another way," I manage to say.

"Another way to what?"

"Spreading terror."

"Is that what you think I'm doing?" Ravi snaps his fingers. The fire rolls off his sleeves and becomes a fire ball. "You still believe their narrative? That we're all psychopaths or walking liabilities?"

I'm confused and overwhelmed. What else am I to believe when he's ranting and playing with his fire like that? "What are you trying to accomplish, then?"

"I'll show you." He marches off without waiting for me to get up, the fireball hovering in front of him.

I scramble to my feet and run after him. "Ravi, don't!"

"Relax, Millie!" he snaps. "Contrary to mages, I don't run around and murder people for who they are."

For someone intent on not being a crazy murderer, he's sure acting like one. "What are you going to do?"

"Set us free."

The words send a shiver down my spine. "Ravi, please."

We've reached the courtyard. Everything's quiet out here with most people already in bed. The only sounds are the howling wind and the crackle of Ravi's fireball. He leads me straight to the portal building.

"Stop your fretting, Millie. I'm not going to kill anyone."

"Then what *are* you doing?"

"I'm going to show them how useless they are. Did you see how many guardians were necessary to capture *one* elemental? I'm going to open that portal tonight. Slip through if you must, but I'd rather have you stay and watch them scramble, see how weak they are, how much they *need* us. Because we're more than a risk factor. Our connection to the Wyld Lands runs so much deeper than theirs."

His plan is so convoluted it makes my head hurt. Taking into consideration he's adamant he's not trying to hurt anyone, I believe he wants to build himself up to be a hero. Cause destruction, then swoop in and save the day. It's utterly insane.

"The Wyld Lands are just like us, something they fear and shut away. Not after tonight." He snaps his fingers again and suddenly, the fireball explodes outward, gathering strength from Ravi's anger as it engulfs the building.

Panicked, I run forward. I have no idea what I'm planning on doing, only that I need to stop this. As much as I love the Wyld Lands, I know it'll be absolute havoc if the gates between our world are thrown open. Ravi has no idea what powers he's inviting. We witches might be strong, but we're not *that* powerful.

Heat blasts my face, sending me further into panic mode. The wind picks up, nearly blowing me into the inferno. Behind me, I hear Ravi shouting, "Leave it be, Millie! Just step back and watch this glorious blaze."

Hard no! Somehow, I have to stop this. Blow out the flames before they can eat through the wood of the door.

And then it happens: one incredibly strong gust sends me sprawling to the ground. When I look up, the fire is gone, leaving nothing but soot. I want to exhale in relief, but the crackling is still in my ear. If anything, it's intensified.

"Call it back!" Ravi suddenly shouts. "Call back your storm! Milena! Quick!"

It's too late, I can't control the storm. It's mixed with Ravi's fire, carrying it from the portal to the buildings behind it—the dining hall, the recreation centre, the dorms.

Within seconds, half the school's caught fire.

37

A fire storm of epic proportions engulfs the dorms. Heat blasts my face and dries out my throat. My lungs start stinging.

Something slams into my shoulders. "Do something!" Ravi says. His eyes are wide with horror, his face pale.

"Me?"

"This is *your* storm."

"And *your* fire!"

My head's swimming with all the horrible consequences: everybody's in bed. They're all trapped. People will die. Lots of them. And it'll all be my fault.

"I've never dealt with so much heat," Ravi admits. He lets go of my shoulders as he stumbles back, then sinks to the ground. "I didn't want this."

Does he think *I* wanted this? I wanted to stop him, not make it disproportionately worse! Looking at my hands I find it unfathomable how so much destruction can come from my wind. Why am I cursed like this? What's the point of it all?

Angrily, I slap my cheeks. There's no time for woe-is-me. People are in immediate danger and I put them there. If I can't trust my wind to make things right, I need to do it the old-fashioned way.

Ignoring Ravi's whimpers, I sprint to the entrance, ducking under a lick of flame, and barrelling through the door. Quickly, I locate the fire alarm, knock the glass out, and press the button. Instantly, a siren blares through the dorms. Despite the ear-deafening sound, I start running and crying out, "Fire! Fire!"

Doors slam open as students stumble into the corridor, some still dressed, others in their pyjamas. They look confused, but the heat and orange shimmer outside their windows is undeniable. Panic ensues as they scramble straight for the emergency exits or head back inside to grab essential items. Only a handful try to use their power against the threat, end even those give up instantly when a fiery gust blows through the corridor.

I shriek and throw myself to the ground as fire blows over my head. People scream, and somewhere, a window bursts. When I look back up, a group of students are trapped by the flames.

There must be something I can do. If I can't stop the fire storm, I need to redirect it. Determined, I get to my feet and push out my hands. The wind follows my lead, forcing the flames to the side. "Run!"

Without hesitation, the students take their chance and use my wind channel to reach the exit. Someone grabs my elbow to make me follow them, but I shake them off and head the opposite way.

Whenever I come to a door that's still closed, I bang my fists against it until the inhabitants are roused. I come across a group of water students that have banded together to fight the fire and rescue two others. I use their vicinity for a quick respite before continuing on.

There's my room, never used. I don't stop to save any of my belongings and keep going. More windows burst. There are flames ahead, quickly coming my direction. Students pass me, some supporting others.

Pavlína's door is closed. Without thinking, I burst inside, just in time for another gust to blow through the corridor. "Pavlína?"

I can't see her. Flames are dancing outside the window, dipping the room into a ghastly orange. I'm just about to turn away when I hear a soft whimper.

"Pavlína!" I throw myself on the floor to look under the beds. And there she is, half covered with earth. "What are you doing?"

"What does it look like?" she shouts back, tears streaming down her face.

"As if you're intending to bake yourself!"

She stops, her eyes wide. *"Bake* myself?"

"You can't escape this by burying your head in the sand. That'll just turn it into an oven." I stretch out my hand. "Come here!"

For a moment longer, she hesitates, but then common sense returns to her and she crawls out of her hiding space.

I take her hand and pull her up. "Come with me."

In the few short minutes it took me to find her, the corridor has transformed into a nightmare. Flames are licking on the walls, eating away at the beautiful pictures in between. Smoke is developing fast now. I swallow a handful of it and start coughing violently.

Pavlína drags me back down to the ground. "Stay low."

Right. But if we're down here, it'll take us ages to reach the exit. I can't even see clearly anymore.

The cough remains, tormenting my lungs, while my eyes start stinging. What was I thinking, running into a burning building? How am I going to save anyone if I die here? I very nearly slap myself again.

Somehow, I need to make right what I did wrong. If I perish, so be it. As long as no one else dies.

The wind whirls around me, bringing heat and smoke. I try to get a hold of it, ignoring how the fire is singeing the hairs on my arms. If I can turn this around...

It works. A fresh wind blows around me, clearing both smoke and flames in our vicinity. I grab Pavlína's arm. "Come with me!"

She moans softly but follows without complaint, entrusting her life to me. "Does this help or hinder you?"

Under her touch, a thick layer of mud coats part of my arm. It's nice to have this protective layer between my skin and the heat, but I already feel my grasp on the wind waning. "Hinders."

"Okay." The mud vanishes. "Sorry." She's coated from head to toe. I envy the protection but know I need full control over the storm if I want to get us out of here.

The wind is fickle yet somehow I manage to stay on its good side. The corridor is impassable, so I kick open doors instead. At last, we find a room not already in flames. "Get in here."

As soon as we're both in, I barricade the door, buying us a few more seconds to follow the plan I've just hatched. I point at the window. On this side of the building, there are no flames on the outside. "I don't want to touch it in case it's hot, can you break it?"

"Easily," Pavlína says, quickly going through her mage motions. Spikes of earth fly at the window, shattering the panes.

"Hurry!" I don't know how much longer I can hold back the storm outside the room. Smoke is already curling under the door.

Pavlína runs towards the window, swipes everything off the desk in front, and climbs on top. As she grabs the window frame, she cries out.

She must have forgotten about the glass splinters still stuck in the wood. That only keeps her for a hot second though. After a moment of intense concentration, the frame turns rock solid, covering the danger. Without further hesitation, she swings out of the room.

I follow her much less elegantly when the fire storm blows the door open behind me. A gust goes over my head as I fall to the ground, landing in the rapidly melting snow. The impact slams the air out of my lungs, then something hits me heavily on the back several times.

It takes me a moment to realise it's Pavlína, and another to think I must've caught on fire during that last stunt.

"Let's get out of here," she shouts, already dragging me up. The next second, she lets go with a shriek and cowers next to me.

Fire surrounds us on all sides as the storm rages on. The hot air burns my lungs and I sprawl back on the ground, trying to escape all of it, the smoke, the heat, the flames, and the storm.

Just then, a wave of water washes over me. The cold film clings to my body, rapidly cooling my body temperature. At the same time, a flow of fresh air reaches my lungs. Something heavy drops on the ground next to us.

"Pavlína!" Then, more surprised, "Milena!"

I look up in disbelief. "Jin?"

He's wearing some sort of protective gear, a piece of cloth covering his mouth. His bright eyes are wide with horror. A wavering wall of water surrounds us, momentarily shielding us from the fire. "You need to get out of here." He grabs my arm and pulls me to my knees.

Just then, the water splashes as the wind presses down on us. Jin lets go and turns outward to perform his magic. Despite his best efforts, the only water he manages to procure evaporates within seconds.

We're going to die.

"Do something!" Pavlína screams, hiding behind Jin like a little child. It's no use. The fire's everywhere.

With a grunt, Jin gives up. He grabs both of us by the elbows. "Run!"

Together, we stumble through the flames. Somehow, we get lucky, and the wind presses the fire away from us. Smoke descends on us, only to be blown away again. Meanwhile, the trees around us are catching fire.

Then we're suddenly outside of the blaze. Jin hauls us a good twenty metres more before he collapses to his knees, coughing and sputtering. Next to him, Pavlína does the same.

My lungs are stinging and my throat feels as if it's coated with a layer of mud, but with each breath, the pain lessens a little more. Instead of an asthma attack, I breathe freely. Not that it helps my panic.

There are still people in the building. I hear their cries, and now the flames have caught in the park.

Jin gasps suddenly. "You!" He looks me straight in the eye.

Oh god, he knows.

"Me?" I whisper.

"You need to calm down."

"What?" How am I supposed to do that when there's a freaking fire storm blazing through the school?

His hands land heavily on my shoulders as his gaze bores itself into my eyes. "The wind makes it impossible for us to gain control over the fire. It will carry beyond the school and spread all across town if *you* don't call it back." His face softens. "Please, Milena, you've got to try."

When I whimper, he pulls me into his arms, pressing my body against his. "We do it together. Inhale. Exhale. Inhale..."

Exhale. I close my eyes, concentrating on nothing but the rise and fall of his chest against mine, his voice providing the rhythm, and the feel of him by my side.

As my breathing slows, I feel the wind in turmoil around me. Hesitantly, I reach out to it. With each inhale, I pull it back inside. Bit by bit, I seal it away.

"Keep going," Jin whispers, his voice carrying awe. "Whatever you're doing, keep doing it."

I don't dare open my eyes for fears of spoiling it. *Inhale. Exhale. Grab the wind. Seal it tight.*

Time stretches as I lose myself in the rhythm. I control the storm. The storm doesn't control me. It's mine to wield, and I choose not to.

When not even the slightest breeze blows through my hair, I open my eyes. Disoriented, I blink several times. "Where's the fire?"

The tell-tale orange flicker is gone. It's so dark I need a few minutes to see anything beyond the heavy shadow that's Jin. Before that changes, he runs his hands through my hair and showers my face with kisses.

"You did it," he exclaims proudly. "You beautiful, amazing woman. You did it."

I still don't understand. All I did was call the wind back to my side. The fire should still be burning. I wasn't out that long. "What happened?"

Jin laughs, the relief palpable in each peal. "Oxygen. You starved the fire. I don't know how you managed to do that and not kill us in the process. I didn't even know it was possible, but you did it. It's over."

Slowly, I'm able to make out other silhouettes. Next to us, Pavlína is still on the ground. She's breathing heavily, supporting her head with both hands. "What a nightmare," she whispers.

Instantly, I feel bad. After all, it would've never got this far if I'd had better control over my power. "I'm sorry."

Jin hugs me tight. "This wasn't your fault."

I know better than that, but I bite my tongue. Hopefully, my turn of luck came in time. If someone died, I could never forgive myself.

"You're an air mage," Pavlína says. "A wind witch—not a lick of flame in you."

Ravi. Without his risky act of rebellion, it would've never got that far either. I'm finding it incredibly hard not to disagree with everyone who thinks witches need to be locked up right now.

Suddenly, a bright light washes over us, making us wince. The flashlight is followed by a rough call. "Are you guys okay?"

Jin shields his eyes with a hand. "As far as we can tell." Then he whispers, only for me to hear, "Guardians."

A cold spike of fear rips into my chest.

"Can you walk?"

As our eyes adjust, we pull ourselves to our feet. I see the guardian now, a man in his thirties with a heavy scowl on his sooty face. He nods at us. A second guardian stands in the shadows behind him. "We're going to bring you to the courtyard. You'll receive medical attention there." His voice leaves room for something more, something bad.

My legs are too wobbly to walk and the breeze returns.

Jin puts an arm around me before I fall back on the ground. "Easy now. We've made it. It's all going to be good now." He throws the guardians a glance. "That was quite the shock."

The man's eyes narrow, making me feel like he's already seen right through me. *Easy.* I try concentrating on my breathing, just like before.

"Just get over there," he says in a gruff but not unkind way. "And don't worry—we're going to find the witches who did this. You're safe now."

I'm glad Jin's already steadying me, because I suddenly find it hard to breathe. The reality of what I am has finally caught up. I want to run, though my legs will never carry me. Not anymore.

"You hear that?" Jin says softly. "We're *safe* now. One step in front of the other. And another one." Even *his* voice is shaking.

Tears swim in my eyes as I try to hold it together. If a storm breaks out now, it's game over.

38

Everybody's checked over by the rescue services under the watchful eyes of at least sixty guardians. As soon as we're cleared, we're made to stand in the courtyard because it isn't safe to return to the house, is the official message, but that's not how it feels to me.

Together with Jin and Pavlína, I stand right in the middle of the crowd, and still, I feel exposed. I can't hold a single guardian's gaze for longer than a split-second, my stomach rolling every time it happens. A rather hefty breeze blows over our head. It's innocent enough. Only I know how close to a storm it is; a storm I can't allow to happen.

"Milena!" Ester throws her arms around me, distracting me from my plight. She's crying as she hugs me tight. "You're alive."

"Of course, I'm alive." But not for long. I close my eyes, taking a couple of deep breaths through my nose.

When I open them again, I find Jamila watching me. Their eyes seem to ask whether it was me, and I feel compelled to nod. They sigh softly, then pull on Ester's arm. "Come on, I want to check on Claudia."

Ester sniffles and squares her shoulder. "It's terrible," I hear her babble as Jamila drags her away; away from the danger.

All the witches keep their distance. Not just from me but from each other. Ravi sits on the ground, his head buried in his hands, ignoring anyone's attempt to talk to him. A boy I don't know is undeterred by this and repeatedly claps his shoulder in support. Louise has her arms wrapped around her belly as if she's got cramps, but makes light chat with some other guys from air class. Meanwhile, Egon sits on the edge of the fountain, looking as if he's about to lose his mind. In a time of crisis, we're all on our own.

The last of the ambulances leaves the compound, while the police chief follows Ms Martínková to her office to finalise his report. Only mages and witches are left in the courtyard. The guardians begin to coral everybody, forcing us to stand when a car rolls in. Next to me, Pavlína inhales sharply.

The door opens and a woman I've only seen in pictures before gets out. Pavlína's mother: Guardian Captain Sokolová. She's in full guardian regalia with a chest full of awards.

She receives an instant report from one of the guardians and nods ominously. Then she raises her voice for all of us to hear, "Everyone get into a single line." She claps her hands to hurry us on. "Come on, quick. The sooner we get this over with, the quicker you can all go to bed."

"Where?" a boy in my vicinity mutters. It's about one in the morning and the dorms are inaccessible.

That's not my concern, though. I know what's going to happen. A storm will break loose and the guardians will seize me, rightfully assuming it was me who brought on this disaster. As much as I might deserve the punishment, I can't bring myself to face it.

Jin grabs my hand as we line up, silently offering his support. While he looks straight ahead like a good little soldier, he makes a great show of inhaling and exhaling. It's a subtle reminder it's more important than ever I get my wind magic under control, and that means controlling this panic.

When the guardians have finished lining us up in front of Captain Sokolová, she throws us all a stern glance. "Tonight, something terrible happened." Her voice is so sharp it even cuts through the howling of the wind. "You became victims of a witch attack." She lets the word sunder through the line.

People glance at each other, horrified and curious. A multitude of gasps can be heard. Someone whimpers. My knees nearly give way. I want to throw up, and my grip on the wind starts to fall.

"Always look up," a quiet voice next to me says. Pavlína clasps my other hand, her chin raised defiantly. "She hates weakness."

"I..."

"Such a shame that smoke triggered your asthma, right?"

Confused, I turn to her, but she's looking straight ahead. I feel a sudden tightness around my chest. My breath gets caught in my throat, and I hear the distinct wheezing sound of my asthma brought upon by sudden earth weighting.

I notice Jin glancing at us, but he quickly snaps his attention back to the front, not interfering with Pavlína's plan. It takes my panic-addled brain a whole minute to figure out what she's doing. My first instinct is to ask Jin for help, but then it clicks, and I gasp for breath, coming up short. She's using her power to protect me from her mother.

"The witches in question may be among us," Captain Sokolová explains. "But don't fear. We'll find them. Every single one of them."

I shudder, still grappling with my failing lungs. About now, a storm would've formed, but the wind has decreased. Pavlína's plan is working.

Jin's grip on my hand intensifies when Captain Sokolová starts walking down the line, examining each student for an uncomfortable amount of time. Every student has to identify themselves by name and affinity. The earth and water students get a little less attention, but she's not letting anyone off the hook. Not even her own daughter.

"Pavlína Sokolová. Earth mage." Pavlína's voice is stone cold. She's let go of my hand and has her chin up, never once wavering.

Captain Sokolová regards her like any other student, though her stance is slightly more relaxed than with the others. She doesn't truly suspect her daughter, just measures her to the same standards.

I cough, struggling for breath. As her attention drifts to me, my first instinct is to look at the ground, as if she'd go away if I pretend I'm not there. Instead, I fight the instinct and take Pavlína's advice. My chin isn't as rigid as hers but I look Captain Sokolová in the eye. "Milena…" I have to pause to catch my breath. The earth is really doing me in. "Šimková. I'm an… air… mage." I almost said witch, like a dumbass.

"Are you okay?" Captain Sokolová asks, raising an eyebrow.

I swallow, fighting the urge to lower my gaze. "Asthma. The smoke…"

She dismisses me with a flick of her hand and walks on.

Next to me, Jin strikes an impressive pose. "Jin…"

"Čermák." Captain Sokolová's voice softens ever so slightly. "I know you, Jin. Thanks for helping with the rescue efforts. You did well."

On my other side, Pavlína gnashes her teeth, her jaw so rigid I fear it might break. I'm struck by how differently her mother treats Pavlína and Jin, and I'm starting to realise there was never any real chance Pavlína would've run to her mother about me. On the contrary, she's prevented my exposure. I shudder to think what would happen to her if she was found complicit in my protection. That only makes me think about what would happen to me, and a whimper escapes me.

Captain Sokolová throws me another glance and then the sky. As the wind has died down almost completely, she dismisses me yet again. When she keeps going, I decide that once the weather improves, I'll treat Pavlína to the biggest sundae I can find.

My panic eases a bit the further Captain Sokolová gets down the line, but the atmosphere is still oppressive. Despite her speech regarding our safety, we're all under observation. No one dares move and quite a few mages whimper or moan in distress. I see tears streaming down several faces.

And then I notice Egon further down. He's sweating profusely. His shoulders rise and fall rapidly as he tries to summon the mental strength to get through this. My breath catches in my throat when I see the puddle forming under his feet.

"Name," Captain Sokolová prompts him when he fails to report on his own.

"E-Egon Menzel. I-I'm a water m-mage."

The captain moves closer, pushing her face into Egon's. "Are you?"

Too many people are straining their necks, so I can't watch what's going on. Then someone screams. And the next thing I see is two guardians pulling Egon from the line. A rivulet of water bubbles to his feet as he's dragged towards the guardian base. His panic kicks into full gear as he kicks and screams, "I didn't do anything. I didn't do anything!"

My stomach turns into a tight knot that nearly makes me double over. I don't notice I'm moving until Jin jerks me back and turns me into him. "Don't look." He holds me so tight I don't get the choice.

Even though I can't see, I hear Egon. There's a hollow thump, followed by a skin-turning moan. Then whimpers, increasingly whiny begging, and the rush of water.

"He's water," I mutter again and again. "He had nothing to do with this."

Fire crackles and Egon screams. Another thump. Two. Silence.

Jin lets go of me, but when I turn, Egon is gone. I have no idea where they've brought him or if he's even still alive. For all I know, they could've killed him right in front of everyone.

"He's going to be fine," Jin whispers, but even he sounds shaken, and I don't believe a word he says.

Captain Sokolová throws another long glance down the line to see if any of us might be breaking before announcing, "Where there's one, there's usually more. We still haven't found the fire witch." And then she continues with her inspection as if nothing ever happened.

"She's a monster," Pavlína whispers, and for once I wholeheartedly agree.

The next witch she gets to is Jamila, with Ravi standing at the very end of the line. Next to Jamila, Ester is sobbing uncontrollably, but since she's a mage, that's all the water she leaks. Meanwhile, Jamila passes the inspection as easily as any of the mages, never once twitching under the captain's stare, despite her carrying the wanted affinity. All those years of meditation are paying off.

The same can't be said for Ravi. Not so soon after that gigantic fuck up. When things turned south, Ravi crumbled. If he recovers now, after they've already taken Egon, he's a bigger psychopath than I'd thought.

Captain Sokolová is nearing the end, and I mentally prepare myself for the inevitable. The panic and earth magic combined are robbing me of my last shred of composure, and my knees give way. I cling to Jin's hand like a drowning woman while desperately trying to pump air into my chest.

Three more people until Ravi.

Two.

"What the hell are you doing there?"

Everybody's heads turn as Ms Martínková crosses the courtyard with long strides. She must've been held up by the police, but she's out in a fury now. "These are children, Vanda!"

"Ilona." Captain Sokolová turns to her, for now turning her back on Ravi. "There was a witch attack. I'm just doing my job."

"By terrifying and traumatising a bunch of innocent children?"

"A witch is never innocent."

The words fall like a blow. The worst thing is they're true. We *did* cause the fire. Ravi and *I* did. Still, there's something so damning and unforgiving about it.

Ms Martínková crosses her arms, glowering at Captain Sokolová. "Rubbish. That's an archaic notion that has done us more harm than it ever did good."

I'm in awe of her guts to openly defy public opinion. Surely, she can't be the only adult who supports that idea.

"These children are innocent. I will personally vouch for every one of them."

Captain Sokolová smiles slyly. "We've already found a witch."

Ms Martínková pales. "Who?"

"A water witch," Captain Sokolová answers with a shoulder shrug. She doesn't give a hot damn about Egon, having already forgotten his name.

"A *water* witch?" Ms Martínková repeats, finding her fury again. "You arrested a water witch for a fire?"

Only I seem to notice how she deliberately left out the storm component of the disaster. Even now, she's protecting me.

"I arrested a witch for being a witch. It was a fire today, it could be a flood tomorrow." Captain Sokolová's eyes narrow. "I might have to start a more thorough investigation if it turns out you've been harbouring multiple witches."

Flames flicker behind Captain Sokolová in the darkness. Ravi's lost it.

Ms Martínková snaps her fingers and the fire responds to her, swirling around the Guardian Captain like a Chinese dragon. "The only witch you should be worrying about is me." She snaps again, and the fire extinguishes before it does any harm. "It was my fire that burnt down the dorms."

"No!" I cry out. I shoot to my feet but Jin's grip is relentless.

"Let them handle it," he hisses audibly.

I'm far from the only one who's reacted badly to Ms Martínková's confession. Some physically recoil, while others break down and cry. The entire line is in disarray. Confusion spreads, and more and more people raise their voices. It's pure mayhem.

Suddenly, the earth shakes, sending us sprawling on the ground. "Quiet!" Captain Sokolová shouts before raising her foot to stomp once more. Instantly, everything quiets down.

Only a few are still standing, among them Ms Martínková. In the flicker of the flames, she looks almost regal. "Are you done with your little tantrum? One day you'll have to explain to me how this *intentional* violence"—she points at us—"is better than when a witch accidentally loses control."

"Who was your partner?" Captain Sokolová asks, ignoring the criticism. As she closes in on Ms Martínková, several guardians, those of water affinity, surround them. "There was a storm. Which student did you use?"

Ms Martínková laughs. "Student? You think a student could've caused this level of destruction?" Spirals of water wrap around her, and she gasps in pain. Despite that, she forces herself to smile. "Think a little harder, Vanda. You know who I was friends with at school. Isn't that why you always distrusted me?"

Who she was *friends* with at school?

Now it's Vanda who pales. "He's still alive?"

"Of course, he's alive. You didn't catch him, did you?"

Captain Sokolová nods sharply at the guardians surrounding Ms Martínková and they double their efforts. The principal is completely enclosed in water, her fire extinguishes as she gasps for air. Horrified, we all watch her struggle, but the guardians are relentless. They don't stop their assault until Ms Martínková stills.

The moment she loses consciousness, the guardians let go, catch her, and put her arms into restraints. Under Captain Sokolová's supervision, they carry her off.

When that's dealt with, the captain turns to us again. At first, she looks disgusted by the lack of discipline—none of us have tried to stand up—but then her face softens. I don't believe the following smile for one second. "Well, that was a surprise. I'm sorry you had to witness that. I'm even more sorry you've had to live with a witch for all these years. Rest assured, we will launch a lengthy investigation into how this could've happened and what sinister ploys were hatched here. We'll revisit the curriculum and interview every single teacher. Until the investigation has concluded, *I* will lead the school. Now. There will be bedding in the library. So, make your way over there and get some rest."

Some students practically run towards the deceptively safe walls of the library, while others need to be helped up by their peers. Next to me, Pavlína stands and dusts herself off. If she's shaken, she doesn't show it. Not out here.

I try to emulate her but can't shake the horrific images of what I've just seen, when the mages practically drowned Ms Martínková—not because they lost control, but because they knew it'd hurt her the most.

"You should find the school nurse and get her to give you some steroids."

I nearly jump when Captain Sokolová appears in front of me. She must've sought out her daughter or Jin, who's currently helping me up, but her gaze rests on me. Before I can stop myself, I mutter, "Why did you do that?"

Jin's hand around mine tightens almost painfully.

"Because she was a witch."

"But she was…" Innocent, I want to say, but I know I can't. Ms Martínková sacrificed herself for Ravi. And for me. "So nice."

Captain Sokolová's face softens, though her smile still makes my stomach turn. "She tricked you. The whole lot of you. It's what witches do best. They sneak into our inner circles, earning our trust, until the perfect moment arrives and they strike. Ms Martínková managed to get control of this school and then she attempted to wipe out an entire generation. She will be tried and punished for her crimes."

As horrible as every single word out of her mouth is, I draw hope from them. If they want to put Ms Martínková on trial, she must be still alive. The relief washes through me, oddly fitting Captain Sokolová's awful promises.

"There you go. Now get some medical attention. Be a good boy, Jin, and take her there, okay? I want to see you at the base tomorrow. It's time to get you started on your career path."

It's only because I'm so close to Jin I notice his sharp intake. Almost instantly, he stands to attention and nods. "Yes, Captain."

"Pavlína." That's all Pavlína gets before her mother walks away and follows the guardians who took Ms Martínková.

"Now, there, breathe easy," Pavlína mutters, stroking my back and releasing me from her tight grip. "You survived your first meeting with my mum."

I'm not so sure I did.

<h1 style="text-align:center">39</h1>

The night in the library is one of the worst I've ever lived through—there's too many people in the room, and most are crying or talking. The guardians guard each exit, keeping watch on us all through the night, in case any more witches reveal themselves. For that reason, and because we're suddenly comrades or something, Pavlína stays close, covering me with a lighter version of her earth spell to counteract my heightened emotions.

I lie completely still until the wee hours of the morning, the images of the last day replaying in an endless loop: the shock of the fire jumping to the dorms, the danger I willingly ran into, and the terror that was the guardian roundup to Egon's and Ms Martínková's arrest. Because of the principal's selfless sacrifice, Ravi and I got away. At least for now.

It sits wrong with me. Even though it was all a terrible accident, Ms Martínková shouldn't have taken the fall. I know why she did it, but that doesn't make it any better. She was building a safe haven at this school. Other witches, present and future ones, need her. She won't be able to fulfil her vision from behind bars—or worse.

At some time in the morning, exhaustion sends me tumbling into sleep at last. It's such a heavy one, I hardly remember anything, just the wind of the Wyld Lands calling me. If only Ravi had opened the door for me instead of trying to burn it all down.

When I wake, Jin's bedroll is already empty, his raven-black hair nowhere to be seen. With a pang, I remember Captain Sokolová's words last night. She asked him to join the guardians and Jin accepted. Not that he had a choice. I just wish I could've talked to him to see if his opinion of witches, and most importantly the guardians, has changed. I'm sure it has, but it makes me uneasy when I remember the familiarity with Pavlína's mother he showed. She treated him like a lost son compared to the coldness she showed her own daughter.

I check on Pavlína, but she's still asleep. In the sunlight filtering in from the high windows, I see her arms reddened by the fire, instantly feeling bad again. It's hard to believe that just sixteen hours ago, we had a massive fight. Then a few hours later, she saved my life.

Much to the librarian's dismay, the guardians have provided bread rolls and tea and coffee for breakfast. I grab a cup and some food and try to find my fellow witches. Louise glowers when I come near, making it very clear I should stay away. Jamila gives a quick shake with their head before doting on Ester, who hasn't noticed me.

I don't even try to approach Ravi. He's awake but still lying on the ground, staring at the ceiling, likely replaying the horrifying events of last night and finding his own role in it as despicable as mine.

A small bout of anger overcomes me when I look at him. He started it all—not just the fire itself but the needless attacks on the school when he let the elementals in. And for what? Stomping his feet and shouting, *here we are? We're not going away?* Well, turns out, we absolutely *do* go away when the guardians catch us. He's lucky Ms Martínková is the angel she is and shares his affinity.

That reminds me of the short exchange she and Captain Sokolová had, the one referencing Ms Martínková's high school friend. It struck me as weird yesterday, and now even more. I know who they were talking about. It's clear my storm was blamed on the Stormwitch, the man who killed Jin's father. It was an excuse Captain Sokolová swallowed only too readily because she already knew about Ms Martínková's connection.

I deposit my untouched breakfast on a table and make my way around the shelves, carefully stepping over bedrolls on the floor. I reach the modern history department and scan the titles for the most likely hit. *Witch Terrorism in the 21st Century* should do it.

With the book under my arm, I find a place in a secluded corner at the back of the library. I miss my coffee now, but it's probably better I don't have it with me in case I spill some on the book.

As expected, there's a whole chapter on Jarek Janda, the Stormwitch of Prague. It doesn't take me long to find what I'm looking for: a portrait of Jarek Janda. *Jarek.* He's a good-looking man with a prominent nose and sharp grey eyes. His sandy hair is unruly, as if permanently tousled by a cheeky wind. The portrait shows him clean-shaven, but it's not too hard to imagine him with a beard. A beard to protect him from immediate identification. One that tickled terribly on my cheeks.

I close the book with a heavy sigh.

The man everybody fears, Ms Martínková's school friend, is my father.

Afterword

Thank you for reading *Wyld Witch Weather*! I hope you enjoyed this first glimpse into Milena's world.

This book has become one of my absolute favourites, but it hasn't always been that way. When I wrote the first draft during *NaNoWriMo* in 2023, I *hated* it. No kidding! I was so glad to be done with it because I felt it didn't really fit with my other books – hello, Spirit Seeker series! – and I thought I'd wasted all my time. Then, a year later, I reread the book and was completely blown away. I don't know what I was thinking in 2023, but I was wrong.

Fast-forward to January 2025 and there are fires all over the world. The far right is on the rise, not just in America but all around the world, and it's scary. I wanted to write a book that deals with similar themes and offers a hopeful ending, reflecting how we want this period to end: with a world committed to being more inclusive, open-minded, and better.

Well, *Wyld Lands Academy* is that series. The next one, *Wyld Witch Tempest,* is dark. Not only does Milena carry a terrible truth, but the guardians have taken over the school and are keeping a close eye on any potential witches. That scene in the courtyard was just the beginning. Milena will have to navigate her own dangerous potential, her father's legacy and propaganda favouring mages. But, of course, she's still a teenager. Her relationship with Jin will be tested, she'll form a beautiful new friendship and learn more about herself, her father and witches in general. And, of course, there's magic! A lot of it!

This book series wouldn't have been possible without the help of my own little elemental cohort. Firstly, I'd like to thank the members of my *Tintenzirkel* writer's forum, especially Rajou, Ixys, Sunflower, and Kamen, who supported me during the *NaNoWriMo* months of writing books one and two, and who are already preparing to cheer me on as I tackle book three next month.

My beta reader team: Paula, Tina, Mariaan, Mathilde, and Perri – you're all awesome! I love receiving your initial feedback, which is always so passionate and supportive, even when you flag up serious shortcomings! These books would be nothing without you!

Jackie, my trusted proofreader: you really whip this book into shape and catch all my German expressions when they try to sneak into the English text.

Natalie, my cover designer: thank you for stepping in and saving the cover when it was clear it wasn't going to pass muster. You not only gave *Wyld Witch Weather* a beautiful cover, but also took it upon yourself to mentor me. Maybe one day I'll reach your level. Until then, I'm eager to learn as much as I can!

To my husband and three sons: you're always so incredibly patient with my writing obsession and workaholic tendencies. You're my biggest fans, and I couldn't love you more. Thank you for putting up with me talking about plots, arcs, and cool scenes.

And last but certainly not least, thank you, the reader, for taking a chance on this new series. I'd be nowhere without your support. If you enjoyed this book, please consider writing a review, posting about it on social media, or telling your friends about it. Being an indie author is hard, so every little bit helps. Plus, reviews also help other readers determine whether a series is for them.

If you're keen to support me or would like access to extra scenes, art, behind-the-scenes content, and much more, you can join my *Patreon* community here: . You can join the free tier or any of the others. Patreon allows me to sleep a little easier, and, most importantly, work on all those extras, like art, without feeling guilty. There's also a Discord server if you want to chat!

I'll see you again for *Wyld Witch Tempest!*

Love,
Janna

Magic, Demons and High School Drama

A supernatural adventure through Europe

Ghosts of the Catacombs (Parisian Ghosts 1)

Urban Fantasy with French Flair

About Janna Ruth

Once upon a time, Janna Ruth studied the plate boundaries of this world. Now, she's creating her own worlds. Born in Berlin, Germany, Janna lives in Wellington, New Zealand, writing both English and German books.

Janna's writing career kicked off when she won a writing competition for German publisher Ueberreuter. Her first self-published novel "Im Bann der zertanzten Schuhe" (Melody of a Curse) went on to win the 2018 SERAPH for "Best Independent Title". She debuted in English with her witchy novella "Witching with Dolphins" in 2020 and has since published urban fantasy, YA sci-fi, and contemporary coming-of-age novels and series.

When Janna isn't writing, she has a plethora of hobbies, such as aerial acrobatics, cake decorating, drawing, reading, and anything crafty you can throw her way.

Find out more about Janna and her books here:

Website: www.janna-ruth.com

Patreon: https://www.patreon.com/c/jannaruth

BookBub: www.bookbub.com/authors/janna-ruth

Facebook: www.facebook.com/authorjannaruth

Reader Group: www.facebook.com/groups/storyseeker

Goodreads:

www.goodreads.com/author/show/16513923.Janna_Ruth

BlueSky: https://bsky.app/profile/janna-ruth.bsky.social

Instagram: www.instagram.com/janna_ruth

TikTok: www.tiktok.com/@jannaruthwrites

Pinterest: www.pinterest.com/jannaruthwrites

www.ingramcontent.com/pod-product-compliance
Lightning Source LLC
Chambersburg PA
CBHW061228310726
48971CB00007B/1987